PENGUIN CANADA

THE PENGUIN BOOK OF CHRISTMAS STORIES

Internationally acclaimed as an anthologist, translator, essayist, novelist, and editor, ALBERTO MANGUEL is the author of several award-winning books, including *The Dictionary of Imaginary Places, A History of Reading,* and *With Borges.* He was born in Buenos Aires, moved to Canada in 1982, and now lives in France, where he was named Officer of the Order of Arts and Letters.

Also by Alberto Manguel

NON-FICTION

A Reading Diary

With Borges

Reading Pictures

Into the Looking-Glass Wood

Bride of Frankenstein

The Dictionary of Imaginary Places (*with Gianni Guadalupi*)

A History of Reading

Magic Land of Toys (*with Michel Pintado*)

The Library at Night

FICTION

Stevenson Under the Palm Trees

News from a Foreign Country Came

ANTHOLOGIES

Black Water

Dark Arrows

Other Fires

Evening Games

The Oxford Book of Canadian Ghost Stories

Seasons

Black Water II

Canadian Mystery Stories

The Gates of Paradise

The Second Gates of Paradise

Meanwhile, In Another Part of the Forest (*with Craig Stephenson*)

Lost Words

Why Are You Telling Me This?

Mothers and Daughters

Fathers and Sons

The Ark in the Garden

By the Light of the Glow-Worm's Lamp

God's Spies

The Penguin Book of Summer Stories

The Penguin Book of Christmas Stories

Edited by
ALBERTO MANGUEL

PENGUIN
CANADA

PENGUIN CANADA

Published by the Penguin Group

Penguin Group (Canada), 90 Eglinton Avenue East, Suite 700, Toronto, Ontario, Canada M4P 2Y3
(a division of Pearson Canada Inc.)

Penguin Group (USA) Inc., 375 Hudson Street, New York, New York 10014, U.S.A.
Penguin Books Ltd, 80 Strand, London WC2R 0RL, England
Penguin Ireland, 25 St Stephen's Green, Dublin 2, Ireland (a division of Penguin Books Ltd)
Penguin Group (Australia), 250 Camberwell Road, Camberwell, Victoria 3124, Australia
(a division of Pearson Australia Group Pty Ltd)
Penguin Books India Pvt Ltd, 11 Community Centre, Panchsheel Park, New Delhi – 110 017, India
Penguin Group (NZ), 67 Apollo Drive, Rosedale, North Shore 0632, New Zealand
(a division of Pearson New Zealand Ltd)
Penguin Books (South Africa) (Pty) Ltd, 24 Sturdee Avenue, Rosebank, Johannesburg 2196,
South Africa

Penguin Books Ltd, Registered Offices: 80 Strand, London WC2R 0RL, England

First published in a Viking Canada hardcover by Penguin Group (Canada),
a division of Pearson Canada Inc., 2005
Published in this edition, 2007

3 4 5 6 7 8 9 10   (WEB)

Introduction, author biographies, and selection copyright © Alberto Manguel, 2005.
The Copyright Acknowledgments on pages 315-317 constitute an extension of this copyright page.

Manufactured in Canada.

ISBN-13: 978-0-14-305425-2
ISBN-10: 0-14-305425-2

Library and Archives Canada Cataloguing in Publication data available upon request.

Visit the Penguin Group (Canada) website at **www.penguin.ca**

Special and corporate bulk purchase rates available; please see
www.penguin.ca/corporatesales or call 1-800-810-3104, ext. 477 or 474

To Katherine Ashenburg,
in memory of Sinter Klaas

Contents

Introduction

by

ALBERTO MANGUEL

In Christmas I no more desire a rose
Than wish a snow in May's new-fangled mirth;
But like of each thing that in season grows.

LOVE'S LABOUR'S LOST I:1

WE ARE SEASONAL CREATURES. We advance in age toward the promised six feet of earth, not along the straight path recommended by the preacher but in a sequence of identical loops that carry us, year after year, from the illusion of beginning to the illusion of end. The Pythagoreans, who believed that all things will return and every life will be lived again, took their cue from the sun rising every morning and from winter announcing the arrival of spring. Like a child who wants the same story told over and over again, the universe seems to take delight in repetition.

Our earliest celebrations mark such repeated moments. Whether in the deserts where writing was invented or, even before, in the primeval steppes where the first human societies came into being, our most ancient grandparents feasted the anniversary of the earth that announced the coming season when crops could again be planted. The Romans marked the passing of midwinter by drinking and dancing on December 17, the feast of Saturnalia, and the Persians honoured the birth of the goddess Mithra, Sun of Righteousness, by carousing and parading on December 25. The Celts adorned their winter trees with garlands to ready them for the New Year, and the Germanic tribes lit huge bonfires on the longest night of all, to coax the hidden rays of the sun into appearing. When the coming of the Saviour was announced to the Jewish people, the celebratory December mood was already well established, and the three kings who came to Bethlehem from the Orient were no doubt aware of the Persian custom of offering gifts on the winter solstice. Under all manner of guises, Christmas was celebrated long before the birth of Christ.

In the beginning, the Christian Church cared little for calendars, fixed holidays, and appointed sacred feasts, since the only date that mattered was that of Christ's Second Coming, and that date lay in the unknowable future. "Let no man therefore judge you," wrote Saint Peter to the Colossians, "in respect of an holiday, or of the new moon, or of the Sabbath days, which are a shadow of things to come." But the seasons came and went, and Christ did not return, and eventually it became necessary for the Church to establish its own timeline, allowing each of us "to put his household in order" (as is told in 2 Samuel) to prepare for our foreseeable end. Even though the first notice we have of Christmas being celebrated by Christians appears in a Roman almanac from the year 336, the official recognition of a specific date for Christ's birth occurs later, in 354, when the date was made to coincide with that of the winter solstice, the birthday of the sun.

But of what year? More than a century and a half later, in 525, Pope John I commissioned the learned abbot Dionysus Exiguus (or "Little Dennis") to calculate the Easter date for the following year. The abbot not only calculated the date of the coming Easter but, for the next six years, worked on a series of tables that charted future Easters as well as several other Church anniversaries, starting, of course, with the birth of the Saviour himself. Inspired (he said) by the Holy Spirit, Little Dennis calculated that Christ had been born 531 years earlier, and called that first year *anno Domini*, or, as it would be written from then on, the year 1 AD. The Armenian Church, however, never accepted December 25 as the day on which to celebrate the birth of Christ, preferring instead to honour the Saviour's birth on Epiphany, January 6, which for the other Christian churches marked either the baptism of Jesus (in the East) or the visit of the Magi (in the West).

Quite early on, the day of the birth of Christ acquired, both in the Eastern and Western churches, a conventional iconography based on the account given in the Gospel of Luke, the same that we recognize today in decorations and greeting cards: Mary and Joseph, the Child born in the manger ("because there was no room for them in the inn"), the adoring shepherds, the announcing angel and, finally, the beasts referred to in Isaiah I:3: "The ox knoweth his owner, and the ass his master's crib."

Already by the second century, the story of the Nativity had become so well known that the Platonic philosopher Celsius was able to mock its tenets in his *True Arguments Against the Christians* (a book which, by an ironic twist, reached us through piecemeal quotations in the works of the Christian censors who condemned it to the flames). "You began by fabricating a fabulous filiation," Celsius wrote as if addressing Christ himself, "pretending that you owed your birth to a virgin."

> In reality, you were born in a small place in Judea, the son of a poor peasant-woman who lived off the land. She, guilty of adultery with a soldier called Panterus, was rejected by her husband, a carpenter by profession. Thus

banished, and ignominiously wandering from one place to another, she gave birth in secret. Later, forced through poverty to emigrate, she travelled to Egypt and there worked for a salary. In the meantime, you learned some of those magic powers of which the Egyptians boast, and returned to your own country where, proud of the reactions you knew how to provoke, you proclaimed yourself a god.

Celsius's is perhaps the first variation on the Christmas story of which examples closer to our time are Nikos Kazantzakis's *The Last Temptation of Christ,* Nino Ricci's *Testament,* Jim Crace's *Quarantine,* José Saramago's *The Gospel According to Jesus Christ*—all efforts to translate the essential narrative into contemporary terms, sometimes stripping it of its obvious religious core, sometimes illuminating that core through a personal expression of faith. Like Luke's story, most of the Christmas stories that followed it attempted to tell, however intimately or allusively, of the experience of hope after despair and redemption after guilt.

Throughout the centuries, the story became enriched with further imaginings that lent it a Northern rather than a Middle Eastern landscape: Yule trees instead of palm trees, reindeer instead of camels and, of course, Father Christmas. St. Nicholas, a fourth-century bishop of Myra in Lycia, Asia Minor, was metamorphosed sometime in the nineteenth century from patron saint of children into the jolly old man who, in the American-Dutch dialect, is called "Sinte Klaas" or Santa Claus. The original Nicholas of Myra was known for both his generosity and his piety, a frugal man who, even as a baby, refused to take his mother's breast except on Wednesdays and Fridays. Legend has it that the young Nicholas, hearing that three young sisters were going to be sold into prostitution by their needy father, wrapped three round pieces of gold in a cloth and, under cover of darkness, threw them through a window of the girls' house, thus saving them from their ignominious fate. For that reason, in Christian iconography, Nicholas is represented holding a gift of three golden balls which (fittingly enough for a saint roped in by the commercial machineries of the season) later became the symbol for a pawnbroker's shop.

But neither belief in the exact date of Christ's birth nor faith in the marvellous Nativity story is necessary to justify our joy when (in the Northern hemisphere) winter starts to end and spring can be soon expected or when (in the Southern hemisphere) the summer holidays begin. Christians will no doubt rejoice in the remembered birth of their Redeemer, while for the secular world Christmas as a season offers the chance to celebrate the rebirth of the world itself—its repeated conclusion as well as its repeated beginning, the end of the working year and the start of a better year to come.

Charles Dickens, perhaps more than any other writer, understood this celebration of "joy and goodwill towards all men" that Christmas entails. His *Christmas Stories* created for the season a mythology that, while never denying its roots in religious faith, lends the notion of Christmas a kind of cosmological state of happiness. More than a consciously understood Church holiday, grounded in astronomy and theological arguments, after Dickens, Christmas became the season in which we must, like Scrooge, echo the generosity of the tired earth and make merry atonement for our selfishness and greed, giving thanks for the gifts that we receive and offering gifts to others as a sign of our allegiance to the beleaguered human family. After Dickens, to set a story at Christmastime is to assume, on the part of the reader, the acknowledgment of a prestigious setting, of a period charged with ancient significance, of a season of promised redemption, however much tinged today with Christmas-card sentimentality and less-than-spiritual mercantile dealings.

In the numberless depictions of the Annunciation, when the Angel comes to tell Mary that the Son of God will be born to her, a small cross or a painting of the Crucifixion is shown on one of the walls of Mary's room. This is not a thoughtless anachronism on the part of the painter, nor merely the conventional representation of a contemporary interior. Like the recurrence of the seasons, its presence affirms the living circularity of time, the promise that birth will follow death which will in turn follow birth. Because all things must end in order to begin again, the knowledge that our efforts and joys and sufferings will have no cut-and-dried conclusions must be cause for rejoicing, not despair, since this must surely mean that a tidy perfection is not expected from us, but rather a stubborn delight in beginning again every day.

The authors of the stories that follow, collected under the merry canopy of Christmas, take for granted the myriad connotations that the mention of Christmas evokes. Something is expected in this season, something hoped for, or feared, or happily awaited, something whose quality remains mysterious to us, because the change that is to come, for all its certainty, gives no indication of its nature. All we know is that darkness will be followed by light, that the days will be longer and brighter, that the commonplaces which mark the change of mood and weather will duly make their appearance, and that, in such expectation, we will begin again, without knowing with what luck or success. Robert Louis Stevenson, writing what he called "A Christmas Sermon" in the last days of 1888, had this to say of our experience:

> There is indeed one element in human destiny that not blindness itself can controvert: whatever else we are intended to do, we are not intended to succeed; failure is the fate allotted. It is so in every art and study; it is so above all in the continent art of living well. Here is a pleasant thought for the year's end.

A pleasant thought indeed, echoed in the stories that follow. Every reader knows that the best stories have no ending but continue beyond the page in the reader's own world. Such inconclusiveness is no doubt a kind of failure, but one that, in all humility and confidence, allows the authors to extend their own landscapes into that of their readers, whose splendid failure it will be never to reach the farthest limit of a memorable voyage through the old Christmas story, imagined all over again for every new generation, "like of each thing that in season grows."

The
Penguin Book
of
Christmas
Stories

Auggie Wren's Christmas Story

by

PAUL AUSTER

I HEARD THIS STORY from Auggie Wren. Since Auggie doesn't come off too well in it, at least not as well as he'd like to, he's asked me not to use his real name. Other than that, the whole business about the lost wallet and the blind woman and the Christmas dinner is just as he told it to me.

Auggie and I have known each other for close to eleven years now. He works behind the counter of a cigar store on Court Street in downtown Brooklyn, and since it's the only store that carries the little Dutch cigars I like to smoke, I go in there fairly often. For a long time, I didn't give much thought to Auggie Wren. He was the strange little man who wore a hooded blue sweatshirt and sold me cigars and magazines, the impish, wisecracking character who always had something funny to say about the weather or the Mets or the politicians in Washington, and that was the extent of it.

But then one day several years ago he happened to be looking through a magazine in the store, and he stumbled across a review of one of my books. He knew it was me because a photograph accompanied the review, and after that things changed between us. I was no longer just another customer to Auggie, I had become a distinguished person. Most people couldn't care less about books and writers, but it turned out that Auggie considered himself an artist. Now that he had cracked the secret of who I was, he embraced me as an ally, a confidant, a brother-in-arms. To tell the truth, I found it rather embarrassing. Then, almost inevitably, a moment came when he asked if I would be willing to look at his photographs. Given his enthusiasm and goodwill, there didn't seem to be any way I could turn him down.

God knows what I was expecting. At the very least, it wasn't what Auggie showed me the next day. In a small, windowless room at the back of the store, he opened a cardboard box and pulled out twelve identical black photo albums. This was his life's work, he said, and it didn't take him more than five minutes a day to do it. Every morning for the past twelve years, he had stood at the corner of Atlantic Avenue and Clinton Street at precisely seven o'clock and had taken a single colour photograph of precisely the same view. The project now ran to more than four thousand photographs. Each album represented a different year, and all the pictures were laid out in sequence, from January 1 to December 31, with the dates carefully recorded under each one.

As I flipped through the albums and began to study Auggie's work, I didn't know what to think. My first impression was that it was the oddest, most bewildering thing I had ever seen. All the pictures were the same. The whole project was a numbing onslaught of repetition, the same street and the same buildings over and over again, an unrelenting delirium of redundant images. I couldn't think of anything to say to Auggie, so I continued turning pages, nodding my head in feigned appreciation. Auggie himself seemed unperturbed, watching me with a broad smile on his face, but after I'd been at it for several minutes, he suddenly interrupted me and said, "You're going too fast. You'll never get it if you don't slow down."

He was right, of course. If you don't take the time to look, you'll never manage to see anything. I picked up another album and forced myself to go more deliberately. I paid closer attention to details, took note of shifts in the weather, watched for the changing angles of light as the seasons advanced. Eventually, I was able to detect subtle differences in the traffic flow, to anticipate the rhythm of the different days (the commotion of workday mornings, the relative stillness of weekends, the contrast between Saturdays and Sundays). And then, little by little, I began to recognize the faces of the people in the background, the passersby on their way to work, the same people in the same spot every morning, living an instant of their lives in the field of Auggie's camera.

Once I got to know them, I began to study their postures, the way they carried themselves from one morning to the next, trying to discover their moods from these surface indications, as if I could imagine stories for them, as if I could penetrate the invisible dramas locked inside their bodies. I picked up another album. I was no longer bored, no longer puzzled as I had been at first. Auggie was photographing time, I realized, both natural time and human time, and he was doing it by planting himself in one tiny corner of the world and willing it to be his own, by standing guard in the space he had chosen for himself. As he watched me pore over his work, Auggie continued to smile with pleasure. Then, almost as if he had been reading my thoughts, he began to recite a line from Shakespeare.

"Tomorrow and tomorrow and tomorrow," he muttered under his breath, "time creeps on its petty pace." I understood then that he knew exactly what he was doing.

That was more than two thousand pictures ago. Since that day, Auggie and I have discussed his work many times, but it was only last week that I learned how he acquired his camera and started taking pictures in the first place. That was the subject of the story he told me, and I'm still struggling to make sense of it.

Earlier that same week, a man from *The New York Times* called me and asked if I would be willing to write a short story that would appear in the paper on Christmas morning. My first impulse was to say no, but the man was very charming and persistent, and by the end of the conversation I told him I would give it a try. The moment I hung up the phone, however, I fell into a deep panic. What did I know about

Christmas? I asked myself. What did I know about writing short stories on commission?

I spent the next several days in despair, warring with the ghosts of Dickens, O. Henry, and other masters of the Yuletide spirit. The very phrase "Christmas story" had unpleasant associations for me, evoking dreadful outpourings of hypocritical mush and treacle. Even at their best, Christmas stories were no more than wish-fulfillment dreams, fairy tales for adults, and I'd be damned if I'd ever allowed myself to write something like that. And yet, how could anyone propose to write an unsentimental Christmas story? It was a contradiction in terms, an impossibility, an out-and-out conundrum. One might just as well try to imagine a racehorse without legs, or a sparrow without wings.

I got nowhere. On Thursday I went out for a long walk, hoping the air would clear my head. Just past noon, I stopped in at the cigar store to replenish my supply, and there was Auggie, standing behind the counter as always. He asked me how I was. Without really meaning to, I found myself unburdening my troubles to him. "A Christmas story?" he said after I had finished. "Is that all? If you buy me lunch, my friend, I'll tell you the best Christmas story you ever heard. And I guarantee that every word of it is true."

We walked down the block to Jack's, a cramped and boisterous delicatessen with good pastrami sandwiches and photographs of old Dodgers teams hanging on the walls. We found a table at the back, ordered our food, and then Auggie launched into his story.

"It was the summer of seventy-two," he said. "A kid came in one morning and started stealing things from the store. He must have been about nineteen or twenty, and I don't think I've ever seen a more pathetic shoplifter in my life. He's standing by the rack of paperbacks along the far wall and stuffing books into the pockets of his raincoat. It was crowded around the counter just then, so I didn't see him at first. But once I noticed what he was up to, I started to shout. He took off like a jackrabbit, and by the time I managed to get out from behind the counter, he was already tearing down Atlantic Avenue. I chased after him for about half a block, and then I gave up. He'd dropped something along the way, and since I didn't feel like running anymore, I bent down to see what it was.

"It turned out to be his wallet. There wasn't any money inside, but his driver's licence was there along with three or four snapshots. I suppose I could have called the cops and had him arrested. I had his name and address from the licence, but I felt kind of sorry for him. He was just a measly little punk, and once I looked at those pictures in his wallet, I couldn't bring myself to feel very angry at him. Robert Goodwin. That was his name. In one of the pictures, I remember, he was standing with his arm around his mother or grandmother. In another one, he was sitting there at age nine or ten dressed in a baseball uniform with a big smile on his face. I just didn't have the heart. He was probably on dope now, I figured. A poor kid from Brooklyn without much going for him, and who cared about a couple of trashy paperbacks anyway?

"So I held on to the wallet. Every once in a while I'd get a little urge to send it back to him, but I kept delaying and never did anything about it. Then Christmas rolls around and I'm stuck with nothing to do. The boss usually invites me over to his house to spend the day, but that year he and his family were down in Florida visiting relatives. So I'm sitting in my apartment that morning feeling a little sorry for myself, and then I see Robert Goodwin's wallet lying on a shelf in the kitchen. I figure what the hell, why not do something nice for once, and I put on my coat and go out to return the wallet in person.

"The address was over in Boerum Hill, somewhere in the projects. It was freezing out that day, and I remember getting lost a few times trying to find the right building. Everything looks the same in that place, and you keep going over the same ground thinking you're somewhere else. Anyway, I finally get to the apartment I'm looking for and ring the bell. Nothing happens. I assume no one's there, but I try again just to make sure. I wait a little longer, and just when I'm about to give up, I hear someone shuffling to the door. An old woman's voice asks who's there, and I say I'm looking for Robert Goodwin. 'Is that you, Robert?' the old woman says, and then she undoes about fifteen locks and opens the door.

"She has to be at least eighty, maybe ninety years old, and the first thing I notice about her is that she's blind. 'I knew you'd come, Robert,' she says. 'I knew you wouldn't forget your Granny Ethel on Christmas.' And then she opens her arms as if she's about to hug me.

"I didn't have much time to think, you understand. I had to say something real fast, and before I knew what was happening, I could hear the words coming out of my mouth. 'That's right, Granny Ethel,' I said. 'I came back to see you on Christmas.' Don't ask me why I did it. I don't have any idea. Maybe I didn't want to disappoint her or something, I don't know. It just came out that way, and then this old woman was suddenly hugging me there in front of the door, and I was hugging her back.

"I didn't exactly say that I was her grandson. Not in so many words, at least, but that was the implication. I wasn't trying to trick her, though. It was like a game we'd both decided to play—without having to discuss the rules. I mean, that woman knew I wasn't her grandson Robert. She was old and dotty, but she wasn't so far gone that she couldn't tell the difference between a stranger and her own flesh and blood. But it made her happy to pretend, and since I had nothing better to do anyway, I was happy to go along with her.

"So we went into the apartment and spent the day together. The place was a real dump, I might add, but what else can you expect from a blind woman who does her own housekeeping? Every time she asked me a question about how I was, I would lie to her. I told her I'd found a good job working in a cigar store, I told her I was about to get married, I told her a hundred pretty stories, and she made like she believed every one of them. 'That's fine, Robert,' she would say, nodding her head and smiling. 'I always knew things would work out for you.'

"After a while, I started getting pretty hungry. There didn't seem to be much food in the house, so I went out to a store in the neighbourhood and brought back a mess of stuff. A precooked chicken, vegetable soup, a bucket of potato salad, a chocolate cake, all kinds of things. Ethel had a couple of bottles of wine stashed in her bedroom, and so between us we managed to put together a fairly decent Christmas dinner. We both got a little tipsy from the wine, I remember, and after the meal was over we went out to sit in the living room, where the chairs were more comfortable. I had to take a pee, so I excused myself and went to the bathroom down the hall. That's where things took yet another turn. It was ditsy enough doing my little jig as Ethel's grandson, but what I did next was positively crazy, and I've never forgiven myself for it.

"I go into the bathroom, and stacked up against the wall next to the shower, I see a pile of six or seven cameras. Brand-new thirty-five-millimetre cameras, still in their boxes, top-quality merchandise. I figure this is the work of the real Robert, a storage place for one of his recent hauls. I've never taken a picture in my life, and I've certainly never stolen anything, but the moment I see those cameras sitting in the bathroom, I decide I want one of them for myself. Just like that. And without even stopping to think about it, I tuck one of the boxes under my arm and go back to the living room.

"I couldn't have been gone for more than a few minutes, but in that time Granny Ethel had fallen asleep in her chair. Too much Chianti, I suppose. I went into the kitchen to wash the dishes, and she slept on through the whole racket, snoring like a baby. There didn't seem to be any point in disturbing her, so I decided to leave. I couldn't even write a note to say good-bye, seeing that she was blind and all, and so I just left. I put her grandson's wallet on the table, picked up the camera again, and walked out of the apartment. And that's the end of the story."

"Did you ever go back to see her?" I asked.

"Once," he said. "About three or four months later. I felt so bad about stealing the camera, I hadn't even used it yet. I finally made up my mind to return it, but Ethel wasn't there anymore. I don't know what happened to her, but someone else had moved into the apartment, and he couldn't tell me where she was."

"She probably died."

"Yeah, probably."

"Which means that she spent her last Christmas with you."

"I guess so. I never thought of it that way."

"It was a good deed, Auggie. It was a nice thing you did for her."

"I lied to her, and then I stole from her. I don't see how you can call that a good deed."

"You made her happy. And the camera was stolen anyway. It's not as if the person you took it from really owned it."

"Anything for art, eh, Paul?"

"I wouldn't say that. But at least you've put the camera to good use."

"And now you've got your Christmas story, don't you?"

"Yes," I said. "I suppose I do."

I paused for a moment, studying Auggie as a wicked grin spread across his face. I couldn't be sure, but the look in his eyes at that moment was so mysterious, so fraught with the glow of some inner delight, that it suddenly occurred to me that he had made the whole thing up. I was about to ask him if he'd been putting me on, but then I realized he would never tell. I had been tricked into believing him, and that was the only thing that mattered. As long as there's one person to believe it, there's no story that can't be true.

"You're an ace, Auggie," I said. "Thanks for being so helpful."

"Any time," he answered, still looking at me with that maniacal light in his eyes. "After all, if you can't share your secrets with your friends, what kind of a friend are you?"

"I guess I owe you one."

"No you don't. Just put it down the way I told it to you, and you don't owe me a thing."

"Except the lunch."

"That's right. Except the lunch."

I returned Auggie's smile with a smile of my own, and then I called out to the waiter and asked for the cheque.

Horatio's Trick

by

ANN BEATTIE

A FEW DAYS BEFORE CHRISTMAS, the U.P.S. truck stopped in front of Charlotte's house. Charlotte's ex-husband, Edward, had sent a package to her and a larger package to their son, Nicholas, who was nineteen. She opened hers immediately. It was the same present she had been sent the year before: a pound of chocolate-covered macadamia nuts, wrapped in silver striped paper, with a card that read "Merry Christmas from Edward Anderson and family." This time, Edward's wife had written the card; it wasn't his handwriting. Charlotte dumped the contents out onto the kitchen floor and played a game of marbles, pinging one nut into another and watching them roll in different directions. She'd had a few bourbons, not too many, while Nicholas was off at the gas station getting an oil change. Before she began the game of chocolate marbles, she pulled the kitchen door closed; otherwise, Horatio, the dog, would come running in at full tilt, as he always did when he heard any sound in the kitchen. Horatio was a newcomer to the house——a holiday visitor. He belonged to Nicholas's girl-friend, Andrea, who had flown to Florida for a Christmas visit with her parents, and since Nicholas was going to drive here for *his* Christmas, he had brought Horatio along, too.

Nicholas was a junior at Notre Dame. He had his father's wavy hair—Edward hated that kind of hair, which he called kinky—but not his blue eyes. Charlotte had always been sad about that. Nicholas had her eyes: ordinary brown eyes that she loved to look at, although she could not say why she found them so interesting. She had to remember not to look at him too long. Only that morning he had said at breakfast, "Charlotte, it's a little unnerving to roll out of bed and be stared at." He often called her Charlotte now. She had moved to Charlottesville six years ago, and although it was a very sociable town and she had met quite a few people (she had finally reached the point with most of them where they had stopped making jokes about a Charlotte coming to live in Charlottesville), she didn't know anyone with a son Nicholas's age. Oddly enough, she knew two women about her age who were having babies. One of them seemed slightly abashed; the other was ecstatic. It was a scandal (people parodied themselves in Charlottesville by calling scandals—which they did not believe in—*"scandales"*) that the ecstatic forty-one-year-old mother-to-be, a recent graduate of the University of Virginia Law School, was not married. Other gossip had it that she was forty-three.

Charlotte worked as a legal secretary for an old and prestigious law firm in town. She had left New York after she and Edward separated a dozen years ago, and had moved to Washington, where she enrolled in American University to resume her B.A. studies in preparation for entering law school. Nicholas went to Lafayette School, and was taken care of on the weekends by her parents, who lived in the Cleveland Park area, while Charlotte sequestered herself and studied almost around the clock. But there were problems: Nicholas had a hard time making friends in his new school; also, the bitterness between Charlotte and Edward seemed to escalate when there was actual distance between them, so Charlotte was constantly distracted by Edward's accusatory phone calls and his total lack of faith in her ability to get a degree. It had all been too much, and finally she decided to abandon her plans of becoming a lawyer and became a legal secretary instead. Edward began to make visits, taking the Metroliner from New York to Washington; one day he turned up with a dark-haired, dark-eyed young woman who wore a bit too much jewellery. Soon after that they were married. The "and family" part of the gift card referred to her daughter from a previous marriage. Charlotte had never met the child.

Charlotte looked out the back window. Horatio was in the yard, sniffing the wind. Nicholas had stopped on the way south and bought a stake and a chain to keep Horatio under control during the visit. Actually, the dog seemed happy enough, and wasn't very interested in the birds or the occasional cat that turned up in Charlotte's yard. Right now, Nicholas was upstairs, talking to Andrea on the phone. Someone throwing a life ring to a drowning child could not have been more energetic and more dedicated than Nicholas was to the girl.

Charlotte poured another bourbon, into which she plopped three ice cubes, and sat on the stool facing the counter, where she kept the telephone and pads of paper and bills to be paid and whatever odd button needed to be sewn back on. There were also two batteries there that were either dead or unused (she couldn't remember anymore) and paper clips (although she could not remember the last time she used a paper clip at home), a few corks, a little bottle of Visine, some loose Aspirins, and a broken bracelet. There was a little implement called a lemon zester that she bought from a door-to-door salesman. She suddenly picked it up and pretended to be conducting, because Nicholas had just put on Handel upstairs. He always played music to drown out his phone conversations.

"For the Lord God omni-potent ..." She had forgotten to get back to the Tazewells about Father Curnan's birthday party. She had promised that she would find out whether Nicholas would come, and then call back. She had meant to ask Nicholas at breakfast but had forgotten. Now she suddenly saw that Horatio might be her salvation. Whenever he came indoors he ran through the house in an excited fashion, and if that happened to get Nicholas off the phone, who would blame her? She went outdoors and, shivering, quickly unhitched the dog and led him in. His fur was soft and cold.

He was glad to see her, as usual. The minute they were inside, he bounded up the stairs. She stood at the bottom, listening to Horatio's panting outside Nicholas's door, and then, sure enough, the door banged open. Nicholas was at the top of the stairs, staring down. He did look as if he had been rescuing a drowning child: dishevelled, with not an extra second to spare. "What's he doing inside?" he asked.

"It's cold out," she said. "Nicky, the Tazewells are having a dinner for Father Curnan's birthday tonight. Will you go with me?"

The sopranos soared in unison. She must have looked alarmed—surely he noticed that she had suddenly put both hands on the banister railing—and perhaps that was why he quickly nodded yes and turned away.

Back in the kitchen, with her boots off, Charlotte stroked the dog with one stockinged foot, and in response he shot up and went into his little routine, his famous trick. Almost complacently, he sat and extended his right paw. Then he rubbed his snout down that leg, put the paw back on the floor, and lifted and rubbed the left paw in the same fashion. He sneezed, turned twice in a circle to his left, and then came over to be patted. The trick meant nothing, of course, but it never failed as a crowd pleaser. Sometimes Charlotte had even come into a room and found him doing it all by himself. "Okay, you're wonderful," she whispered to Horatio now, scratching his ears.

She heard Nicholas's footsteps on the stairs and called, "Where are you going?" It dismayed her that he kept to himself so much.

He stayed upstairs most of the day studying, or he talked on the telephone. He already had on his coat and scarf.

Instead of hanging them in the hall closet, he kept them up in his room. He kept everything there, as if he were forever on the point of packing up for some quick journey.

"Back to the garage," he said. "Don't get upset. It's no big thing. I asked them yesterday if they had time to line the rear brakes, and they said they could fit me in this afternoon."

"Why would that upset me?" she said.

"Because you'd think the car was unsafe. You've always got your images of disaster."

"What are you talking about?" she said. She was addressing Christmas cards, trying to convince herself that there might be some truth to Better late than never.

"When I had the broken thumb, you carried on as if I was a quadriplegic."

He was talking about the year before—a bicycling injury, when he'd skidded on some icy pavement. She shouldn't have flown out to Indiana, but she missed him and she hated the idea of his being hurt. College was the first time he had ever lived away from her. She hadn't made a scene—she had just gone there and called from a motel. (It was in the back of her mind, she had to admit now, that the trip might also be a chance for her to meet Andrea, the off-campus student who had begun to turn up in Nicholas's letters.) Nicholas was horrified that she'd come all that distance. He was fine, of course—he had a cast on his left hand was all—and he had said almost angrily that he couldn't tell her anything without eliciting a huge overreaction.

"You didn't forget the dinner, did you?" she said now.

He turned and looked at her, "We already talked about that," he said. "Seven o'clock—is that right?"

"Right," she said. She began to address another envelope, trying to pass it off.

"It will take approximately one hour at the garage," he said.

Then he left—the way his father so often had left—without saying good-bye.

She wrote a few more cards, then called the florist's to see whether they had been able to locate bird-of-paradise flowers in New York. She wanted to send them to Martine, her oldest friend, who had just returned from a vacation in Key West to the cold winds of the Upper East Side. Charlotte was happy to hear that someone had them, and that a dozen had gone out. "I thought we'd have good luck," the woman at the florist's said. "If we couldn't locate some paradise in New York, I don't know where paradise *could* be tracked down." She had a young voice—and after Charlotte hung up it occurred to her that she might have been the VanZells' daughter, who had just been hired by a florist in town after having been suspended from college because of some trouble with drugs. Charlotte clasped her hands and touched them to her lips, in one of her silent prayers to the Virgin: No drugs for Nicholas, ever. Protect my Nicholas from harm.

The Tazewells' sunken dining room was done in Chinese red, and against the far wall there was an enormous glass china press edged in brass, illuminated from within in a way that flooded the cut glass with light. The shelves were also glass, and their edges sparkled and gleamed with a prism-bright clarity. Charlotte was not surprised to see that Martin Smith, who ran the Jefferson Dreams catering service, was there himself to oversee things. People in Charlottesville followed through—even fun wasn't left totally to chance—and

Charlotte liked that. Edith Stanton, the host's cousin, almost Charlotte's first friend when she had moved here to Charlottesville (she could remember their first lunch together, and Edith's considering gaze above the seafood salad: was this nice-looking new single woman who was working down at Burwell, McKee going to *fit in?*), was talking with Father Curnan. Charlotte looked hard at his face—the round, open face of an adolescent, except that there were deep lines around his eyes—and saw on it the look she called Bemused Monsignor. He could nod and smile and murmur his "not to be *believed*" as Edith went on in her breathless way (surely she was telling him again about her session in a bodybuilding shop for women out in Santa Barbara last summer), but his interest was feigned. Edith was not a Catholic, and she could not know the sort of complicated, surprising man Philip Curnan really was. He had told Charlotte once that after working his way through Cornell (his father had an auto-repair garage in upstate New York somewhere), he had ridden across the country on a Harley-Davidson, while searching his soul about his desire to enter the priesthood. Charlotte smiled now, remembering the confidence. Just last week he had told her that there were still times when he longed to get back on a motorcycle; his helmet was still on the top shelf in his bedroom closet.

A server passed by, and Charlotte finally got a drink. Surveying the room, she was pleased to see that Nicholas was talking to the McKays' daughter, Angela, home from Choate for Christmas. Charlotte thought of the day, a month before, when Angela's mother, Janet, had consulted with the head of Burwell, McKee about filing for legal separation from Chaz, her husband. Chaz, a lawyer himself, stood with his arm around his wife's waist, talking to a couple Charlotte didn't know. Perhaps Chaz still did not know that she had made inquiries about getting a divorce. M.L., the hostess, passed in her peach-coloured gown, and Charlotte touched her shoulder and whispered, "It's wonderful. Thank you for having us." M.L. gave her a hug and said, "I must be somewhere *else* if I didn't even say hello." As she moved away, Charlotte smelled her perfume—at night, M.L. always wore Joy—and heard the rustle of silk.

Martin VanZell came up to Charlotte and began talking to her about his arthritic knee. He tapped a bottle in his breast pocket. "All doctors dote on Advil," he said. "Ask any of them. Their eyes light up. You'd think it was Lourdes in a bottle. Pull off the top, take out the cotton, and worship. I'm not kidding you." He noticed that he seemed to have caught Father Curnan's attention. "Meaning no disrespect," he said.

"Who was being slighted?" Father Curnan said. "The pharmaceutical company?" His eyes met Charlotte's for a second, and he winked before he looked away. He speared a shrimp and ate it, waving away the napkin a server extended in her other hand.

Frankie Melkins suddenly swooped in front of Charlotte, kissing the air above her cheek. Frankie had been in a bad car accident last New Year's, and had returned to the Church after Father Curnan's hospital visits. That had been much talked about, as well as the fact that the case was settled out of court, which led people to believe that Frankie had got a lot of money. As Frankie and Martin began to compare painkiller stories, Charlotte drifted away and went to the side door, where someone had been knocking for quite some time. Oren and Billy! Oren could be such a devil. He gave drums to his nephews for Christmas and once threw rice during a party that wasn't at all like a wedding. The minute she opened the door, he gave her a bear hug.

"What on earth!" M.L. said, staring out the door after the two men had come in. "Why, I'll bet Frankie has left the cabdriver out there waiting." She began to wave her arms wildly, whistling to him. She turned to Charlotte. "Can you believe it?" she said. She looked beyond Charlotte to Frankie. "Frankie!" she called. "Were you going to leave your cabdriver out in the driveway all night? There's plenty of food. Tell him to come in and have something to eat."

Father Curnan stood talking to the host, Dan Tazewell. They were looking at the mantel, discussing a small drawing of a nude that was framed and propped there. She overheard Father Curnan lamenting the fact that the artist had recently left the art department at the university and gone back to New York to live. Charlotte accepted another drink from a server, then looked back at Father Curnan. He was scrutinizing the drawing. On her way to the bathroom, Charlotte heard Nicholas telling Angela McKay details about hand surgery, spreading his thumb and first finger wide. Angela looked at the space between his fingers as though staring at some fascinating thing squirming beneath a microscope. His hand? Had Nicholas had hand surgery?

One of the servers was coming out of the bathroom as Charlotte got to the door. She was glad it was empty, because she had had two drinks before she left the house and another at the party. She put her glass on the back of the sink before she used the toilet. What if she left the drink there? Would anybody notice and think things?

The bathroom was tiny, and the little casement window had been flipped open. Still, Charlotte could smell cigarette smoke. She reached up and pulled the window closed, hooked it, and rubbed her hand down her new black shirt. *"Wheet,"* she said, imitating the sound the silk made. "Someone's in there," she heard a voice say. She took a sip of her drink, then unhooked the window and pushed it out again. The sky was black—no stars visible across the small part of the sky she could see. There was a huge wind out there, like an animal loose in the trees. She turned and began to wash her hands. The spigot reminded her of a fountain she had seen years ago in Rome, when she was first married. It had bothered her that so many things there were exaggerated but not full-form: massive marble heads—lions and gargoyles, rippling manes, mythic beasts spewing water—but whole bodies were usually to be found only on the angels and cherubs. She dried her hands. That couldn't be true—that couldn't have been what all the fountains looked like. What am I doing thinking about fountains in Rome, she thought.

When she opened the door, she saw Martin VanZell in the dim hallway, his white face a ghostly contrast to his dark pin-striped suit. "Great party, huh?" he said. She had stopped outside the door, dead centre. It took her a minute to realize that she was staring, and blocking his way. "It is every year," she heard herself saying, and then he passed by and she turned toward the noise of the party. A man whose wife ran one of the nurseries on Route 29 came over as she walked down the two steps into the room. "Charlotte, you just missed my wife here, losing track again. She was telling Father Curnan—hey, he's gone off again—she thought Chernobyl was this year. It was *last* year. It happened in the spring."

"Well, I believe you," his wife said, with a false smile. "Why were you bringing it up, Arthur?"

Nicholas came up to Charlotte just as the host rang a bell and everyone fell silent.

"It's not Santa. It's the annual ringing out of one year for Father Curnan and a ringing in of the new," the host said cheerfully. He rang the bell again. "Because today he's our birthday boy again, and if he's going to keep getting older we're going to keep noticing it."

Father Curnan raised his glass, blushing. "Thank you all—" he began, but the host clanged the bell again, drowning him out. "Oh, no, you don't. You don't make us take time out from the party to hear a speech," the host said. "Time for that on Sunday, Philip, when you've got your captive audience. But happy birthday, Father Phil, and on with the ball!" People laughed and cheered.

Charlotte saw that someone's glass had made a white ring on the tabletop between two mats that had been put there. Janet's husband came up and started to talk about the cost of malpractice insurance, and then Charlotte felt Nicholas's hand on her elbow. "It's late," he said. "We should go." She started to introduce him to Janet's husband, but Nicholas steered them away and into a bedroom where two temporary clothes racks stood bulging with coats and furs. More coats made a great mound on the bed. Then suddenly she and Nicholas were standing with M.L. at the courtyard door, saying good-bye as they struggled into their coats and scarves. It was not until the door closed that Charlotte realized that she had not said a single word to Father Curnan. She turned and looked back at the house.

"Come on," Nicholas said. "He didn't even notice."

"Did you speak to him?" Charlotte said.

"No," Nicholas said. "I have nothing to say to him." He was walking toward their car, at the foot of the drive. She looked up.

"I only asked," she said.

He was too far ahead of her to hear. He held open the car door, and she got inside. He crossed in front of the car, and she realized that for some reason he was upset.

"All right," he said, getting in and slamming his door. "You're wronged. You're always wronged. Would you like it if I left the engine running and we both went back in and said good night to Father Curnan? Because that would be entirely proper. I could bow and you could curtsy."

Charlotte wouldn't have thought that at that moment there was an emotion she could feel stronger than frustration. Wouldn't have thought it until she realized that what was smothering her was sadness. "No," she said quietly. "You're entirely right. He didn't even notice that we left."

The telephone rang twice, interrupting their Christmas Eve ceremony of tea and presents. Nicholas had been nice to her all day—even taking her out to lunch and trying to make her laugh by telling her stories about a professor of his who delivered all his lectures in the interrogative—because he knew he had jumped on her the night before, leaving the party. Each time the phone rang, Charlotte hoped it wasn't Andrea, because then he would drift away and be gone for ages. The first call was from Martine in New York, overjoyed by the flowers; the next was from M.L., to wish them a good Christmas and to say that she was sorry she had not really got to talk to them amid the confusion of the party.

Nicholas gave her a cashmere scarf and light-blue leather gloves. She gave him subscriptions to *Granta* and *Manhattan, inc.,* a heavy sweater with a hood, and a hundred-dollar cheque to get whatever else he wanted. His father gave him a paperweight that had belonged to his grandfather, and a wrist-watch that would apparently function even when launched from a rocket pad. When Nicholas went into the kitchen to boil up more water, she slid over on the couch and glanced at the gift card. It said, "Love, Dad," in Edward's nearly illegible script. Nicholas returned and opened his last present, which was from Melissa, his stepsister. It was a cheap ballpoint pen with a picture of a woman inside. When you turned the pen upside down her clothes disappeared.

"How old is Melissa?" Charlotte asked.

"Twelve or thirteen," he said.

"Does she look like her mother?"

"Not much," Nicholas said. "But she's really her sister's kid, and I never saw her sister."

"Her sister's child?" Charlotte took a sip of her tea, which was laced with bourbon. She held it in her mouth a second before swallowing.

"Melissa's mother killed herself when Melissa was just a baby. I guess her father didn't want her. Anyway, he gave her up."

"Her sister killed herself?" Charlotte said. She could feel her eyes widening. Suddenly she remembered the night before, the open window in the bathroom, the black sky, wind smacking her in the face.

"Awful, huh?" Nicholas said, lifting the tea bag out of the mug and lowering it to the saucer. "Hey, did I shock you? How come you didn't know that? I thought you were the one with a sense for disaster."

"What do you mean? I don't expect disaster. I don't know anything at all about Melissa. Naturally—"

"I know you don't know anything about her," he said, cutting her off. "Look—don't get mad at me, but I'm going to say this, because I think you aren't aware of what you do. You don't ask anything, because you're afraid of what every answer might be. It makes people reluctant to talk to you. Nobody wants to tell you things."

She took another sip of tea, which had gone tepid. Specks of loose tea leaves had floated to the top. "People talk to me," she said.

"I know they do," he said. "I'm not criticizing you. I'm just telling you that if you give off those vibes people are going to back off."

"Who backs off?" she said.

"Charlotte, I don't know everything about your life. I'm just telling you that you've never asked one thing about Dad's family in—what is it? Eleven years. You don't even mention my stepmother by name, ever. Her name is Joan. You don't want to know things, that's all."

He kicked a ball of wrapping paper away from his foot. "Let's drop it," he said. "What I'm saying is that you're always worried. You always think something's going to happen."

She started to speak, but took another drink instead. Maybe all mothers seemed oppressive when their children were teenagers. Didn't everyone say that parents could hardly do anything right during those years? That was what Father Curnan said—that although we may always try to do our best, we can't always expect to succeed. She wished Father Curnan were here right now. The whole evening would be different.

"Don't start sulking," Nicholas said. "You've been pissed off at me since last night, because I wouldn't go over and glad-hand Father Curnan. I hardly know him. I went to the party with you because you wanted me to. I don't practise anymore. I'm not a Catholic anymore. I don't believe what Father Curnan believes. Just because twenty years ago he had some doubt in his life and sorted it out, you think he's a hero. I don't think he's a hero. I don't care what he decided. That's fine for him, but it doesn't have anything to do with me."

"I never mention your loss of faith," she said. "Never. We don't discuss it."

"You don't have to say anything. What's awful is that you let me know that I've scared you. It's like I deliberately did something to you."

"What would you have me do?" she said. "How good an actress do you think I can be? I *do* worry. You don't give me credit for trying."

"You don't give *me* credit," he said. "I don't get credit for putting up with Dad's crap because I came to Virginia to be with you instead of going to his house. If I go to a stupid party for some priest who condescends to me by letter and says he'll pray for my soul, I don't get credit from you for going because you wanted me there. It never occurs to you. Instead I get told that I didn't shake his hand on the way out. If I had told you that the car was driving funny before I got it fixed, you would have bitten your nails some more and refused to ride in it. I wish you'd stop being scared. I wish you'd just stop."

She put the mug on the table and looked at him. He's a grown man, she thought. Taller than his father. Nicholas shook his head and walked out of the room. She heard him stomp upstairs. In a few minutes, the music began. He was playing rock, not Christmas music, and her heart seemed to pick up the relentless beat of the bass. Nicholas had scored his point. She was just sitting there, scared to death.

The sound jolted through her dream: once, twice, again. And then it awakened her. When she opened her eyes, it took her a minute to realize that she was in the living room in a chair, not in bed, and that she had been dreaming. The loud music had become part of her dream. She was squinting. Light flooded part of the living room—a painful brightness as constant as the noise. Out of the area of light she saw the shapes of crumpled gift wrappings by the tree. She passed one hand over her forehead, attempting to soothe the pain. The dog looked up from across the room. He yawned and walked over to the footstool beside her, wagging his tail.

The noise continued. It was from outside. A high-pitched squeal resonated in her chest. It had been snowing earlier. It must have gone on snowing. Someone's car was stuck out there.

The dog padded with her to the front window. Beyond the huge oak tree in the front yard, there was a car at an odd angle, with its headlights aimed toward the house. A front and back wheel were up on the hill. Whoever was driving had missed the turn and skidded onto her property. There was a man bending over by the side of the car. Somebody else, in the driver's seat, gunned the engine and wheels spun again. "Wait for me to move! Wait till I'm out of the way, for Christ's sake," the man outside the car hollered. The wheels screamed again, drowning out the rest of what he said.

Charlotte got her coat from the hall closet and snapped on the outside light. She nudged the dog back inside, and went carefully down the front walkway. Snow seeped into one shoe.

"What's going on?" she called, clasping her hands across her chest.

"Nothin'," the man said, as if all this were the most normal thing in the world. "I'm trying to give us something to roll back on, so's we can get some traction."

She looked down and saw a large piece of flagstone from her wall jammed under one back wheel. Again the man raced the engine.

"He's gonna get it," the man said.

"Do you want me to call a tow truck?" she said, shivering.

There were no lights in any nearby windows. She could not believe that she was alone in this, that half the neighbourhood was not awake.

"We got it! We got it!" the man said, crouching as the driver raced the engine again. The tire screamed on the flagstone, but the car did not move. Suddenly she smelled something sweet—liquor on the man's breath. The man sprang up and banged on the car window. "Ease up, ease up, God damn it," he said. "Don't you know how to drive?"

The driver rolled down the window and began to curse. The other man hit his hand on the roof of the car. Again, the driver gassed it and tires spun and screamed.

For the first time, she felt frightened. The man began to tug at the door on the driver's side, and Charlotte turned away and walked quickly toward the house. This has got to stop, she thought. *It has got to stop.* She opened the door. Horatio was looking at her. It was as though he had been waiting and now he simply wanted an answer.

Above the screeching of tires, she heard her voice, speaking into the telephone, giving the police the information and her address. Then she stepped farther back into the dark kitchen, over on the left side, where she could not be seen through the front windows or through the glass panels that stretched to each side of the front door. She could hear both men yelling. Where was Nicholas? How could he still be asleep? She hoped that the dog wouldn't bark and wake him, now that he'd managed to sleep through so much. She took a glass out of the cabinet and started toward the shelf where she kept the bourbon, but then stopped, realizing that she might he seen. She pulled open the refrigerator door and found an opened bottle of wine. She pulled the cork out and filled the glass half full and took a long drink.

Someone knocked on the door. Could it be the police—so soon? How could they have come so quickly and silently? She wasn't sure until, long after the knocking stopped, she peered down the hallway and saw, through the narrow rectangle of glass, a police car with its revolving red and blue lights.

At almost the same instant, she touched something on her lapel and looked down, surprised. It was Santa: a small pin, in the shape of Santa's head, complete with a little red hat, pudgy cheeks, and a ripply white plastic beard. A tiny cord with a bell at the bottom dangled from it. Nicholas must have gone back to the store where they had seen it on his first day home. She had pointed it out on a tray of Christmas pins and ornaments. She told him she'd had the exact same pin—the Santa's head, with a bell—back when she was a girl. He must have gone back to the store later to buy it.

She tiptoed upstairs in the dark, and the dog followed. Nicholas was snoring in his bedroom. She went down the hall to her room, at the front of the house, and without turning on the light, sat on her bed to look out the nearest window at the scene below. The man she had spoken to was emptying his pockets onto the hood of the police car. She saw the beam of the policeman's flashlight sweep up and down his body, watched while he unbuttoned his coat and pulled it open wide in response to something the policeman said. The other man was being led to the police car. She could hear his words—"my car, *it's my car, I tell you*"—but she couldn't make out whole sentences, couldn't figure out what the driver was objecting to so strongly. When both men were in the car, one of the policemen turned and began to walk toward the house. She got up quickly and went downstairs, one hand sliding along the slick banister; the dog came padding down behind her.

She opened the door just before the policeman knocked. Cold flooded the hallway. She saw steam coming out of the car's exhaust pipe. There was steam from her own breath, and the policeman's.

"Could I come in, ma'am?" he asked, and she stood back and then shut the door behind him, closing out the cold. The dog was on the landing.

"He's real good, or else he's not a guard dog to begin with," the policeman said. His cheeks were red. He was younger than she had thought at first.

"They were going to keep that racket up all night," she said.

"You did the right thing," he said. His head bent, he began to fill out a form on his clipboard. "I put down about fifty dollars of damage to your wall," he said.

She said nothing.

"It didn't do too much damage," the policeman said. "You can call in the morning and get a copy of this report if you need it."

"Thank you," she said.

He touched his cap. "Less fun than digging out Santa and his reindeer," he said, looking back at the car, tilted onto the lawn. "Have a good Christmas, ma'am," he said.

He turned and left, and she closed the door. With the click, she remembered everything. Earlier in the evening she had gone upstairs to tell Nicholas that she was sorry they had ended up in a quarrel on Christmas Eve. She had said she wanted him to come back downstairs. She had said it through the closed door, pleading with him, with her mouth close to the blank white panel of wood. When the door opened at last, and she saw Nicholas standing there in his pajamas, she had braced herself by touching her fingers to the doorframe, shocked to realize that he was real, and that he was there. He was looking into her eyes—a person she had helped to create—and yet, when he wasn't present, seeing him in her mind would have been as strange as visualizing a Christmas ornament out of season.

Nicholas's hair was rumpled, and he looked at her with a tired, exasperated frown. "Charlotte," he said, "why didn't you come up hours ago? I went down and let the dog in. You've been out like a light half the night. Nobody's supposed to say that you drink. Nobody's supposed to see you. If you don't ask any questions, we're supposed to stop noticing you. Nobody's supposed to put you on the spot, are they? You only talk to Father Curnan, and he prays for you."

Downstairs in the dark hallway now, she shuddered, remembering how she had felt when he said that. She had gone back downstairs and huddled in the chair—all right, she had had too much to drink—but it was she who had woken up and been alert to squealing tires and people screaming, and Nicholas who had slept. Also, she thought, relief suddenly sweeping through her, he couldn't have been as angry as he seemed. He must have put the pin on her coat after the party—after their words in the car—or even when he had come downstairs to let Horatio in and had seen her asleep or passed out in the chair. He must have pinned it onto her lapel when the coat still hung in the closet, so she would find it there the next day. She had found it early, inadvertently, when she went out to investigate the car and the noise.

She looked at the dog. He was watching her, as usual.

"Are you real good, or not a guard dog to begin with?" she whispered. Then she pulled the cord. Santa's face lit up. She pulled the cord again, several times, smiling as the dog watched. Over her shoulder, she looked at the kitchen clock. It was three-fifty Christmas morning.

"Come on," she whispered, pulling the cord another time. "I've done my trick. Now you do yours."

Christmas Is a Sad Season for the Poor

by

JOHN CHEEVER

CHRISTMAS IS A SAD SEASON. The phrase came to Charlie an instant after the alarm clock had waked him, and named for him an amorphous depression that had troubled him all the previous evening. The sky outside his window was black. He sat up in bed and pulled the light chain that hung in front of his nose. Christmas is a very sad day of the year, he thought. Of all the millions of people in New York, I am practically the only one who has to get up in the cold black of 6 A.M. on Christmas Day in the morning; I am practically the only one.

He dressed, and when he went downstairs from the top floor of the rooming house in which he lived, the only sounds he heard were the coarse sounds of sleep; the only lights burning were lights that had been forgotten. Charlie ate some breakfast in an all-night lunchwagon and took an Elevated train uptown. From Third Avenue, he walked over to Sutton Place. The neighbourhood was dark. House after house put into the shine of the street lights a wall of black windows. Millions and millions were sleeping, and this general loss of consciousness generated an impression of abandonment, as if this were the fall of the city, the end of time. He opened the iron-and-glass doors of the apartment building where he had been working for six months as an elevator operator, and went through the elegant lobby to a locker room at the back. He put on a striped vest with brass buttons, a false ascot, a pair of pants with a light-blue stripe on the seam, and a coat. The night elevator man was dozing on the little bench in the car. Charlie woke him. The night elevator man told him thickly that the day doorman had been taken sick and wouldn't be in that day. With the doorman sick, Charlie wouldn't have any relief for lunch, and a lot of people would expect him to whistle for cabs.

CHARLIE had been on duty a few minutes when 14 rang—a Mrs. Hewing, who, he happened to know, was kind of immoral. Mrs. Hewing hadn't been to bed yet, and she got into the elevator wearing a long dress under her fur coat. She was followed by her two funny-looking dogs. He took her down and watched her go out into the dark and take her dogs to the curb. She was outside for only a few minutes. Then she came in and he took her up to 14 again. When she got off the elevator, she said, "Merry Christmas, Charlie."

"Well, it isn't much of a holiday for me, Mrs. Hewing," he said. "I think Christmas is a very sad season of the year. It isn't that people around here ain't generous—I mean, I got plenty of tips—but, you see, I live alone in a furnished room and I don't have any family or anything, and Christmas isn't much of a holiday for me."

"I'm sorry, Charlie," Mrs. Hewing said. "I don't have any family myself. It is kind of sad when you're alone, isn't it?" She called her dogs and followed them into her apartment. He went down.

It was quiet then, and Charlie lighted a cigarette. The heating plant in the basement encompassed the building at that hour in a regular and profound vibration, and the sullen noises of arriving steam heat began to resound, first in the lobby and then to reverberate up through all the sixteen stories, but this was a mechanical awakening, and it didn't lighten his loneliness or his petulance. The black air outside the glass doors had begun to turn blue, but the blue light seemed to have no source; it appeared in the middle of the air. It was a tearful light, and as it picked out the empty street he wanted to cry. Then a cab drove up, and the Walsers got out, drunk and dressed in evening clothes, and he took them up to their penthouse. The Walsers got him to brooding about the difference between his life in a furnished room and the lives of the people overhead. It was terrible.

Then the early churchgoers began to ring, but there were only three of these that morning. A few more went off to church at eight o'clock, but the majority of the building remained unconscious, although the smell of bacon and coffee had begun to drift into the elevator shaft.

At a little after nine, a nursemaid came down with a child. Both the nursemaid and the child had a deep tan and had just returned, he knew, from Bermuda. He had never been to Bermuda. He, Charlie, was a prisoner, confined eight hours a day to a six-by-eight elevator cage, which was confined, in turn, to a sixteen-story shaft. In one building or another, he had made his living as an elevator operator for ten years. He estimated the average trip at about an eighth of a mile, and where he thought of the thousands of miles he had travelled, when he thought that he might have driven the car through the mists above the Caribbean and set it down on some coral beach in Bermuda, he held the narrowness of his travels against his passengers, as if it were not the nature of the elevator but the pressure of their lives that confined him, as if they had clipped his wings.

He was thinking about this when the DePauls, on 9, rang. They wished him a merry Christmas.

"Well, it's nice of you to think of me," he said as they descended, "but it isn't much of a holiday for me. Christmas is a sad season when you're poor. I live alone in a furnished room. I don't have any family."

"Who do you have dinner with, Charlie?" Mrs. DePaul asked.

"I don't have any Christmas dinner," Charlie said. "I just get a sandwich."

"Oh, Charlie!" Mrs. DePaul was a stout woman with an impulsive heart, and Charlie's plaint struck at her holiday mood as if she had been caught in a cloudburst. "I do wish we could share our Christmas dinner with you, you know," she said. "I come from Vermont, you know, and when I was a child, you know, we always used to have a great many people at our table. The mailman, you know, and the schoolteacher, and just anybody who didn't have any family of their own, you know, and I wish we could share our dinner with you the way we used to, you know, and I don't see any reason why we can't. We can't have you at the table, you know, because you couldn't leave the elevator—could you?—but just as soon as Mr. DePaul has carved the goose, I'll give you a ring, and I'll arrange a tray for you, you know, and I want you to come up and at least share our Christmas dinner."

Charlie thanked them, and their generosity surprised him, but he wondered if, with the arrival of friends and relatives, they wouldn't forget their offer.

Then old Mrs. Gadshill rang, and when she wished him a merry Christmas, he hung his head.

"It isn't much of a holiday for me, Mrs. Gadshill," he said. "Christmas is a sad season if you're poor. You see, I don't have any family. I live alone in a furnished room."

"I don't have any family either, Charlie," Mrs. Gadshill said. She spoke with a pointed lack of petulance, but her grace was forced. "That is, I don't have any children with me today. I have three children and seven grandchildren, but none of them can see their way to coming East for Christmas with me. Of course, I understand their problems. I know that it's diffi-cult to travel with children during the holidays, although I always seemed to manage it when I was their age, but people feel differently, and we mustn't condemn them for the things we can't understand. But I know how you feel, Charlie. I haven't any family either. I'm just as lonely as you."

Mrs. Gadshill's speech didn't move him. Maybe she was lonely, but she had a ten-room apartment and three servants and bucks and bucks and diamonds and diamonds, and there were plenty of poor kids in the slums who would be happy at a chance at the food her cook threw away. Then he thought about poor kids. He sat down on a chair in the lobby and thought about them.

They got the worst of it. Beginning in the fall, there was all this excitement about Christmas and how it was a day for them. After Thanksgiving, they couldn't miss it. It was fixed so they couldn't miss it. The wreaths and decorations everywhere, and bells ringing, and trees in the park, and Santa Clauses on every corner, and pictures in the magazines and newspapers and on every wall and window in the city told them that if they were good, they would get what they wanted. Even if they couldn't read, they couldn't miss it. They couldn't miss it even if they were blind. It got into the air the poor kids inhaled. Every time they took a walk, they'd see all the expensive toys in the store windows, and they'd write letters to Santa Claus, and their mothers and fathers would promise to mail them, and after the kids had gone to sleep, they'd burn the letters in the stove. And when it came Christmas morning, how could you explain it, how could you tell them that Santa Claus only visited the rich, that he didn't know about the good? How could you face them when all you had to give them was a balloon or a lollipop?

On the way home from work a few nights earlier, Charlie had seen a woman and a little girl going down Fifty-ninth

Street. The little girl was crying. He guessed she was crying, he knew she was crying, because she'd seen all the things in the toy-store windows and couldn't understand why none of them were for her. Her mother did housework, he guessed, or maybe was a waitress, and he saw them going back to a room like his, with green walls and no heat, on Christmas Eve, to eat a can of soup. And he saw the little girl hang up her ragged stocking and fall asleep, and he saw the mother looking through her purse for something to put into the stocking— This reverie was interrupted by a bell on 11. He went up, and Mr. and Mrs. Fuller were waiting. When they wished him a merry Christmas, he said, "Well, it isn't much of a holiday for me, Mrs. Fuller. Christmas is a sad season when you're poor."

"Do you have any children, Charlie?" Mrs. Fuller asked.

"Four living," he said. "Two in the grave." The majesty of his lie overwhelmed him. "Mrs. Leary's a cripple," he added.

"How sad, Charlie," Mrs. Fuller said. She started out of the elevator when it reached the lobby, and then she turned. "I want to give your children some presents, Charlie," she said. "Mr. Fuller and I are going to pay a call now, but when we come back, I want to give you some things for your children."

He thanked her. Then the bell rang on 4, and he went up to get the Westons.

"It isn't much of a holiday for me," he told them when they wished him a merry Christmas. "Christmas is a sad season when you're poor. You see, I live alone in a furnished room."

"Poor Charlie," Mrs. Weston said. "I know just how you feel. During the war, when Mr. Weston was away, I was all alone at Christmas. I didn't have any Christmas dinner or a tree or anything. I just scrambled myself some eggs and sat there and cried." Mr. Weston, who had gone into the lobby, called impatiently to his wife. "I know just how you feel, Charlie," Mrs. Weston said.

BY NOON, the climate in the elevator shaft had changed from bacon and coffee to poultry and game, and the house, like an enormous and complex homestead, was absorbed in the preparations for a domestic feast. The children and their nursemaids had all returned from the Park. Grandmothers and aunts were arriving in limousines. Most of the people who came through the lobby were carrying packages wrapped in coloured paper, and were wearing their best furs and new clothes. Charlie continued to complain to most of the tenants when they wished him a merry Christmas, changing his story from the lonely bachelor to the poor father, and back again, as his mood changed, but this outpouring of melancholy, and the sympathy it aroused, didn't make him feel any better.

At half past one, 9 rang, and when he went up, Mr. DePaul was standing in the door of their apartment holding a cocktail shaker and a glass. "Here's a little Christmas cheer, Charlie," he said, and he poured Charlie a drink. Then a maid appeared with a tray of covered dishes, and Mrs. DePaul came out of the living room. "Merry Christmas, Charlie," she said. "I had Mr. DePaul carve the goose early, so that you could have some, you know. I didn't want to put the dessert on the tray, because I was afraid it would melt, you know, so when we have our dessert, we'll call you."

"And what is Christmas without presents?" Mr. DePaul said, and he brought a large, flat box from the hall and laid it on top of the covered dishes.

"You people make it seem like a real Christmas to me," Charlie said. Tears started into his eyes. "Thank you, thank you."

"Merry Christmas! Merry Christmas!" they called, and they watched him carry his dinner and his present into the elevator. He took the tray and the box into the locker room when he got down. On the tray, there was a soup, some kind of creamed fish, and a serving of goose. The bell rang again, but before he answered it, he tore open the DePauls' box and saw that it held a dressing gown. Their generosity and their cocktail had begun to work on his brain, and he went jubilantly up to 12. Mrs. Gadshill's maid was standing in the door with a tray, and Mrs. Gadshill stood behind her. "Merry Christmas, Charlie!" she said. He thanked her, and tears came into his eyes again. On the way down, he drank off the glass of sherry on Mrs. Gadshill's tray. Mrs. Gadshill's contribution was a mixed grill. He ate the lamb chop with his fingers. The bell was ringing again, and he wiped his face with a paper towel and went up to 11. "Merry Christmas, Charlie," Mrs. Fuller said, and she was standing in the door with her arms full of packages wrapped in silver paper, just like a picture in an advertisement, and Mr. Fuller was beside her with an arm around her, and they both looked as if they were going to cry. "Here are some things I want you to take home to your children," Mrs. Fuller said. "And here's something for Mrs. Leary and here's something for you. And if you want to take these things out to the elevator, we'll have your dinner ready for you in a minute." He carried the things into the elevator and came back for the tray. "Merry Christmas, Charlie!" both of the Fullers called after him as he closed the door. He took their dinner and their presents into the locker room and tore open the box that was marked for him. There was an alligator wallet in it, with Mr. Fuller's initials in the corner. Their dinner was also goose, and he ate a piece of the meat with his fingers and was washing it down with a cocktail when the bell rang. He went up again. This time it was the Westons. "Merry Christmas, Charlie!" they said, and they gave him a cup of eggnog, a turkey dinner, and a present. Their gift was also a dressing gown. Then 7 rang, and when he went up, there was another dinner and some more toys. Then 14 rang, and when he went up, Mrs. Hewing was standing in the hall, in a kind of negligee, holding a pair of riding boots in one hand and some neckties in the other. She had been crying and drinking. "Merry Christmas, Charlie," she said tenderly. "I wanted to give you something, and I've been thinking about you all morning, and I've been all over the apartment, and these are the only things I could find that a man might want. These are the only things that Mr. Brewer left. I don't suppose you'd have any use for the riding boots, but wouldn't you like the neckties?" Charlie took the neckties and thanked her and hurried back to the car, for the elevator bell had rung three times.

BY THREE O'CLOCK, Charlie had fourteen dinners spread on the table and the floor of the locker room, and the bell kept ringing. Just as he started to eat one, he would have to go up and get another, and he was in the middle of the Parsons' roast beef when he had to go up and get the DePauls' dessert. He kept the door of the locker room closed, for he sensed that the quality of charity is exclusive and that his friends would have been disappointed to find that they were not the only ones to try to lessen his loneliness. There were goose, turkey, chicken, pheasant, grouse, and pigeon. There were trout and salmon, creamed scallops and oysters, lobster, crab meat, whitebait, and clams. There were plum puddings, mince pies, mousses, puddles of melted ice cream, layer cakes, *Torten,* éclairs, and two slices of Bavarian cream. He had dressing gowns, neckties, cuff links, socks, and handkerchiefs, and one of the tenants had asked for his neck size and then given him three green shirts. There were a glass teapot filled, the label said, with jasmine honey, four bottles of after-shave lotion, some alabaster bookends, and a dozen steak knives. The avalanche of charity he had precipitated filled the locker room and made him hesitant, now and then, as if he had touched some well-spring in the female heart that would bury him alive in food and dressing gowns. He had made almost no headway on the food, for all the servings were preternaturally large, as if loneliness had been counted on to generate in him a brutish appetite. Nor had he opened any of the presents that had been given to him for his imaginary children, but he had drunk everything they sent down, and around him were the dregs of Martinis, Manhattans, Old-Fashioneds, champagne-and-raspberry-shrub cocktails, eggnogs, Bronxes, and Side Cars.

His face was blazing. He loved the world, and the world loved him. When he thought back over his life, it appeared to him in a rich and wonderful light, full of astonishing experiences and unusual friends. He thought that his job as an elevator operator—cruising up and down through hundreds of feet of perilous space—demanded the nerve and the intellect of a birdman. All the constraints of his life—the green walls of his room and the months of unemployment—dissolved. No one was ringing, but he got into the elevator and shot it at full speed up to the penthouse and down again, up and down, to test his wonderful mastery of space.

A bell rang on 12 while he was cruising, and he stopped in his flight long enough to pick up Mrs. Gadshill. As the car started to fall, he took his hands off the controls in a paroxysm of joy and shouted, "Strap on your safety belt, Mrs. Gadshill! We're going to make a loop-the-loop!" Mrs. Gadshill shrieked. Then, for some reason, she sat down on the floor of the elevator. Why was her face so pale, he wondered; why was she sitting on the floor? She shrieked again. He grounded the car gently, and cleverly, he thought, and opened the door. "I'm sorry if I scared you, Mrs. Gadshill," he said meekly. "I was only fooling." She shrieked again. Then she ran out into the lobby, screaming for the superintendent.

The superintendent fired Charlie and took over the elevator himself. The news that he was out of work stung Charlie for a minute. It was his first contact with human meanness that day. He sat down in the locker room and gnawed on a drumstick. His drinks were beginning to let him down, and while it had not reached him yet, he felt a miserable soberness in the offing. The excess of food and presents around him began to make him feel guilty and unworthy. He regretted bitterly the lie he had told about his children. He was a single man with simple needs. He had abused the goodness of the people upstairs. He was unworthy.

Then up through this drunken train of thought surged the sharp figure of his landlady and her three skinny children. He thought of them sitting in their basement room. The cheer of

Christmas had passed them by. This image got him to his feet. The realization that he was in a position to give, that he could bring happiness easily to someone else, sobered him. He took a big burlap sack, which was used for collecting waste, and began to stuff it, first with his presents and then with the presents for his imaginary children. He worked with the haste of a man whose train is approaching the station, for he could hardly wait to see those long faces light up when he came in the door. He changed his clothes, and, fired by a wonderful and unfamiliar sense of power, he slung his bag over his shoulder like a regular Santa Claus, went out the back way, and took a taxi to the Lower East Side.

The landlady and her children had just finished off a turkey, which had been sent to them by the local Democratic Club, and they were stuffed and uncomfortable when Charlie began pounding on the door, shouting "Merry Christmas!" He dragged the bag in after him and dumped the presents for the children onto the floor. There were dolls and musical toys, blocks, sewing kits, an Indian suit, and a loom, and it appeared to him that, as he had hoped, his arrival in the basement dispelled its gloom. When half the presents had been opened, he gave the landlady a bathrobe and went upstairs to look over the things he had been given for himself.

NOW, the landlady's children had already received so many presents by the time Charlie arrived that they were confused with receiving, and it was only the landlady's intuitive grasp of the nature of charity that made her allow the children to open some of the presents while Charlie was still in the room, but as soon as he had gone, she stood between the children and the presents that were still unopened. "Now, you kids have had enough already," she said. "You kids have got your share. Just look at the things you got there. Why, you ain't even played with the half of them. Mary Anne, you ain't even looked at that doll the Fire Department give you. Now, a nice thing to do would be to take all this stuff that's left over to those poor people on Hudson Street—them Deckkers. They ain't got nothing." A beatific light came into her face when she realized that she could give, that she could bring cheer, that she could put a healing finger on a case needier than hers, and—like Mrs. DePaul and Mrs. Weston, like Charlie himself and like Mrs. Deckker, when Mrs. Deckker was to think, subsequently, of the poor Shannons—first love, then charity, and then a sense of power drove her. "Now, you kids help me get all this stuff together. Hurry; hurry, hurry," she said, for it was dark then, and she knew that we are bound, one to another, in licentious benevolence for only a single day, and that day was nearly over. She was tired, but she couldn't rest, she couldn't rest.

Crèche

by

RICHARD FORD

FAITH IS NOT DRIVING THEM, her mother, Esther is.

In the car, it's the five of them. The family, on their way to
Snow Mountain Highlands, to ski. Sandusky, Ohio, to northern Michigan. It's Christmas, or nearly. No one wants to
spend Christmas alone.

The five include Faith, who's the motion-picture lawyer,
arrived from California; her mother, Esther, who's sixty-four
and has, over the years, become much too fat. There's Roger,

Faith's sister Daisy's estranged husband, a guidance counsellor at Sandusky JFK; and Roger's two girls: Jane and Marjorie, ages eight and six. Daisy—the girls' mom—is a presence, but not along. She's in rehab in a large Midwestern city that is not Chicago or Detroit.

Outside, beyond the long, treeless expanse of whitely-frozen winterscape, Lake Michigan itself becomes suddenly visible, pale-blue with a thin veneer of fog just above its metallic surface. The girls are chatting in the back seat. Roger is beside them reading *Skier* magazine.

Florida would've been a much nicer holiday alternative, Faith thinks. EPCOT for the girls. The Space Center. Satellite Beach. Fresh pompano. The ocean. She's paying for everything and doesn't even like to ski. But it's been a hard year for everyone, and somebody has to take charge. If they'd gone to Florida, she'd have ended up broke.

Her basic character strength, Faith thinks, watching what seems to be a nuclear power plant coming up on the left, is the same feature that makes her a first-rate lawyer; an undeterrable willingness to see things as capable of being made better, and an addiction to thoroughness. If someone at the studio, a V.P. in marketing, for example, wishes to exit from a totally binding yet surprisingly uncomfortable obligation—say, a legal contract—then Faith's your girl. Faith the doer. Faith the blond beauty with smarts. Your very own optimist. A client's dream with great tits. Her own tits. Just give her a day on your problem.

Her sister Daisy is the perfect case in point. Daisy has been able to admit her serious methamphetamine problem, but only after her biker boyfriend, Vince, had been made a guest of the state of Ohio. And here Faith has had a role to play, beginning with phone calls to attorneys, a restraining order, then later the police and handcuffs for Vince. Daisy, strung out and thoroughly bruised, finally proved to be a credible witness, once convinced she would not be killed.

Going through Daisy's apartment with their mother, in search for clothes Daisy could wear with dignity into rehab, Faith found dildos; six in all—one even under the kitchen sink. These she put in a plastic Grand Union bag and left in the neighbour's street garbage just so her mother wouldn't know. Her mother is up-to-date, but not necessarily interested in dildos. For Daisy's going-in outfit, they eventually settled on a nice, dark jersey shift and some new white Adidas.

The downside of the character issue, the non-lawyer side, Faith understands, is the fact that she's almost thirty-seven and nothing's very solid in her life. She is very patient (with assholes), very good to help behind the scenes (with assholes). Her glass is always half full. Stand and ameliorate could be her motto. Anticipate change. The skills of the law, again, only partly in synch with the requirements of life.

A tall silver smokestack with blinking white lights on top and several grey megaphone-shaped cooling pots around it, now pass on the left. Dense, chalky smoke drifts out of each pot. Lake Michigan, beyond, looks like a blue-white desert. It has snowed for three days, but has stopped now.

"What's that big thing?" Jane or possibly Marjorie says, peering out the back-seat window. It is too warm in the cranberry-coloured Suburban Faith rented at the Cleveland airport especially for the trip. The girls are both chewing watermelon-smelling gum. Everyone could get carsick.

"That's a rocket ship ready to blast off to outer space. Would you girls like to hitch a ride on it?" Roger, the brother-in-law says to his daughters. Roger is the friendly-funny neighbour in a family sit-com, although not that funny. He is small and blandly handsome and wears a brush cut and black horn-rimmed glasses. And he is loathsome—though in subtle ways, like some TV actors Faith has known. He is also thirty-seven and prefers pastel cardigans and Hush Puppies. Daisy has been very, very unfaithful to him.

"It is *not* a rocket ship," says Jane, the older child, putting her forehead to the foggy window then pulling back to consider the smudge mark she's left.

"It's a pickle," Marjorie says.

"And shut up," Jane says. "That's a nasty expression."

"No it's not," Marjorie says.

"Is that a word your mother taught you?" Roger asks and smirks. He is in the back seat with them. "I bet it is. That's her legacy. Pickle." On the cover of *Skier* is a photograph of Hermann Maier, wearing an electric red outfit, slaloming down Mount Everest. The headline says, "GOING TO EXTREMES."

"It better not be," Faith's mother says from behind the wheel. She has her seat pushed way back to accommodate her stomach.

"Okay. Two more guesses," Roger says.

"It's an atom plant where they make electricity," Faith says, and smiles back at the nieces, who are staring at the smoke-stacks, losing interest. "We use it to heat our houses."

"But we don't like them," Esther says. Esther's been green since before it was chic.

"Why?" Jane says.

"Because they threaten our precious environment, that's why," Esther answers.

"What's 'our precious environment'?" Jane says insincerely.

"The air we breathe, the ground we stand on, the water we drink." Once Esther taught eighth grade science, but not in years.

"Don't you girls learn anything in school?" Roger is flipping pages in his *Skier*. For some mysterious reason, Faith has noticed, Roger is quite tanned.

"Their father could always instruct them," Esther says. "He's in education."

"Guidance," Roger says. "But touché."

"What's touché?" Jane says, wrinkling her nose.

"It's a term used in fencing," Faith says. She likes both girls immensely, and would happily punish Roger for speaking to them with sarcasm.

"What's fencing," Marjorie asks.

"It's a town in Michigan where they make fences," Roger says. "Fencing, Michigan. It's near Lansing."

"No it's not," Faith says.

"Well then, you tell them," Roger says. "You know everything. You're the lawyer."

"It's a game you play with swords," Faith says. "Only no one gets killed. It's fun." In every respect, she despises Roger and wishes he'd stayed in Sandusky. But she couldn't ask the little girls without him. Letting her pay for everything is Roger's way of saying thanks.

"So. There you are, little girls. You heard it here first," Roger says in a nice-nasty voice, continuing to read. "All your lives now you'll remember where you heard fencing explained first and by whom. When you're at Harvard …"

"You didn't know," Jane says.

"That's wrong. I did know. I absolutely knew," Roger says. "I was just having some fun. Christmas is a fun time, don't you know?"

FAITH'S LOVE LIFE has not been going well. She has always wanted children-with-marriage, but neither of these things has quite happened. Either the men she's liked haven't liked children, or else the men who loved her and wanted to give her all she longed for haven't seemed worth it. Practising law for a movie studio has therefore become very engrossing. Time has gone by. A series of mostly courteous men has entered but then departed—all for one reason or another unworkable: married, frightened, divorced, all three together. "Lucky" is how she has chiefly seen herself. She goes to the gym every day, drives an expensive car, lives alone in Venice Beach in a rental owned by a teenage movie star who is a friend's brother and who has HIV. A deal.

Late last spring she met a man. A stock market hotsy-totsy with a house on Nantucket. Jack. Jack flew to Nantucket from the city in his own plane, had never been married at age roughly forty-six. She came east a few times and flew up with him, met his stern-looking sisters, the pretty, socialite mom. There was a big blue rambling beach house facing the sea, with rose hedges, sandy pathways to secret dunes where you could swim naked—something she especially enjoyed, though the sisters were astounded. The father was there, but was sick and would soon die. So life and plans were generally on hold.

Jack did beaucoup business in London. Money was not a problem. Maybe when the father departed they could be married, Jack had almost suggested. But until then, she could travel with him whenever she could get away—scale back a little on the expectation side. He wanted children, could get to California often. It could work.

One night a woman called. Greta, she said her name was. Greta was in love with Jack. She and Jack had had a fight, but he still loved her, she said. It turned out Greta had pictures of Faith and Jack together. Who knew who took them? A little bird. One was a picture of Faith and Jack exiting Jack's building on Beckman Place. Another was of Jack helping Faith out of a yellow taxi. One was of Faith, alone, at the Park Avenue Café eating seared swordfish. One was of Jack and Faith kissing in the front seat of an unrecognizable car—also in New York.

Jack liked particular kinds of sex in very particular kinds of ways, Greta said on the phone. She guessed Faith knew all about that by now. But "best not make long-range plans" was somehow the message. Other calls were placed, messages left on her voicemail, prints arrived by Fed-Ex.

When asked, Jack conceded there was a problem. But he would solve it, *tout de suite* (though she needed to understand he was preoccupied with his father's approaching death). Jack was a tall, smooth-faced, handsome man with a shock of lustrous, mahogany-coloured hair. Like a clothing model. He smiled and everyone felt better. He'd gone to public high school, Harvard, played squash, rowed, debated, looked good in a brown suit and oldish shoes. He was trustworthy. It still seemed workable.

But Greta called more times. She sent pictures of herself and Jack together. Recent pictures, since Faith had come on board. It was harder than he'd imagined to get untangled, Jack admitted. Faith would need to be patient. Greta was, after all, someone he'd once "cared about very much." Might've even married. Didn't wish to hurt. She had problems, yes. But he wouldn't just throw her over. He wasn't that kind of man, something she, Faith, would be glad about in the long run. Meanwhile, there was the sick patriarch. And his mother. And the sisters. That had been plenty.

SNOW MOUNTAIN HIGHLANDS is a smaller ski resort, but nice. Family, not flash. Faith's mother found it as a "Holiday Getaway" in the *Erie Weekly*. The package includes a condo, weekend lift tickets, and coupons for three days of Swedish smorgasbord in the Bavarian-style lodge. The deal, however, is for two people only. The rest have to pay. Faith will sleep with her mother in the "Master Suite." Roger can share the twin with the girls.

Two years ago, when sister Daisy began to take an interest in Vince, the biker, Roger simply "receded." Her and Roger's sex life had long ago lost its effervescence, Daisy confided. They had started off well enough as a model couple in a suburb of Sandusky, but eventually—after some years and two kids—happiness ended and Daisy had been won over by Vince, who liked amphetamines and more importantly sold them. Vince's arrival was when sex had gotten really good, Daisy said. Faith believes Daisy envied her movie connections and movie lifestyle and the Jaguar convertible, and basically threw her own life away (at least until rehab) as a way of simulating Faith's, only with a biker. Eventually Daisy left home and gained forty-five pounds on a body that was already voluptuous, if short. Last summer, at the beach at Middle Bass, Daisy in a rage actually punched Faith in the chest when she suggested that Daisy might lose some weight, ditch Vince and consider coming home to her family. Not a diplomatic suggestion, she later decided. "I'm not like you," Daisy screamed, right out on the sandy beach. "I fuck for pleasure. Not for business." Then she waddled into the tepid surf of Lake Erie, wearing a pink one-piece that boasted a frilly skirt-let. By then, Roger had the girls, courtesy of a court order.

IN THE CONDO NOW, Esther has been watching her soaps, but has stopped to play double solitaire and have a glass of wine by the big picture window that looks down toward the crowded ski slope and the ice rink. Roger is actually there on the bunny slope with Jane and Marjorie, though it's impossi-ble to distinguish them. Red suits. Yellow suits. Lots of dads with kids. All of it soundless.

Faith has had a sauna and is now thinking about phoning Jack, wherever Jack is. Nantucket. New York. London. She has no particular message to leave. Later she plans to do the Nordic Trail under moonlight. Just to be a full participant, to set a good example. For this she has brought LA purchases: loden knickers, a green-and-brown-and-red sweater knitted in the Himalayas, socks from Norway. No way does she plan to get cold.

Esther plays cards at high speed with two decks, her short fat fingers flipping cards and snapping them down as if she hates the game and wants it to be over. Her eyes are intent. She has put on a cream-coloured neck brace because the tension of driving has aggravated an old work-related injury. And she is now wearing a big Hawaii-print orange muumuu. How long, Faith wonders, has she been wearing these tents. Twenty years, at least. Since Faith's own father—Esther's husband—kicked the bucket.

"Maybe I'll go to Europe," Esther says, flicking cards ferociously. "That'd be nice, wouldn't it?"

Faith is at the window, observing the expert slope. Smooth, wide pastures of snow, framed by copses of beautiful spruces. Several skiers are zigzagging their way down, doing their best to appear stylish. Years ago, she came here with her high-school boyfriend, Eddie, a.k.a. "Fast Eddie," which in some respects he was. Neither of them liked to ski, nor did they get out of bed to try. Now, skiing reminds her of golf—a golf course made of snow.

"Maybe I'll take the girls out of school and treat us all to Venice," Esther goes on. "I'm sure Roger would be relieved."

Faith has spotted Roger and the girls on the bunny slope. Blue, green and yellow suits, respectively. He is pointing, giving detailed instructions to his daughters about ski etiquette. Just like any dad. She thinks she sees him laughing. It is hard to think of Roger as an average parent.

"They're too young for Venice," Faith says, putting her small, good-looking nose near the surprisingly warm window-pane. From outside, she hears the rasp of a snow shovel and muffled voices.

"Maybe I'll take *you* to Europe, then," Esther says. "Maybe when Daisy clears rehab we can all three take in Europe. I always planned for that."

Faith likes her mother. Her mother is no fool, yet still seeks ways to be generous. But Faith cannot complete a picture that includes herself, her enlarged mother and Daisy on the Champs Elysées or the Grand Canal. "That's a nice idea," she says. She is standing beside her mother's chair, looking down at the top of her head, hearing her breathe. Her mother's head is small. Its hair is dark grey and short and sparse, and not especially clean. She has affected a very wide part straight down the middle. Her mother looks like the fat lady in the circus, but wearing a neck brace.

"I was reading what it takes to live to a hundred," Esther says, neatening the cards on the glass table top in front of her belly. Faith has begun thinking of Jack and what a peculiar species of creep he is. Jack Matthews still wears the Lobb cap-toe shoes he had made for him in college. Ugly, pretentious English shoes. "You have to be physically active," her mother continues. "And you have to be an optimist, which I am. You have to stay interested in things, which I more or less do. And you have to handle loss well."

With all her concentration Faith tries not to wonder how she ranks on this scale. "Do you want to be a hundred?"

"Oh, yes," her mother says. "*You* just can't imagine it, that's all. You're too young. And beautiful. And talented." No irony. Irony is not her mother's specialty.

Outside, one of the men shovelling snow can be heard to say, "Hi, we're the Weather Channel." He's speaking to someone watching them through another window from yet another condo.

"Colder'n a well-digger's dick, you bet," a second man's voice says. "That's today's forecast."

"Dicks, dicks, and more dicks," her mother says pleasantly. "That's it, isn't it? The male appliance. The whole mystery."

"So I'm told," Faith says, and thinks about Fast Eddie.

"They were all women, though," her mother says.

"Who?"

"All the people who lived to be a hundred. You could do all the other things right. But you still needed to be a woman to survive."

"Good for us," Faith says.

"Right. The lucky few."

THIS WILL BE THE GIRLS' FIRST Christmas without a tree or their mother. Though Faith has attempted to improvise around this by arranging presents at the base of the large, plastic rubber-tree plant stationed against one of the empty white walls of the small living room. The tree was already here. She has brought with her a few Christmas balls, a gold star and a string of lights that promise to blink. "Christmas in Manila," could be a possible theme.

Outside, the day is growing dim. Faith's mother is napping. Following his ski lesson, Roger has gone down to "The Warming Shed" for a mulled wine. The girls are seated on the couch side by side, wearing their Lanz of Salzburg flannel nighties with matching smiling monkey-face slippers. Green and yellow again, but with printed white snowflakes. They have taken their baths together, with Faith to supervise, then insisted on putting on their nighties early for their nap. They seem perfect angels and perfectly wasted on their parents. Faith has decided to pay their college tuitions. Even to Harvard.

"We know how to ski now," Jane says primly. They're watching Faith trim the plastic rubber-tree plant. First the blinking lights, though there's no plug-in close enough, then the six balls (one for each family member). Last will come the gold star. Faith understands she is trying for too much. Though why not try for too much. It's Christmas. "Marjorie wants to go to the Olympics," Jane adds.

Jane has watched the Olympics on TV, but Marjorie was too young. It is Jane's power position. Marjorie looks at her sister without expression, as if no one can observe her staring.

"I'm sure she'll win a medal," Faith says, on her knees, fiddling with the fragile strand of tiny peaked bulbs she already knows will not light up. "Would you two like to help me?" She smiles at both of them.

"No," Jane says.

"No," Marjorie says immediately after.

"I don't blame you," Faith says.

"Is Mommy coming here?" Marjorie blinks, then crosses her tiny, pale ankles. She is sleepy and could possibly cry.

"No, sweet," Faith says. "This Christmas Mommy is doing *herself* a favour. So she can't do one for us."

"What about Vince?" Jane says authoritatively. Vince is ground that has been gone over several times before now, and carefully. Mrs. Argenbright, the girls' therapist, has taken special pains with the Vince subject. The girls have the skinny on Mr. Vince but want to be given it again, since they like Vince more than their father.

"Vince is a guest of state of Ohio, right now," Faith says. "You remember that? It's like he's in college."

"He's not in college," Jane says.

"Does he have a tree where he is," Marjorie asks.

"Not in any real sense, at least not in his room like you do," Faith says. "Let's talk about happier things than our friend Vince, okay?" She is stringing bulbs now, on her knees.

The room doesn't include much furniture, and what there is conforms to the Danish modern style. A raised, metal-hooded, red-enamel fireplace device has a paper message from the condo owners taped to it, advising that smoke damage will cause renters to lose their security deposit and subject them to legal actions. These particular owners, Esther has learned, are residents of Grosse Pointe Farms, and are people of Russian extraction. There's, of course, no firewood except what the Danish furniture could offer. So smoke is unlikely. Baseboards supply everything.

"I think you two should guess what you're getting for Christmas," Faith says, carefully draping lightless lights onto the stiff plastic branches of the rubber tree. Taking pains.

"In-lines. I already know," Jane says and crosses her ankles like her sister. They are a jury disguised as an audience. "I don't have to wear a helmet, though."

"But are you sure of that?" Faith glances over her shoulder and gives them a smile she's seen movie stars give to strangers. "You could always be wrong."

"I'd better be right," Jane says unpleasantly, with a frown very much like her mom's.

"Santa's bringing me a disk player," Marjorie says. "It'll come in a small box. I won't even recognize it."

"You two're too smart for your britches," Faith says. She is quickly finished stringing Christmas lights. "But you don't know what *I* brought you." Among other things, she has brought a disk player and an expensive pair of in-line skates. They are in the Suburban and will be returned back in LA. She has also brought movie videos. Twenty in all, including *Star Wars* and *Sleeping Beauty*. Daisy has sent them each $50.

"You know," Faith says, "I remember once a long, long time ago, my dad and I and your mom went out in the woods and cut a tree for Christmas. We didn't buy a tree, we cut one down with an axe."

Jane and Marjorie stare at her as if they've read this story someplace. The TV is not turned on in the room. Perhaps, Faith thinks, they don't understand someone talking to them— live action presenting its own unique continuity problems.

"Do you want to hear the story?"

"Yes," Marjorie, the younger sister, says. Jane sits watchful and silent on the green Danish sofa. Behind her on the bare white wall is a framed print of Bruegel's *Return of the Hunters,* which is, after all, Christmas-y.

"Well," Faith says. "Your mother and I—we were only nine and ten—picked out the tree we desperately wanted to be our tree, but our dad said no, that tree was too tall to fit inside our house. We should choose another one. But we both said, 'No, this one's perfect. This is the best one.' It was green and pretty and had a perfect Christmas shape. So our dad cut it down with his axe, and we dragged it out through the woods and tied it on top of our car and brought it back to Sandusky." Both girls are sleepy now. There has been too much excitement, or else not enough. Their mother is in rehab. Their dad's an asshole. They're in someplace called Michigan. Who wouldn't be sleepy?

"Do you want to know what happened after that?" Faith says. "When we got the tree inside?"

"Yes," Marjorie says politely.

"It *was* too big," Faith says. "It was much, much too tall. It couldn't even stand up in our living room. And it was too wide. And our dad got really mad at us because we'd killed a beautiful living tree for a selfish reason, and because we hadn't listened to him and thought we knew everything just because we knew what we wanted."

Faith suddenly doesn't know why she's telling this story to these innocent sweeties who do not need another object lesson. So she simply stops. In the real story, of course, her father took the tree and threw it out the door into the back yard where it stayed for a week and turned brown. There was crying and accusations. Her father went straight to a bar and got drunk. Later, their mother went to the Kiwanis lot and bought a small tree that fit and which the three of them trimmed without the aid of their father. It was waiting, all lighted, when he came home smashed. The story had always been one others found humour in. This time the humour seems lacking.

"Do you want to know how the story turned out?" Faith says, smiling brightly for the girls' benefit, but feeling defeated.

"I do," Marjorie says. Jane says nothing.

"Well, we put it outside in the yard and put lights on it so our neighbours could share our big tree with us. And we bought a smaller tree for the house at the Kiwanis. It was a sad story that turned out good."

"I don't believe that," Jane says.

"Well you should believe it," Faith says, "because it's true. Christmases are special. They always turn out wonderfully if you just give them a chance and use your imagination."

Jane shakes her head as Marjorie nods hers. Marjorie wants to believe. Jane, Faith thinks, is a classic older child. Like herself.

"DID YOU KNOW,"—this was one of Greta's cute messages left for her on her voicemail in Los Angeles—"did you know that Jack hates—*hates*—to have his dick sucked? Hates it with a passion. Of course you didn't. How could you? He always lies about it. Oh well. But if you're wondering why he never comes, that's why. It's a big turn-off for him. I personally think it's his mother's fault, not that *she* ever did it to him, of course. By the way, that was a nice dress last Friday. Really great tits. I can see why Jack likes you. Take care."

AT SEVEN, when the girls wake up from their naps and everyone is hungry at once, Faith's mother offers to take the two hostile Indians for a pizza then on to the skating rink, while Roger and Faith share the smorgasbord coupons in the Lodge.

Very few diners have chosen the long, harshly-lit rather sour-smelling Tyrol Room. Most guests are outside awaiting the Pageant of the Lights, in which members of the ski patrol descend the expert slope each night, holding flaming torches. It is a thing of beauty but takes time getting started. At the very top of the hill a giant Norway spruce has been illuminated in the Yuletide tradition, just as in the untrue version of Faith's story. All of this is viewable from inside the Tyrol Room via a great picture window.

Faith does not want to eat with Roger, who is hungover from his gluhwein and a nap. Conversation that she would find offensive could easily occur; something on the subject of her sister, the girls' mother—Roger's (still) wife. But she's trying to keep up a Christmas spirit. Do for others, etc.

Roger, she knows, dislikes her, possibly envies her, and also is attracted to her. Once, several years ago, he confided to her that he'd very much like to fuck her ears flat. He was drunk, and Daisy hadn't long before had Jane. Faith found a way not to specifically acknowledge his offer. Later he told her he thought she was a lesbian. Having her know that just must've seemed like a good idea. A class act is The Roger.

The long, echoing dining hall has criss-crossed ceiling beams painted pink and light green and purple, a scheme apparently appropriate to Bavaria. There are long green-painted tables with pink and purple plastic folding chairs meant to promote an informal good time and family fun. Somewhere else in the lodge, Faith is certain, there is a better place to eat where you don't pay with coupons and nothing's pink or purple.

Faith is wearing a shiny black Lycra bodysuit, over which she has put on her loden knickers and Norway socks. She looks superb, she believes. With anyone but Roger this would be fun, or at least a hoot.

Roger sits across the long table, too far away to talk easily. In a room that can conveniently hold five hundred souls, there are perhaps fifteen scattered diners. No one is eating family style, only solos and twos. Young lodge employees in paper caps wait dismally behind the long smorgasbord steam table. Metal heat lamps with orange beams are steadily over-cooking the prime rib, of which Roger has taken a goodly portion. Faith has chosen only a few green lettuce leaves, a beet round, two tiny ears of yellow corn and no salad dressing. The sour smell of the Tyrol Room makes eating almost impossible.

"Do you know what I worry about?" Roger says, sawing around a triangle of glaucal grey roast beef fat, using a comically small knife. His tone implies he and Faith eat here together often and are just picking up where they've left off; as if they didn't hold each other in complete contempt.

"No," Faith says. "What?" Roger, she notices, has managed to hang on to his red smorgasbord coupon. The rule is you leave your coupon in the basket by the bread sticks. Clever Roger. Why, she wonders, is Roger tanned?

Roger smiles as though there's a lewd aspect to whatever it is that worries him. "I worry that Daisy's going to get so fixed up in rehab that she'll forget everything that's happened and want to be married again. To me, I mean. You know?" Roger chews as he talks. He wishes to seem earnest, his smile a serious, imploring, vacuous smile. This is Roger levelling. Roger owning up.

"That probably won't happen," Faith says. "I just have a feeling." She no longer wishes to look at her fragmentary salad. She does not have an eating disorder and could never have one.

"Maybe not." Roger nods. "I'd like to get out of guidance pretty soon, though. Start something new. Turn the page."

In truth, Roger is not bad-looking, only oppressively regular: small chin, small nose, small hands, small straight teeth—nothing unusual except his brown eyes are too narrow, as if he had Ukrainian blood. Daisy married him—she said—

because of his alarmingly big dick. That—or more importantly, the lack of that—was in her view why many other marriages failed. When all else gave way, that would be there. Vince's, she'd shared, was even bigger. Ergo. It was to this particular quest that Daisy had dedicated her life. This, instead of college.

"What exactly would you like to do next?" Faith says. She is thinking how nice it would be if Daisy came out of rehab and *had* forgotten everything. A return to how things were when they still sort of worked often seemed a good solution.

"Well, it probably sounds crazy," Roger says, chewing, "but there's a company in Tennessee that takes apart jetliners for scrap. There's big money in it. I imagine it's how the movie business got started. Just some hair-brained scheme." Roger pokes at macaroni salad with his fork. A single Swedish meatball remains on his plate.

"It doesn't sound crazy," Faith lies, then looks longingly at the smorgasbord table. Maybe she's hungry, after all. But is the table full of food the smorgasbord, or is eating the food the smorgasbord?

Roger, she notices, has casually slipped his meal coupon into a pocket.

"Well, do you think you're going to do that?" Faith asks with reference to the genius plan of dismantling jet airplanes for big bucks.

"With the girls in school, it'd be hard," Roger admits soberly, ignoring what would seem to be the obvious—that it is not a genius plan.

Faith gazes away again. She realizes no one else in the big room is dressed the way she is, which reminds her of who she is. She is not Snow Mountain Highlands (even if she once was). She is not Sandusky. She is not even Ohio. She is Hollywood. A fortress.

"I could take the girls for a while," she suddenly says. "I really wouldn't mind." She thinks of sweet Marjorie and sweet, unhappy Jane sitting on the Danish modern couch in their sweet nighties and monkey-face slippers, watching her trim the plastic rubber-tree plant. At the same moment, she thinks of Roger and Daisy being killed in an automobile crash on their triumphant way back from rehab. You can't help what you think.

"Where would they go to school?" Roger says, becoming alert to something unexpected. Something he might like.

"I'm sorry?" Faith says and flashes Roger, big-dick, narrow-eyed Roger a second movie star's smile. She has let herself become distracted by the thought of his timely death.

"I mean, like, where would they go to school?" Roger blinks. He is that alert.

"I don't know. Hollywood High, I guess. They have schools in California. I could find one."

"I'd have to think about it," Roger lies decisively.

"Okay, do," Faith says. Now that she has said this, without any previous thought of ever saying it, it becomes part of everyday reality. Soon she will become Jane and Marjorie's parent. Easy as that. "When you get settled in Tennessee you could have them back," she says without conviction.

"They probably wouldn't want to come back by then," Roger says. "Tennessee'd seem pretty dull."

"Ohio's dull. They like that."

"True," Roger says.

No one has thought to mention Daisy in promoting this new arrangement. Though Daisy, the mother, is committed elsewhere for the next little patch. And Roger needs to get his life jump-started, needs to put "guidance" in the rearview mirror. First things first.

The Pageant of the Lights has gotten underway outside now—a ribbon of swaying torches gliding soundlessly down the expert slope like an overflow of human lava. All is preternaturally visible through the panoramic window. A large, bundled crowd of spectators has assembled at the bottom of the slope behind some snow fences, many holding candles in scraps of paper like at a Grateful Dead concert. All other artificial light is extinguished, except for the Yuletide spruce at the top. The young smorgasbord attendants, in their aprons and paper caps, have gathered at the window to witness the event yet again. Some are snickering. Someone remembers to turn the lights off in the Tyrol Room. Dinner is suspended.

"Do you downhill," Roger asks, leaning over his empty plate in the half darkness. He is whispering, for some reason. Things could really turn out great, Faith understands him to be thinking: Eighty-six the girls. Dismantle plenty jets. Just be friendly and it'll happen.

"No, never," Faith says, dreamily watching the torchbearers schussing side to side, a gradual, sinuous, drama-less tour downward. "It scares me."

"You'd get used to it," Roger unexpectedly reaches across the table to where her hands rest on either side of her uneaten salad. He touches, then pats, one of these hands. "And by the way," Roger says. "Thanks. I mean it. Thanks a lot."

BACK IN THE CONDO all is serene. Esther and the girls are still at the skating rink. Roger has wandered back to "The Warming Shed." He has a girlfriend in Port Clinton, a former high school counsellee, now divorced. He will be calling her, telling her about his new Tennessee plans, adding that he wishes she were here at Snow Mountain Highlands with him and that his family could be in Rwanda. Bobbie, her name is.

A call to Jack is definitely in order. But first Faith decides to slide the newly-trimmed rubber tree plant nearer the window, where there's an outlet. When she plugs in, most of the little white lights pop cheerily on. Only a few do not, and in the box are replacements. This is progress. Later, tomorrow, they can affix the star on top—her father's favourite ritual. "Now it's time for the star," he'd always say. "The star of the wise men." Her father had been a musician, a woodwind specialist. A man of talents, and of course a drunk. A specialist also in women who were not his wife. He had taught committedly at a junior college to make all their ends meet. He had wanted Faith to become a lawyer, so naturally she became one. Daisy he had no specific plans for, so naturally she became a drunk and sometime later, an energetic nymphomaniac. Eventually he died, at home. The paterfamilias. After that, but not until, her mother began to put weight on. "Well, there's my size, of course," was how she usually expressed it. She took it as a given: increase being the natural consequence of loss.

Whether to call Jack, though, in London or New York. (Nantucket is out, and Jack never keeps his cell phone on except for business hours.) Where is Jack? In London it was after midnight. In New York it was the same as here. Half past eight. And what message to leave? She could just say she was lonely; or that she had chest pains, or worrisome test results. (These would need to clear up mysteriously.)

But London, first. The flat in Sloane Terrace, half a block from the tube. They'd eaten breakfast at the Oriel, then Jack had gone off to work in the City while she did the Tate, the Bacons her specialty. So far from Snow Mountain Highlands— this being her sensation when dialling—a call going a great, great distance.

Ring-jing, ring-jing, ring-jing, ring-jing, ring-jing. Nothing.

There was a second number, for messages only, but she'd forgotten it. Call again to allow for a misdial. Ring-jing, ring-jing, ring-jing …

New York, then. East 50th. Far, far east. The nice, small slice of river view. The bolthole he'd had since college. His freshman numerals framed. 1971. She'd gone to the trouble to have the bedroom re-done. White everything. A smiling and tanned picture of herself from the boat, framed in red leather. Another of the two of them together at Cabo, on the beach. All similarly long distances from Snow Mountain Highlands.

Ring, ring, ring, ring. Then click. "Hi, this is Jack."—she almost says "Hi" back—"I'm not here right now, etc., etc., etc.," then a beep.

"Merry Christmas, it's me. Ummmm, Faith." She's stuck, but not at all flustered. She could just as well tell him everything. This happened today: the atomic energy smokestacks, the plastic rubber-tree plant, the Pageant of the Lights, the smorgasbord, Eddie from years back, the girls' planned move to California. All things Christmas-y. "Ummm, I just wanted to say that I'm … fine, and that I trust—make that *hope*—that

I *hope* you are too. I'll be back home—at the beach, that is—after Christmas. I'd love—make that like—to hear from you. I'm in Snow Mountain Highlands. In Michigan." She pauses, discussing with herself if there was further news worth relating. There isn't. Then she realizes (too late) she's treating his voicemail like her dictaphone: There's no revising. Too bad. Her mistake. "Well, good-bye," she says, realizing this sounds a bit stiff, but doesn't revise. With them it's all over anyway. Who cares? She called.

OUT ON THE NORDIC TRAIL 1, lights, soft white ones not unlike the Christmas tree lights in the condo, have been strung in selected fir boughs—bright enough that you'd never get lost in the dark, dim enough not to spoil the mysterious effect.

She does not actually enjoy this kind of skiing either. Not really. Not with all the tiresome waxing, the stiff rental shoes, the long inconvenient skis, the sweaty underneath, the chance that all this could eventuate in catching cold and missing work. The gym is better. Major heat, then quick you're clean and back in the car, back in the office. Back on the phone. She is a sport, but definitely not a sports nut. Still, this is not terrifying.

No one accompanies her on nighttime Nordic Trail 1, the Pageant of the Lights having lured away the other skiers. Two Japanese were conversing at the trail head, small beige men in bright chartreuse Lycras—smooth, serious faces, giant thighs, blunt, no-nonsense arms—commencing the rigorous course, "The Beast," Nordic Trail 3. On their rounded, stocking-capped heads they'd worn tiny lights like coal miners to light their way. They have disappeared immediately.

Here the snow virtually hums to the sound of her sliding strokes. A full moon rides behind filigree clouds as she strides forward in the near-darkness of crusted woods. There is wind she can hear high up in the tallest pines and hemlocks, but at ground level there's none, just cold radiating off the metallic snow. Only her ears actually feel cold, that and the sweat line of her hair. Her heartbeat barely registers. She is in shape.

For an instant she hears distant music, a singing voice with orchestral accompaniment. She pauses to listen. The music's pulse travels through the trees. Strange. Possibly it's Roger, she thinks, between deep breaths; Roger on stage in the karaoke bar, singing his greatest hits to other lonelies in the dark. "Blue Bayou," "Layla," "Tommy," "Try To Remember." Roger at a safe distance. Her hair, she realizes, is shining in the moonlight. If she were being watched, she would at least look good.

But wouldn't it be romantic to peer down from these woods through the dark and spy some shining, many-winged lodge lying below, windows ablaze, like an exotic casino from some Paul Muni movie. Graceful skaters adrift on a lighted rink. A garlanded lift still in stately motion, a few, last alpinists taking their silken, torchless float before lights-out. The great tree shining from the summit.

Except, this is not a particularly pretty part of Michigan. Nothing's to see—dark trunks, cold dead falls, swags of heavy snow hung in the spruce boughs.

And she is stiffening. Just that fast. New muscles being visited. Best not to go so far.

Daisy, her sister, comes to mind. Daisy, who will soon exit the hospital with a whole new view of life. Inside, there's of course been the 12-step ritual to accompany the normal curriculum of deprivation and regret. And someone, somewhere, at some time possibly even decades back, will definitely turn out to have touched Daisy in ways inappropriate and detrimental to her well being, and at an all-too-tender age. And not just once, but many times, over a series of terrible, silent years. The culprit possibly an older, suspicious neighbourhood youth—a loner—or a far too avuncular school librarian. Even the paterfamilias will come under posthumous scrutiny (the historical perspective, as always, unprovable and therefore indisputable).

And certain sacrifices of dignity will naturally be requested of everyone then, due to this rich new news from the past: a world so much more lethal than anyone believed, nothing being the way we thought it was; so much hidden from view; if anyone had only known, could've spoken out and opened up the lines of communication, could've trusted, confided, blah, blah, blah. Their mother will, necessarily, have suspected nothing, but unquestionably should've. Perhaps Daisy, herself, will have suggested that Faith is a lesbian. The snowball effect. No one safe, no one innocent.

Up ahead, in the shadows, a mile into the trek, Shelter I sits to the right of Nordic Trail I—a darkened clump in a small clearing, a place to rest and wait for the others to catch up (if there were others). A perfect place to turn back.

Shelter I is nothing fancy, a simple rustic school-bus enclosure open on one side and hewn from logs. Out on the snow lie crusts of dinner rolls, a wedge of pizza, some wadded tissues, three beer cans—treats for the forest creatures—each casting its tiny shadow upon the white surface.

Although seated in the gloomy inside on a plank bench are

not school kids, but Roger, the brother-in-law, in his powder-blue ski suit and hiking hoots. He is not singing karaoke after all. She noticed no boot tracks up the trail. Roger is more resourceful than at first he seems.

"It's eff-ing cold up here." Roger speaks from within the shadows of Shelter I. He is not wearing his black glasses now, and is barely visible, though she senses he's smiling—his brown eyes even narrower.

"What are you doing up here, Roger," Faith asks.

"Oh," Roger says out of the gloom. "I just thought I'd come up." He crosses his arms and extends his hiking boots into the snow-light like some species of high-school toughie.

"What for?" Her knees are both knotted and weak from exertion. Her heart has begun thumping. Perspiration is cold on her lip. Temperatures are in the low twenties. In winter the most innocent places turn lethal.

"Nothing ventured," Roger says. He is mocking her.

"This is where I'm turning around," Faith ventures. "Would you like to go back down the hill with me?" What she wishes for is more light. Much more light. A bulb in the shelter would be very good. Bad things happen in the dark that would prove unthinkable in the light.

"Life leads you to some pretty interesting places, doesn't it, Faith?"

She would like to smile and not feel menaced by Roger, who should be with his daughters.

"I guess," she says. She can smell alcohol in the dry air. He is drunk and is winging all of this. A bad concurrence.

"You're very pretty. *Very* pretty. The big lawyer," Roger says. "Why don't you come in here?"

"Oh, no thank you," Faith says. Roger is loathsome, but he is also family, and she feels paralyzed by not knowing what to do—a most unusual situation. She wishes to be more agile on her skis, to leap upward and discover herself turned around and already gliding away.

"I always thought that in the right situation, we could have some big-time fun," Roger goes on.

"Roger, this isn't a good thing to be doing," whatever he's doing. She wants to glare at him, then understands her knees are quivering. She feels very, very tall on her skis, unusually accessible.

"It *is* a good thing to be doing," Roger says. "It's what I came up here for. Some fun."

"I don't want us to do anything up here, Roger," Faith says. "Is that all right?" This, she realizes, is what fear feels like—the way you'd feel in a late-night parking structure, or jogging alone in an isolated factory area, or entering your house in the wee hours, fumbling for your key. Accessible. And then, suddenly, there would be someone. Bingo. A man with oppressively ordinary looks who lacks a plan.

"Nope, nope. That's absolutely not all right." Roger stands up but stays in the sheltered darkness. "The lawyer," he says again, still grinning.

"I'm just going to turn around," Faith says, and very unsteadily begins to move her long left ski up out of its track, and then, leaning on her poles, her right ski up and out of its track. It is dizzying, and her calves ache, and it is complicated not to cross her ski tips. But it is essential to remain standing. To fall would mean surrender. What is the skiing expression? Tele … Tele-something. She wishes she could tele-something.

Tele-something the hell away from here. Her thighs burn. In California, she thinks, she is an officer of the court. A public official, sworn to uphold the law—though not to enforce it. She is a force for good.

"You look stupid standing there," Roger says stupidly.

She intends to say nothing more. There is nothing really to say. Talk is not cheap now, and she is concentrating very hard. For a moment she thinks she hears music again, music far away. It can't be.

"When you get all the way around," Roger says, "then I want to show you something." He does not say what. In her mind—moving her skis inches at a time, her ankles heavy—in her mind she says "Then what?" but doesn't say that.

"I really hate your eff-ing family," Roger says. His boots go crunch on the snow. She glances over her shoulder, but to look at him is too much. He is approaching. She will fall and then dramatic, regrettable things will happen. In a gesture he possibly deems dramatic, Roger—though she cannot see it—unzips his blue snowsuit front. He intends her to hear this noise. She is three-quarters turned around. She could see him over her left shoulder if she chose to. Have a look, see what all the excitement's about. She is sweating. Underneath she is drenched.

"Yep, life leads you to some pretty interesting situations." He is repeating himself. There is another zipping noise. This is big-time fun in Roger's world-view.

"Yes," she says, "it does." She has come almost fully around now.

She hears Roger laugh a little chuckle, an un-humorous "hunh." Then he says, "Almost." She hears his boots squeeze.

She feels his actual self close beside her. This undoubtedly will help to underscore how much he hates her family.

Then there are voices—saving voices—behind her. She cannot help looking over her left shoulder now and up the trail where it climbs into the dark trees. There is a light, followed by another light, like stars coming down from on high. Voices, words, language she doesn't quite understand. Japanese. She does not look at Roger, but simply slides one ski, her left one, forward into its track, lets her right one follow and find its way, pushes on her poles. And in just that small allotment of time and with that amount of effort she is away. She thinks she hears Roger say something, another "hunh," a kind of grunting sound but she can't be sure.

IN THE CONDO everyone is sleeping. The plastic rubber-tree lights are twinkling. They reflect from the window that faces the ski hill, which now is dark. Someone, Faith notices (her mother) has devoted much time to replacing the spent bulbs so the tree can fully twinkle. The gold star, the star that led the wise men, is lying on the coffee table like a starfish, waiting to be properly affixed.

Marjorie, the younger, sweeter sister, is asleep on the orange couch, under the Bruegel scene. She has left her bed to sleep near the tree, brought her quilted pink coverlet with her.

Naturally Faith has locked Roger out. Roger can die alone and cold in the snow. Or he can sleep in a doorway or by a steam pipe somewhere in the Snow Mountain Highlands complex and explain his situation to the security staff. Roger will not sleep with his pretty daughters this night. She is taking a hand in things now. These girls are hers. Though, how naive of her not to know that an offer to take the girls would immediately be translated by Roger into an invitation to fuck him. She has been in California too long, has fallen out of touch with things middle American. How strange that Roger, too, would say, "Eff-ing." He probably also says "X-mas."

At the ice rink, two teams are playing hockey under high white lights. A red team opposes a black team. Net cages have been brought on, the larger rink walled down to regulation size and shape. A few spectators stand watching—wives and girlfriends. Boyne City versus Petosky; Cadillac versus Sheboygan, or some such. The little girls' own white skates are piled by the door she has now safely locked with a dead bolt.

It would be good to put the star on, she thinks. "Now it's time for the star." Who knows what tomorrow will bring. The arrival of wise men couldn't hurt.

So, with the flimsy star, which is made of slick aluminum paper and is large and gold and weightless and five-pointed, Faith stands on the Danish dining-table chair and fits the slotted fastener onto the topmost leaf of the rubber-tree plant. It is not a perfect fit by any means, there being no sprig at the pinnacle, so that the star doesn't stand up as much as it leans off the top in a sad, comic, but also victorious way. (This use was never envisioned by the Philippine tree-makers.) Tomorrow others can all add to the tree, invent ornaments from absurd or inspirational raw materials. Tomorrow Roger himself will be rehabilitated, and become everyone's best friend. Except hers.

Marjorie's eyes have opened, though she has not stirred on the couch. For a moment, but only for a moment, she appears dead. "I went to sleep," she says softly and blinks her brown eyes.

"Oh, I saw you," Faith smiles. "I thought you were another Christmas present. I thought Santa had been here early and left you for me." She takes a careful seat on the spindly coffee table, close beside Marjorie—in case there would be some worry to express, a gloomy dream to relate. A fear. She smoothes her hand through Marjorie's warm hair.

Marjorie takes a deep breath and lets air go out smoothly through her nostrils. "Jane's asleep," she says.

"And how would you like to go back to bed?" Faith whispers. Possibly she hears a soft tap on the door—the door she has dead bolted. The door she will not open. The door beyond which the world and trouble wait. Marjorie's eyes wander toward the sound, then swim again with sleep. She is safe.

"Leave the tree on," Marjorie instructs, though asleep.

"Sure okay, sure," Faith says. "The tree stays. We keep the tree."

She eases her hand under Marjorie, who, by old habit, reaches, caresses her neck. In an instant she has Marjorie in her arms, pink coverlet and all, carrying her altogether effortlessly into the darkened bedroom where her sister sleeps on one of the twin beds. Carefully she lowers Marjorie onto the empty bed and re-covers her. Again she thinks she hears soft tapping, though it stops. She believes it will not come again this night.

Jane is sleeping with her face to the wall, her breathing deep and audible. Jane is the good sleeper, Marjorie the less reliable one. Faith stands in the middle of the dark, windowless room, between the twin beds, the blinking Christmas lights haunting the stillness that has come at such expense. The room smells musty and dank, as if it's been closed for months and opened just for this purpose, this night, these children. If only briefly she is reminded of Christmases she might've once called her own. "Okay," she whispers. "Okay, okay, okay."

FAITH UNDRESSES in the Master Suite, too tired to shower. Her mother sleeps on one side of their shared bed. She is a small mountain, visibly breathing beneath the covers. A glass of red wine, half-drunk, sits on the bed table beside her moulded neck brace. A picture of a white sailboat on a calm blue ocean hangs over the bed. Faith half-closes the door to undress, the blinking Christmas lights shielded.

She will wear pajamas tonight, for her mother's sake. She has bought a new pair. White, pure silk, smooth as water. Blue silk piping.

And here is the unexpected sight of herself in the cheap, wavy door mirror. All good. Just the small pale scar where a cyst was notched from her left breast, a meaningless scar no one would see. But a good effect still. Thin, hard thighs. A small nice belly. Boy's hips. The whole package, nothing to complain about.

There's need of a glass of water. Always take a glass of water to bed, never a glass of red wine. When she passes through the living-room window, her destination the tiny kitchen, she sees that the hockey game is now over. It is after midnight. The players are shaking hands on the ice, others are skating in wide circles. On the expert slope above the rink, lights have been turned on again. Machines with headlights groom the snow at treacherous angles and great risk.

And she sees Roger. He is halfway between the ice rink and the condos, walking back in his powder-blue suit. He has watched the hockey game, no doubt. Roger stops and looks up at her where she stands in the window in her white pjs, the Christmas tree lights blinking as her background. He stops and stares. He has found his black-frame glasses. His mouth is moving, but he makes no gesture. There is no room at this inn for Roger.

In bed, her mother is even larger. A great heat source, vaguely damp when Faith touches her back. Her mother is wearing blue gingham, a nightdress not so different from the muumuu she wears in daylight. She smells unexpectedly good. Rich.

How long, Faith wonders, has it been since she's slept with her mother. A hundred years? Twenty? But good that it would seem so normal.

She has left the door open in case the girls should call, in case they wake up and are afraid, in case they miss their father. The Christmas lights blink off and on merrily beyond the doorway. She can hear snow slide off the roof, an automobile with chains jingling softly somewhere out of sight. She has intended to call for messages but let it slip.

And how long ago, she wonders, was her mother slim and pretty? The sixties? Not so long ago, really. She had been a girl then. They—the sixties—always seem so close. Though to her mother probably not.

Blink, blink, blink, the lights blink.

Marriage. Yes, naturally she would think of that now. Though maybe marriage was only a long plain of self-preservation at the end of which here's someone else who doesn't know you very well. That would be a message she could've left for Jack. "Dear Jack, I now know that marriage is a long plain at the end of which there's etc., etc., etc." You always thought of these things too late. Somewhere, Faith hears more faint music, "Away in a Manger" played prettily on chimes. It is music to sleep to.

And how would they deal with tomorrow? Not the eternal tomorrow, but the promised, practical one. Her thighs feel stiff, yet she is slowly relaxing. Her mother, the mountain beside her, is facing away. How indeed? Roger would be rehabilitated tomorrow, yes, yes. There will be board games. Changes of outfits. Phone calls placed. She will find the time to ask her mother if anyone had ever been abused, and find out, happily, not. Unusual looks will be passed between and among everyone. Certain names, words will be in short supply, for the sake of all. The girls will again learn to ski and to enjoy it. Jokes will be told. They will feel better, be a family again. Christmas takes care of its own.

The Sunday
After Christmas

by

MAVIS GALLANT

AT A QUARTER TO FOUR the sun moved behind a mountain.
The valley below us went dark, as if an enormous bird had just
spread its wings. For a moment I understood what my mother
means when she complains I give her the feeling of being
outside life. The two of us, and the American girl my mother
had picked up, were still on the terrace between the ski-lift
and a restaurant. I saw, as the lights of the restaurant welled
up, how the girl looked quickly, wistfully almost, at the

steamed windows and the hissing coffee machine.

"Don't you want to go in?" said my mother's new friend. "It's kind of cold now the sun's gone."

My mother made a wild, gay movement of turning to me, as if this were only one of a hundred light-hearted decisions we made together. It is extraordinary how, in Italy, she becomes the eccentric Englishwoman—hair flying, sunglasses askew, too friendly with the waiter at breakfast, but unexpectedly waspish if a child brushes against her chair: "Harold, didn't you notice? The little brute deliberately barged into me!" An hour later she will be ready to tell the little brute my life's story and what I was like when I was his age. Her greed for people makes her want to seem attractive to almost anyone—a child, or a waiter, or this girl, whose absence of charm and mystery made her seem, to me, something like a large coloured poster. My mother dreads being alone with me. In the last of the afternoon, when she suddenly says, "You must be cold," meaning that she is, and we gather everything together and start the slow progression back to the hotel, I sense her panic. The dark minutes between afternoon and night creep by; she looks surreptitiously at her watch; she imagines she has been walking beside me down a twilit street for years on end. To engage and hold my attention on the way home she will comment on everything she sees—the patches of snow so curiously preserved on a shutter, the late skiers in the distance like matchstick figures, the expressiveness of those matchsticks. "Look," she says, at red berries, green moss, beeches, a juniper, reeds frozen in a black stream, the plumed grasses above the snow. I am not an old man in a fur-lined pelisse; she is not pushing me along in a wheelchair (I may, in fact, be carrying her skis); I am not snow-blind. I must be all those things in her eyes. I am crippled, aged, in the dark, an old man she diverts with the crumbs of life because part of him is dying, and even a partial death is like her own. "Why don't you talk to me?" she used to say. She is past that kind of pleading now. She knows that I can hear her thinking, so that speech isn't needed. To answer the silent sentences in her mind, I answer, "Yes, but if that little old man died, you would at least be free, wouldn't you?"

"Oh. Harold," she replies. "Your father *is* dead, darling, and he was never old."

IT HAD RAINED until shortly before Christmas. There was deep snow only on the upper slopes, which were marked *"difficile"* on the map in our hotel. We took the chair-lift to the very top every day and came down at four o'clock. I heard her telling her newest American friend how she used to come to this village years ago, with my father, without me. She could remember electric cars shaped like the swan boats she used to be taken for rides in when she was a child. She would have liked to ski all the way down to the village, but hardly anyone did. The runs were too short, broken by stone walls and the boundaries of close-set trees, and lower down no snow at all except on a mule path, which was hard and icy and followed the course of a mountain stream. She would have tried it, she said, had there been anyone to go with. She was not confident enough alone. Suppose she were to fracture a leg and lie for hours without help? At fifty a break is a serious matter; she might never walk without limping again. Her hands shook as she lighted the girl's cigarette and then her own.

"Harold sits for hours, as long as there's sun," she said. "He doesn't feel heat or cold. He wanted marvellous equipment; now he won't use it. I don't insist."

The new girl, who had said her name was Sylvia, pulled off her knitted cap. Her hair, dark, fell over the shoulders of a white sweater. An exchange of intimate gossip, my mother's alternative to friendship, was under way. The girl said quite easily, "There doesn't seem to be any friction between you two, but my mother never lets me alone. I've travelled with her sometimes and it's no joke. She drinks too much and she gets loud. She'll have her breakfast in the bar and ask the bartender a whole lot of questions—things she wouldn't do at home."

"I think I'm always the same," my mother cried—like something screamed at a party.

"I am sorry for her," the girl went on. "She needs all of somebody's life and she hasn't ever had that."

"Not even your father's?"

"He looked after her, but he didn't give her all his life. No one has the right to a whole extra life." Her pure, humourless regard rested on each of us. Her look preached to us; one of us was being warned. "I lived with her for a year after my father died. I've got to leave her now. I came all this way just so as not to spend Christmas at home. She's got to get used to it. It's a sort of shock treatment."

"Well, that's very strong of you," said my mother. "Isn't that so, Harold? But are you really leaving so soon? Can't you stay until after New Year's Eve? You may never be here again."

I could hear her thinking, *Don't go. Stay. Are two or three days so much to give me? You gave your mother a year.*

I love my mother and I don't care two pins about you, I heard the girl answer.

She said, "No, I've got to get back."

I looked at the lights strung along the street, and the lights slowly moving out of the car park at the foot of the lift. I saw the girl shiver, as if she felt that great wing rushing over the valley.

"I can't go down," I said.

"Of course you can't," said my mother. Her little apricot face looked cheerful. "We're going down in the lift."

I said, "I can't go down in the chair either. I can't go down at all."

"It's mountain sickness," said my mother, making round-about movements with her cigarette, as if to show what vertigo means. "It will be over in a minute. It just means a wait. What a bother for you!" She was taking it for granted, of course, that the girl would not feel free to leave us there.

"Shouldn't we go in?" said the girl, again attracted by the warm light.

"He'll want to stay out, I'm afraid."

"Oh. Well, we can have coffee, anyway," said the girl. "We're all freezing." She went into the restaurant and I saw her leaning on the counter, fingering chocolate bars, wishing she had never talked to us. A ski club from Turin filled the place. They were noisy as monkeys, ordering hot drinks and food and combing their hair before a little mirror. I saw the girl smiling at them, waiting for the coffee, but they were too full of themselves to notice a stranger.

"I don't believe this," my mother said to me. "There's nothing wrong with you today. You're perfectly well. You're shamming, shamming." Her voice broke on her habit of repeating the same word twice. She was disappointed as a child over the girl. I tried to reason with her: Was Sylvia her real name? It did not seem an American name to me; it was, in fact, the name of one of my aunts. But by now my mother had left me and joined the girl. I could see her back, and the girl's face. On the counter was a tray and three cups. My mother was telling her about me: "He had an unusual experience, you know," she was saying. "He was one of a group of university students visiting a large hospital. While they were waiting for their conducted tour, a nurse told Harold that the place was run by a most eccentric doctor who did experiments on children and on young people, and that Harold and his friends were the new victims. The patients, when they survived, were so changed in character that they were no longer fit for life in the outside world. 'Didn't you notice the scars on the necks of the little boys playing football outside?' the nurse said. She advised him not to fight, as there was nothing he could do. Harold argued for his freedom. His argument centred on two things—that he was young and had a right to live, and that he still hadn't decided what he wanted to do, and needed time to find out. It seemed impossible to him that she shouldn't understand this. She was a serious person—a nice girl. They went outside and sat discussing his life on a bench overlooking the playing field. Suddenly, in a second, it was clear that the nurse had been convinced by Harold's arguments and had purposely brought him out-of-doors, and, just as he understood, she said, 'Run for it.' His reflexes are very slow, but he must have pulled himself together, and he did run, through the players, to liberty, and the road outside, and to his own home—safe, safe."

She bobbed her head as she repeated the last word. I did not think, or guess, or imagine what she was saying; I *knew*. She must have then said, "Pretend it is funny," because the girl laughed, and was still remembering her laughter as she picked up the tray and brought it out to me.

My mother said, "I was telling Sylvia about that midnight Mass where they had the live animals, and how the priest said the goat was an incarnation of the Devil and had to be taken out, and then the goat broke loose, and all the villagers said later they had seen the Devil, really seen him, with his flaming eyes."

"I wish I had seen that," said the girl, with a lift to the sentence, as if it were half a question, as if giving me a reason to speak. I was already thinking about the trip down, and the slight sighing of the cable.

"He's fine now," my mother said.

BELOW, because it was Sunday, everyone except the visitors looked awkward and solemn. It seemed an unnatural day, that had to be lived through in formal, festive clothes. The men wore thick moustaches turned up at the ends, and black felt hats, and knee breeches. They looked distinguished and calm, and not like any idea the girl had ever had about Italians, I heard her say. She drew near my mother. She repeated that she had not known before coming here that Italians could be patient, or naturally elegant, any more than she had known they possessed an educated middle class. In her mind (she had not really given it thought) she had been coming to a Rossellini, a De Sica country.

While she was saying this, she was also saying to me, *Was it a dream? Did you really have an experience like that? If it was a dream, why didn't she say so?*

I answered, "It was a long experience, lasting well over a year."

"Harold, Harold!" my mother said, looking not at me but at the girl. We had reached the girl's hotel, and the long goodbye my mother would now insist upon would be, in her eyes, one minute's friendship more. "Are you leaving because there isn't enough snow?" she said. "There will be a Mass for snow on New Year's Eve. All the hotel owners and all the shop-keepers are contributing, they say." In my mother's poor, immediate vision of future events (never more than three or four days in span), she and her new friend walked in moon-light. Vega was bright and blue as a diamond; their shadows were hard and black as if cut out with knives.

"The goat, of course, the goat," I said. "'Don't move,' I said to Mother. 'When he sees the Cross he's sure to panic.'"

"I never move anyway," said my mother to Sylvia, to prolong the goodbye. "Nothing makes *me* move." She smiled, and even when the girl had turned aside forever, kept the smile alive.

The Zoo
at Christmas

by

JANE GARDAM

Christmas Eve, and twelve of the clock.
　"Now they are all on their knees,"
　An elder said as we sat in a flock
　By the embers in hearthside ease.

We pictured the meek mild creatures where
　They dwelt in their strawy pen,
　Nor did it occur to one of us there
　To doubt they were kneeling then.

So fair a fancy few would weave
In these years! Yet, I feel,
If someone said on Christmas Eve,
"Come; see the oxen kneel,

"In the lonely barton by yonder coomb
Our childhood used to know,"
I should go with him in the gloom,
Hoping it might be so.

—*The Oxen,* Thomas Hardy

A PALE, STILL DAY, the sky hanging white and low. It is the morning of Christmas Eve. The girl on the gate locks up at noon and waits around for the cleaner over in Refreshments. They go off together through the main gates, chatting down the lane to the pub. Over the other side of the Zoo, near Birds and Reptiles, the two resident keepers finish checking things and go off towards mince pies and a glass, the telly and the tree.

No human life stirs now within the Zoo. The toilets are locked; the kitchen of the cafeteria is washed down. Metallic, cold and colourless. The tigers look across. At it. Through it. Past it. Into the hoofstock enclosure. The tigers are fed on Tuesdays. Their weekly meal. This is Thursday. Not an urgent day. A flake or two of snow falls.

Word goes round. Electricity passes between cages without visible device. Ears can be switched on and off from within, out of boredom or pique or from the need for higher ruminations, particularly if we are talking tigers.

Tigers listen to other voices.

The feebler animals, the almost-humanoids, are always fussing to get through to the tigers. The tigers don't notice them. They pace. They pace and pace, turning on their own tails, on their own dilemmas. Pace and pace.

Suddenly they speak. The Zoo listens. It is like Jove talking in the heavens. Whoever Jove is. The tigers stop pacing and listen to their own echo, flick the tongue. Yawn. Great sabres glisten. Then they flow lightly up the walkways kindly provided by the management, liquefy themselves along them, turn on to their long, striped, brush-stroked backs, raise their great paws, expose the loose material that hangs below the abdomen, silk and fluff, close their eyes. They ponder in their hearts the problem of the hoofstock.

The domestic hoofstock is recent. It consists of cattle, givers of milk and meat. Oxen and asses and silly great cows; farm-yard creatures who have been introduced to the outskirts of the Zoo to familiarize children with the idea that all creatures are one. Ha!

The tigers drowse.

The less domestic hoofstock, the great bison, have been penned nearby, their mountainous necks like deformed oak trees. They look puzzled. Born in captivity, they have never roamed a plain, yet somehow they cannot feel that they are cows. "They'll be giving kids rides on them next," say the tigers. "Look what happened to the elephants."

Over in the sand paddock an elephant trumpets. Two Canadian wolves suddenly come trotting out of their den and stand listening. They run together up to the scrubby roof of the den and lift their noses. They start to howl, first one and then the other, like whales calling under the sea. Long, cold music.

Something's afoot. Here and there throughout the Zoo, other messages pass. Lemurs, little black faces wrapped in granny swan's-down, let out bellows from unlikely lips. The great gibbons whoop. The strange snow leopard runs up and down its high platform on its big fur-soled bedroom slippers. It flings its wonderful misty tail around its neck like Marlene Dietrich.

"Who brought in hoofstock to unsettle us?" muse the tigers. "Farmyard domestics. Thomas Hardy!"

For it is the new hoofstock who have put about this legend of Thomas Hardy's, that animals—particularly oxen, who are the elect—are wont to kneel before their Creator on Christmas Eve. They worship the Christ child. And sing.

"We do it, too," says a Jacob's sheep. "Several kinds of farm animals were present at the Nativity. We *should* worship."

"I wasn't present at the Nativity," says Ackroyd, the Siberian tiger. "And Thomas Hardy was an agnostic."

"Sing?" the other tigers say. *"Sing?"*

"We sing. We worship," say the hoofstock.

"You don't catch me copying anything human," says Ackroyd. Ackroyd is bitter. Ackroyd is not himself. He has not been himself for three months, since he ate his keeper.

The golden-lion tamarins, their black leather faces tiny as a baby's fist, scream and chatter at the idea of kneeling and singing, and worshipping their Creator, but they have been persuaded—oh, weeks ago—by the languid, pleasant cattle to give it a try. In fact, it is they who have organized the whole outing tonight, to the nearby church. They have done all the publicity. They have liaised with visiting squirrels and rabbits who know the neighbourhood. The venue is the farmer's field outside the Zoo; the time, 23.00 hours. A local sheep will lead them. Escape from the Zoo will of course be no problem, for there is an excellent p.o.w. network of tunnels, always has been. The serval cats and bush-dogs make use of it regularly for night-time forages down the M2. The panther is scarcely ever at home. He went off as far as Canterbury the other day (Hallowe'en, the fool) and walked round the Cathedral during evensong. It was in the papers. He was compared to some tomcat on Exmoor. Washed his face in the sacristy.

"But that's panthers for you," trembled the Zoo's one old lion (Theodore). "They like humans. They feel affection."

"Well, so does he," said an elk, nodding at murderous Ackroyd. "*He* feels affection."

Ackroyd looked baffled, but unrepentant. Tigers and penitence do not mingle.

"It's true," called an elephant. "Affection was what started it with that tiger. Up with his dinner-plate paws on the feller's shoulders. Lick, lick … Next thing, the keeper's in bits and Ackroyd's getting bashed with an iron spade, and then put in Solitary. I've seen cats do it with kittens."

"Hit them with spades?"

"Don't be foolish. Licking. Love breeds violence; it's better avoided."

"Only certain kinds of love," said the yearning, ugly tapir with his anal-looking snout. "Not worship."

"Worship!" said the elephants among themselves. "What do any of us know about worship? We're not lapdogs."

"Just what *we* say," fussed the Low-Church wallabies, the Quakerish giraffes, the pacifist bongos. 'What do any of us really know about love? But Thomas Hardy says that once a year, on Christmas Eve, we catch a glimmer. We are enabled to express our love to God and the Christ child. The experience is said to be agreeable."

"God?" thinks Wallace, the gorilla, in the distance. He is the oldest inhabitant. He sits all day in the corner of his empire, the Great Gorillarium. He takes a straw from between his toes and holds it for an hour or two in his fist, pondering. His hand is the hand of an old farmer, purple, square-knuckled, with round grey nails. His domed, grizzled head is the shape of the helmet of the Black Prince. It is set between huge humped shoulders. Carefully he inserts the straw into the syrup bottle attached to the side of his cage, and sucks. He draws it out and re-examines it. Around him silly spider monkeys swing and spring. Two fluffy black baby gorillas, born last year, roll about covered in straw, the cage their world.

But Wallace can remember the rainforest. It returns to him in dreams; horizons beyond the diamond-shaped wire, vistas clear of hairless humans patched about with cloth. Winds and great rains. Scents of a river. Here, the snow is grey. Wallace in his thirty years has seen snow before. It does not excite him. Not as it does the snow leopard, who will now be up on his tree-shelf, purring. Bad luck for the public that it's not an open afternoon. They stand around for hours waiting to hear the snow leopard purr. Purring is his only sound.

Gorillas don't purr.

Pleasure? Happiness? Wallace's ancient eyes, the eyes that humans cannot face, the eyes that say, "I am before The Fall. I am the one that knows"—Wallace's eyes ask: "God? Christ?" Then, hours later, "Worship?"

Yet he goes off with the rest. He accompanies them this night.

Nobody has expected him at all, but he turns up first. Timid antelopes, afraid of being late, come second. They are astounded to see his looming shape. They flicker off into the lane and stand between the farmer's hedge and the Canadian wolves, who, it being Christmas Eve, are uninterested in them. Next, the poor mangy lion, Theodore, comes creeping out of the escape tunnel and lies down with some local lambs. Red Kent cattle are standing about and the panther passes the time of night with them. The tamarins run about everywhere, flexing their tiny black hands, like tour guides with clipboards, and enigmatic langurs, like oriental restaurateurs on their night off, assist them. Where are the elephants?

"The tunnel's too small for them," says a gibbon. "They'll be kneeling at home."

The giraffes?

"Yes. A giraffe has promised to be here. Vera, a nice creature. If her structure permits it."

And, yes, here she is. Her delicate, knobbly, anxious little head emerges from the tunnel like a birth.

Monkeys galore follow her. It is 23.45. A quarter of an hour to go. *"Christmas Eve, and twelve of the clock,"* quotes an old ibex. *"Now they are all on their knees."*

All is silent. Not a cold night. Snow settles lightly on the ground, on fur and hide. The snow leopard moves to a little distance on account of his rarity and distinction. He purrs. He sounds like a distant motorbike.

"This looks like the lot of us," says the most human, the most mistrusted animal, the pied ruffed lemur, a donnish, dangly fellow once thought to be a form of Madagascan man who climbed trees in his pyjamas. "Orl aboard, lads."

But then there paced from the tunnel three tigers: Hilda, Enid—and Ackroyd himself.

NOW ST FRANCIS, Easingbourne, is very close to the Zoo. Like many other old English churches built on pagan sites, it stands on a knoll. It is near the turnoff for the Channel Tunnel, down a wooded lane. Well before the Danes, things of a nasty nature went on here, and although a Christian presence was established in the sixth century the atmosphere is still not altogether settled. There is a sacrificial aroma. Two strange animal heads are carved on either side of the church porch. They're in Pevsner. Tall dark trees stand close.

For many years this church has been closed, but recent guidebooks have drawn attention to the beauty of the setting, especially in the spring when the knoll is covered with blossoming cherries, so that tonight, for the first time in ages, a celebration of the Midnight Mass is to take place, by candlelight. The approaching animals, who had banked on privacy, see the glow from coloured windows, hear the deep chords of an organ within.

"But it's *always* been empty," fusses a sheep. "*Always* quite left to ourselves. Except for the angels. They arrive on the half-hour in the sky above. That's when we go into Latin."

The three tigers stand apart, looking across the graveyard at the church with their terrible eyes. They lie down among the tombs.

One or two people are arriving—not many. They are walking up the path to the porch, passing under a bunch of mistletoe reminiscent of other times.

A woman with a small, muffled-up boy pauses beneath the mistletoe as she straightens him out; Terry Hogbin, thought to be retarded. He looks out over the graveyard and waves at a lynx. His mother pulls him into church.

"So we just wait here, then, do we?" asks a nervous bongo, most beautiful, most fleet of all antelopes, most aristocratic of hoofstock.

"I don't know. This isn't in the poem," says a common sort of nilgai. "Ask the bloody tamarins."

The tamarins confer manically together. They can't say, they can't say. Stay or go?

The gorilla, Wallace, decides it. He sighs, raises his vast grey bottom and lopes on fingers and toes into church, where he sits in one of the empty pews at the back, a space before him and an aisle to his side. The rest, except for the tigers, follow without demur. The old lion Theodore snuffs about and settles by the shelves at the door, flat out, his chin in the hymn books.

The tigers sit out in the graveyard. Their sleek, ringed tails twitch once. Twice. Then first Hilda, followed by Enid, and at last Ackroyd get up and slide seamlessly in.

Melting snow from the pelts of the animals forms pools on the medieval flagstones. A smell arises, like fierce incense.

A parishioner sneezes.

The organ strikes up the first and most glorious Christmas hymn.

"Mum," says Terry Hogbin, "look at all them animals." She says shut up and turn round.

But neither she nor Terry, nor any of them there, ever forgot the music of that night.

The parishioners said it was like a tape. There was a new vicar, a woman. They hadn't got to know her yet and she must have set something up. It was as good as the Bach Choir, they said, or the Nine Lessons and Carols at King's College Chapel. It was like angels.

And they talked of how the candlelight had shone in a most peculiar way. The crib with its holy family, surrounded by cardboard animals, had been bathed in a midnight sunshine. The baby in the hay had stretched out His arms towards a glorious world nobody there had ever suspected. It was a pity that Terry Hogbin had upset his mother by tugging at her sleeve and talking about giraffes.

And there was that stranger, an old hunchback, who came up after the Blessing to look in the crib. And made off. And the doll they had used for the Christ child had disappeared with him.

And, come to that, so had the woman priest. She'd stood out at the church door in the snow after the service saying happy Christmas to everyone, and good night, and nobody ever saw her again. Margaret Bean, her name was. A name with a ring to it, like it might be a martyr's.

And Ackroyd had gone missing, too, the tiger who had eaten his keeper. His tracks had not been among the others making their way home; tracks that were to amaze many people the next morning. Ackroyd wasn't caught until the day after Boxing Day, and in a very confused state. He remained confused, even desolate, ever afterwards. All his life. But tigers are funny.

As for old Wallace, he took the doll from the crib up to his private lodging in the cage top, and would sit staring at it, quite still, for hours. When the silly spider monkeys tried to get hold of it and snatch it about, he would show his might. He would rise up in his terrible strength and beat upon his black, rock-hard breast, though (it has to be said) he hadn't much of a notion why.

Run Silent, Run Deep

by

PETER GOLDSWORTHY

I

He has kept the best gift till last, but his heart is in his mouth as his daughter teases apart the veils of tissue paper. Kneeling beneath the plastic Christmas tree amid a scattering of earlier, disappointing offerings—three-for-the-price-of-two novels, last season's Calvin Klein T-shirt—she lifts out a small leather carry-bag, unzips it and peers inside.

A quick verdict; her thin face is lit—fattened—by a rare smile, and she wraps her arms around him, the failure of the earlier gifts already forgotten. The lurid, green tree—"Is it biodegradable, Nick?"—is also forgotten. Even the disgrace of the previous night, when he drove himself home from Christmas Eve work drinks and she sniffed his breath before declaring him irresponsible, now seems ancient history.

"This is *so* good, Dad."

Having answered to Nick for too many weeks, he feels his heart swell happily at the restoration of proper rank and title. He watches through a dad's moist, sentimental eyes as she fits the compact video camera snugly into her right hand and squints into the viewfinder. It might be some exotic wind instrument, but played with the eye, not the mouth; he marvels as she fingers the various stops and keys without need of manual or sheet music.

"Wicked," she says, still grinning from ear to ear. "Thanks heaps, Dad."

He often worries for her health—vegetarian for the past year, all skin and bone—but again that smile somehow adds a layer of reassuring puppy fat to the lean angles of her nose and cheekbones.

When she smiles she puts on weight.

For the rest of Christmas morning daughter and camcorder are inseparable. She films—tapes? shoots?—Nick as he unwraps his Christmas gifts from her: joke tie, Best of Stones CD.

"How did you know, Emma?"

"Clairvoyant, Dad."

She tapes the bottle of Glenfiddich malt he has wrapped and now unwraps "for the dog," zooming in without passing judgment. She tapes the dog attacking its other present, a rubber bone. She tapes 360-degree sweeps of both small rooms of the small apartment; she tapes herself in the bathroom mirror, videotaping.

Late in the morning, she connects the camcorder to the television and they sit down together to watch. He holds his breath, momentarily anxious again, as the picture flickers and fuzzes, but all is soon smoothly tracking. Not even the handheld jerkiness can dampen her pleasure. She replays several key moments, laughing uproariously as his image Charlie-Chaplins silently about the house, on fast-forward or fast-reverse.

"Look at you, Dad! Sweet!"

The familiar scenes end without warning, an abrupt cut from a sleeping dog, her last shot of the morning, to—what?

"What's this? I didn't shoot *this*."

He sits forward on the edge of the sofa, equally puzzled. At first he thinks it might be a scene from some badly shot and underlit movie: a bed, two pillowed heads, two voices—one male, one female—intimately murmuring.

Emma turns to him, then back to the screen, mystified. "You didn't tape one of your *girl*friends…?" Her words trail off; she realizes even as she speaks that neither of the heads on that pillow belongs to him.

He reaches for the remote and turns up the volume. The man in the bed is whispering something to his partner—June? Jane?—about how much he will miss her.

"It's a used tape," Emma realizes.

For once he is ahead of her, already thinking back. The cassette came with the camera; he assumed it was blank when he tested the machine in the store, tracking about the shelves of merchandise for several minutes, zooming in on the sales assistant, then replaying a few minutes of the tape till he was satisfied.

Emma is hot on his trail. "Is this a second*hand* camcorder, Nick?"

Stripped of rank and title already. "I thought it was new," he murmurs lamely.

"Where did you get it?"

"At, ah, Buy'n'Sell."

"The *pawn*broker's?"

He hasn't yet told her that he has furnished his small apartment almost entirely from Buy'n'Sell. "It's just a secondhand dealer, Em."

"It's a *fence*. And this camera is stolen property."

He stares at her, a little in awe. Sixteen going on sixty. Where does this stuff come from? School lessons, regurgitated? Model Citizenship 1A? Ethics for Parrots?

She is looking intently again at the screen, at the bed and its two ill-defined occupants. An edge of filmy curtain drifts into frame, then billows away, as if eddying in a slight breeze. "The camera is outside a window," she declares. A short pause, then a further conclusion: "It must be a peeping Tom!"

The notion has crossed his mind too, but the gaze of the camera seems too steady, too fixed. "No," he says. "I think it's inside the room. Sitting on the sill."

The man has thrown back the quilt, exposing both bodies, although little detail is visible in the dim light. His partner pulls the covering back up, mumbling something about the cold.

"Then it must have been stolen from those people," Emma decides.

She presses the stop button and sets down the camcorder as if it is toxic. All warmth has vanished from her lean face; with the loss of her smile she also loses weight. Her mouth is as small and tight as an asterisk.

"I can't believe you gave me a *stolen* camcorder for Christmas."

"Maybe they sold it with the cassette still inside," he says, thinking quickly. "Maybe they forgot."

"Nick, *every*thing in Buy'n'Sell is stolen! You know that."

He almost groans. "We don't *know* it's stolen. If I'd known it was stolen, I would never have bought it."

She isn't listening. "Every time you buy something from those people, you're encouraging crime."

"The tape may have nothing to do with the camera, Em. Maybe someone loaded the tape at the shop."

"You don't believe that. A *drug* addict probably stole it. By buying this you're supporting a drug habit!"

"Even if it was stolen, and I'm not saying it was, insurance would have covered it."

"That's not the point," she says. "That's *why* insurance premiums are so high."

A school lesson, certainly. In sixteen sweet-and-sour years she has never once had to fork out an insurance premium.

"Perhaps if we watch the rest of the video," he suggests. "There might be more clues on it."

She gives him a horrified look. "That would be like reading someone's diary. Or spying on them. Especially *that* video."

He stares back at her, helplessly in the wrong. "Emma, I'm sorry if it's a stolen camera. Very sorry. The possibility didn't cross my mind. I was so excited about giving it to you." A pause, a deep breath. The words he is about to utter seem to require extra air to inflate them. "If it *has* been stolen—I say 'if'—there's not much we can do about it."

A car honks in the street, and again, peremptorily. Her mother. Christmas visit over. She rises, leaving the camcorder on the floor, and heads into her bedroom for her bag. When she emerges and walks past him towards the front door, it's without so much as a peck on the cheek.

"See you tomorrow?" he asks hopefully.

"Maybe."

She opens the door, then turns back again. "Love you, Nick. Don't forget to keep the wrapping paper for recycling."

2

He strips and climbs back into bed as soon as she has left. In a world that has largely turned its back on him, bed at least remains inviting. After Emma's visits he will often lie cocooned in the sheets, replaying conversations, trying to learn from his mistakes, a grub hoping for some sort of metamorphosis. Today, thoughts of his daughter are entangled with thoughts of the camera; he feels a growing urge to watch more of the tape.

He casts aside the bandaging bedclothes, wanders naked into the kitchen and fixes a basic breakfast: coffee and toast. Food, also, still returns his affection, warmly enough, although it requires an exhausting amount of work at times. He plonks himself in front of the TV with a tray on his lap and presses play.

The male character in the drama is pleading with his lover. "I want to see you naked. Please. I want to remember you when I'm away. How beautiful you are ..."

Realization strikes: of course! The woman doesn't—didn't—know she was being taped. Yet it was her room, surely: candles, filmy drapes, fancy floral quilt.

"I'll show myself if you leave the lights off, Richard," she says. "I'm no oil painting."

"You are to me," her lover—Richard—tells her, and throws back the covers again.

She climbs reluctantly from the bed and stands naked before him. Her back is to the camera, small hipped, boyishly hipped, and indistinct in the half-light—still clothed, in a sense, in shadows.

"Turn around," Richard is urging. "Twirl for me."

She raises one arm above her head, mock-ballerina style, and pirouettes half-heartedly, yet rapidly enough for her large breasts to lift a little with the centrifugal force. Could it be a movie after all? he hopes. She is beautiful, although not in a standard, actressy sort of way. Sitting in his own room, naked himself, Nick feels a slight stirring in his loins. He glances about guiltily, absurdly, as if someone might be watching *him*. Has he passed beyond the bounds of normal, healthy curiosity and become a voyeur? Enough is enough; he reaches out and stops the tape, presses rewind.

There is much to do, especially in his exhausted state: Christmas wrappings to fold, and recycle; the dog's Glenfiddich malt to sample. There is a body, his, to bathe and dress. There is even another drinks party to attend, later in the day, if he feels courageous enough.

He steps into the bathroom and turns on the shower. Hot fingers of water engulf him, massaging his scalp and stroking his face, as reliably as ever. The shower ceremony, also, offers a cocoon he has come to depend on, morning and evening. A warm cocoon at the turn of a tap. His shower still loves him, he likes to joke to friends. His shower, and his dog.

Cheered by the attentions of hot, pressurized water, he towels himself dry, pulls on some clothes, and steps out of the bathroom to face the world.

3

He had warned Emma when she rang the following morning that the local police station might be closed on Boxing Day. But she'd insisted that he drive her to report the theft—"Mum thinks so, too"—and here, now, the front doors of the station are wide open, although no officers seem to be in attendance.

"Ripe for a burglary," he murmurs, following her inside.

She ignores the mild joke as she jangles a handbell attached to the desk by a tough, stainless-steel chain.

No response.

She jangles the bell again; a plump, bespectacled sergeant wearing a floppy red Santa cap waddles out from the rear room. "Merry Christmas."

"Ho ho ho," Nick says.

Emma has no time for niceties. "I want to report a stolen camcorder."

The sergeant's eyes flick from her to Nick, and back. "When was it stolen?"

Emma seems momentarily flummoxed. "We don't know. That's the point. Nick?"

She turns and gestures to him, the bearer of the stolen goods; he sets the camera down on the counter.

The sergeant looks on from afar, disinterestedly. "How do you know it was stolen?"

Emma reaches over and ejects the cassette. "This was inside. It contains vital clues."

The sergeant picks it up. "What's on it?" he asks, turning it this way and that for a time, squinting, as if he can somehow bring the recording into focus with the naked eye.

"Not much," Nick tells him. "I've watched most of it."

His daughter turns on him, incredulous.

Nick keeps his eyes on the sergeant. "It's a recording. Two people in bed. The previous owners, I guess."

The sergeant looks momentarily interested. "Porn?"

Nick shakes his head. "Home movie."

"Nothing identifying?"

Another shake of the head. The sergeant replaces the tape in the camera, and hands it back to Nick.

"What are you doing?" Emma demands to know. "You don't want to keep it?"

"Serial number will do. If someone has reported it missing, we'll be in contact. It's a Christmas present, right? Enjoy it. Best not to record over the tape, though."

"What happens if you find the owner?"

"Not all that likely with what we have to go on. I think you can safely regard it as your property."

Emma stands fast, refusing to leave, glaring at the sergeant; he shifts his glance away. Nick half smiles to see his own avoidance duplicated, exactly.

"I'll have to find them myself," she finally announces.

The sergeant looks to Nick, then away—another avoidance, this time perhaps of the possibility of a smile.

"Don't make any citizen's arrests," he says. "Merry Christmas."

"Christmas was yesterday," Emma reminds him, and turns on her heel and leaves, trailing Nick in her wake.

4

They watch the tape together again at home that afternoon, after fast-forwarding through Emma's Christmas-morning home movie. Nick sits slightly to one side on the Buy'n'Sell sofa, as much interested in Emma's response as in the tape. She had demanded to visit another police station—"Somewhere staffed by *honest* cops"—he had managed to talk her out of it. Now she sits on the floor at his feet, studying the screen, occasionally pausing the tape to jot notes on a small pad. Only when the tape reaches the point at which he'd stopped watching—the woman, naked, pirouetting—does he begin to pay as much attention to the screen as to his daughter. What might come next? The man called Richard is out of bed, he sees, and suddenly the bedroom light is on. Exposed, his lover wraps her arms around her body, wearing her hands like clothes, covering up.

"Turn it off," she is saying. "I feel embarrassed."

"I want to feast on you," he tells her. "I want to remember this—every detail, every single hair on your beautiful head."

"Turn it off," she repeats, begging. "Please."

His tone becomes more hectoring. "Jane, I'm not asking much. Jesus! Put yourself in my place. Three months at sea!"

A sailor? Nick turns to Emma; her mouth is set in a small, triumphant smile as she jots the vital clue on her notepad.

"Three months without being able to touch you, talk with you."

"You said you'd be able to phone."

"A few minutes each week. It's very costly from the sub."

Nick sits forward a little; this is becoming interesting. A submariner? Emma continues scribbling triumphantly.

The man's tone becomes honeyed again, cajoling. "Turn around and wiggle your lovely arse at me."

She turns reluctantly, and is suddenly staring straight into the frame, straight at Nick.

"What's that on the sill?"

"Come back to bed." Her lover's voice from somewhere behind her.

Instead she steps closer to the camera, filling the frame. Nick shivers, disconcerted. He feels an urge to hide from her eyes, as if she can see him. Watching. Perving. He glances at Emma, her mouth has fallen slightly open, mesmerized.

"Jesus!" the woman is saying. "Are you *recording* this, Richard?" Her hand now reaching towards the camera, and suddenly the field is tilting and shifting, a giddying visual nonsense. Her face swims into view and out, and in, then the room, upside down, walls and door at odd angles. Only the voices still make sense—hers loud and foregrounded, his from somewhere more distant.

"I can't believe you would *do* this," she is saying. "Our last night together."

"That's why I wanted to remember it."

"If you'd *asked* I probably would have allowed it. I'm not that much of a prude, Richard. But to do it without even *asking,* sneakily ..."

The camera seems to be lying on its side. Nick tilts his head, but nothing useful emerges from the blur.

"Actually, I don't think I would have allowed it. Jesus! The more I think about it … I can just see you all down there in your sardine can. Friday-night happy hour in the mess. You show me your tape, I'll show you mine."

"Hardly," he says. "There are women on the boat."

But she is shouting now, beyond argument. "Get out! Get your clothes on and get out! And don't think you're taking *this*! You can leave this. I'm confiscating it!"

Then silence, and nothing but flickering snow, voice and image abruptly terminated.

Emma is staring into the blank screen, stunned. Nick reaches over and presses the stop button. His first thought: he wants to know how the story ends. He wants to know what happens next, what has *already* happened next. One narrative thread seems to have emerged: the woman pawned her lover's camera.

"I guess we know who the thief is," he says.

Emma seems unusually subdued. Eventually: "I hardly think that 'thief' is the word, Nick."

He is tempted, momentarily, to turn the tape into a Topic, a Good Citizenship discussion. Should Jane have allowed Richard to tape her, as a memento, a visual treat to warm him through the long, submerged nights? Should the camera be returned to Richard, its rightful owner? The questions soon became parodies of themselves; kindergarten-primer versions pop into his head, and urge themselves on his tongue. Look, Jane, see Dick's camera. Is Dick naughty? Is Jane naughty? See Dick's *dick*!

Amused, he manages to keep his mouth shut. Emma's silence is only temporary, he knows. Within minutes, she will have the issues boxed and sorted, with or without his help. For the moment, while he waits for her further guidance, it is a pleasure just to be next to her, as she sits in silence, pen poised above pad, in front of the grey, snowing confusion of the screen.

A Visit to Morin

by

GRAHAM GREENE

[1]

Le Diable au Ciel—there it was on a shelf in the Colmar book-shop causing a memory to reach out to me from the past of twenty years ago. One didn't often, in the 1950s, see Pierre Morin's novels on display, and yet here were two copies of his once famous book, and looking along the rows of paper bindings I discovered others, as though there existed in Alsace a secret *cave,* like those hidden cellars where wines were once preserved from the enemy for the days when peace would return.

I had admired Pierre Morin when I was a boy, but I had almost forgotten him. He was even then an older writer on the point of abandonment by his public, but the language-class in an English public school is always a long way behind the Paris fashions. We happened at Collingworth to have a Roman Catholic master who belonged to the generation which Morin had pleased or offended. He had offended the orthodox Catholics in his own country and pleased the liberal Catholics abroad; he had pleased, too, the French Protestants who believed in God with the same intensity he seemed to show, and he found enthusiastic readers among non-Christians who, when once they had accepted imaginatively his premises, perhaps detected in his work the freedom of speculation which put his fellow Catholics on their guard. How fresh and exciting his work had appeared to my schoolmaster's generation; and to me, brought up in a lower form on *Les Misérables* and the poems of Lamartine, he was a revolutionary writer. But it is the fate of revolutionaries that the world accepts them. The excitement has gone from Morin's pages. Only the orthodox read him now, when the whole world seems prepared to believe in a god, except strangely enough—but I will not anticipate the point of my small anecdote which may yet provide a footnote to the literary history of Morin's day. When I publish it no harm can be done. Morin will be dead in the flesh as well as being dead as a writer, and he has left, so far as I am aware, no descendants and no disciples.

I yet recall with pleasure those French classes presided over by a Mr. Strangeways from Chile; his swarthy complexion was said by his enemies to indicate Spanish blood (it was the period of the Spanish Civil War when anything Spanish and Roman was regarded as Fascist) and by his friends, of whom I was one, a dash of Indian. In dull fact his father was an engineer from Wolverhampton and his mother came from Louisiana and was only Latin after three removes. At these senior classes we no longer studied syntax—at which Mr. Strangeways was in any case weak. Mr. Strangeways read aloud to us and we read aloud to him, but after five minutes we would launch into literary criticism, pulling to pieces with youthful daring—Mr. Strangeways like so many schoolmasters remained always youthful—the great established names and building up with exaggerated appreciation those who had not yet "arrived." Of course Morin had arrived years before, but of that we were unaware in our brick prison five hundred miles from the Seine—he hadn't reached the school textbooks; he hadn't yet been mummified by Messrs Hachette et Cie. Where we didn't understand his meaning, there were no editor's notes to kill speculation.

"Can he really believe that?" I remember exclaiming to Mr. Strangeways when a character in *Le Diable au Ciel* made some dark and horrifying statement on the Atonement or the Redemption, and I remember Mr. Strangeways' blunt reply, flapping the sleeves of his short black gown, "But I believe it too, Dunlop." He did not leave it at that or allow himself to get involved in a theological debate, which might have imperilled his post in my Protestant school. He went on to indicate that we were unconcerned with what the author believed. The author had chosen as his viewpoint the character of an orthodox Catholic—all his thoughts therefore must be affected, as they would be in life, by his orthodoxy. Morin's technique forbade him to play a part in the story himself; even to show irony would be to cheat, though perhaps we might detect something of Morin's view from the fact that the orthodoxy of Durobier was extended to the furthest possible limits, so that at the close of the book we had the impression of a man stranded on a long strip of sand from which there was no possibility of advance, and to retreat towards the shore would be to surrender. "Is this true or is it not true?" His whole creed was concerned in the answer.

"You mean," I asked Mr. Strangeways, "that perhaps Morin does not believe?"

"I mean nothing of the kind. No one has seriously questioned his Catholicism, only his prudence. Anyway that's not true criticism. A novel is made up of words and characters. Are the words well chosen and do the characters live? All the rest belongs to literary gossip. You are not in this class to learn how to be gossip-writers."

And yet in those days I would have liked to know. Sometimes Mr. Strangeways, recognizing my interest in Morin, would lend me Roman Catholic literary periodicals which contained notices of the novelist's work that often offended his principle of leaving the author's views out of account. I found Morin was sometimes accused of Jansenism—whatever that might be: others called him an Augustinian—a name which meant as little to me—and in the better printed and bulkier reviews I thought I detected a note of grievance. He believed all the right things, they could find no specific fault, and yet ... it was as though some of his characters accepted a dogma so wholeheartedly that they drew out its implications to the verge of absurdity, while others examined a dogma as though they were constitutional lawyers determined on confining it to a kind of legal minimum. Durobier, I am sure, would have staked his life on a literal Assumption: at some point in history, somewhere in the latter years of the first century A.D., the body of the Virgin had floated skywards, leaving an empty tomb. On the other hand there was a character called Sagrin, in one of the minor novels, perhaps *Le Bien Pensant,* who believed that the holy body had rotted in the grave like other bodies. The strange thing was that both views seemed to possess irritating qualities to Catholic reviewers, and yet both proved to be equally in accordance with the dogmatic pronouncement when it came. One could assert therefore that they were orthodox; yet the orthodox critics seemed to scent heresy like a rat dead somewhere under the boards, at a spot they could not locate.

These, of course, were ancient criticisms, fished out of Mr. Strangeways' cupboard, full of old French magazines dating back to his long-lost sojourn in Paris some time during the late 'twenties, when he had attended lectures at the Sorbonne and drunk beer at the Dôme. The word "paradox" was frequently used with an air of disapproval. Perhaps after all the orthodox were proved right, for I certainly was to discover just how far Morin carried in his own life the sense of paradox.

[2]

I am not one of those who revisit their old school, or what a disappointment I would have proved to Mr. Strangeways, who must by now be on the point of retirement. I think he had pictured me in the future as a distinguished writer for the weeklies on the subject of French literature—perhaps even as the author of a scholarly biography of Corneille. In fact, after an undistinguished war-record, I obtained a post, with the help of influential connections, in a firm of wine-merchants. My French syntax, so neglected by Mr. Strangeways, had been improved by the war and proved useful to the firm, and I suppose I had a certain literary flair which enabled me to improve on the rather old-fashioned style of the catalogues. The directors had been content for too long with the jargon of the Wine and Food Society—"An unimportant but highly sympathetic wine for light occasions among friends." I introduced a more realistic note and substituted knowledge for knowingness. "This wine comes from a small vineyard on the western slopes of the Mont Soleil range. The soil in this region has Jurassic elements, as the vineyard is on the edge of the great Jurassic fissure which extends across Europe from the Urals, and this encourages the cultivation of a small, strong, dark grape with a high sugar-content, less vulnerable than more famous wines to the chances of weather." Of course it was the same "unimportant" wine, but my description gave the host material for his vanity.

Business had brought me to Colmar—we had found it necessary to change our agent there, and as I am a single man and find the lonely Christmases of London sad and regretful, I had chosen to combine my visit with the Christmas holiday. One does not feel alone abroad; I imagined drinking my way through the festival itself in some *bierhaus* decorated with holly, myself invisible behind the fume of cigars. A German Christmas is Christmas *par excellence:* singing, sentiment, gluttony.

I said to the shop assistant, "You seem to have a good supply of M. Morin's books."

"He is very popular," she said.

"I got the impression that in Paris he is no longer much read."

"We are Catholics here," she said with a note of reproof. "Besides, he lives near Colmar, and we are very proud he chose to settle in our neighbourhood."

"How long has he been here?"

"He came immediately after the war. We consider him almost one of us. We have all his books in German also—you will see them over there. Some of us feel he is even finer in German than in French. German," she said, scrutinizing me with contempt as I picked up a French edition of *Le Diable au Ciel,* "has a better vocabulary for the profundities."

I told her I had admired M. Morin's novels since my schooldays. She softened towards me then, and I left the shop with M. Morin's address—a village fifteen miles from Colmar. I was uncertain all the same whether I would call on him. What really had I to say to him to excuse the vulgarity of my curiosity? Writing is the most private of all the arts, and yet few of us hesitate to invade the writer's home. We have all heard of that one caller from Porlock, but hundreds of callers every day are ringing door-bells, lifting receivers, thrusting themselves into the secret room where a writer works and lives.

I doubt whether I should have ventured to ring M. Morin's bell, but I caught sight of him two days later at the Midnight Mass in a village outside Colmar; it was not the village where I had been told he lived, and I wondered why he had come such a distance alone. Midnight Mass is a service which even a non-believer like myself finds inexplicably moving. Perhaps there is some memory of childhood which makes the journey through the darkness, the lighted windows and the frosty night, the slow gathering of silent strangers from the four quarters of the countryside moving and significant. There was a crib to the left of the door as I came in—the plaster-baby sprawled in the plaster-lap, and the cows, the sheep and the shepherd cast long shadows in the candlelight. Among the kneeling women was an old man whose face I seemed to remember: a round head like a peasant's, the skin wrinkled like a stale apple, with the hair gone from the crown. He knelt, bowed his head, and rose again. There had just been time, I suppose, for a formal prayer, but it must have been a short one. His chin was stubbled white like the field outside, and there was so little about him to suggest a member of the French Academy that I might have taken him for the peasant he appeared to be, in his suit of respectable and shiny black and his black tie like a bootlace, if I had not been attracted by the eyes. The eyes gave him away: they seemed to know too much and to have seen further than the season and the fields. Of a very clear pale blue, they continually shifted focus, looking close and looking away, observant, sad and curious like those of a man caught in some great catastrophe which it is his duty to record, but which he cannot bear to contemplate for any length of time. It was not, of course, during his short prayer before the crib that I had time to watch Morin so closely; but when the congregation was shuffling up towards the altar for Communion, Morin and I found ourselves alone among the empty chairs. It was then I recognized him—perhaps from memories of old photographs in Mr. Strangeways' reviews. I do not know, yet I was convinced of his identity, and I wondered what it was that kept this old and distinguished Catholic from going up with the others, at this Mass of all Masses in the year, to receive the Sacrament. Had he perhaps inadvertently broken his fast, or was he a man who suffered from scruples and did he believe that he had been guilty of some act of uncharity or greed? There could not be many serious temptations, I thought, for a man who must be approaching his eightieth year. And yet I would not have believed him scrupulous; it was from his own novels I had learnt of the existence of this malady of the religious, and I would never have supposed the creator of Durobier to have suffered from the same disease as his character. However, a novelist may sometimes write most objectively of his own failings.

We sat there alone at the back of the church. The air was as cold and still as a frozen tree and the candles burned straight on the altar and God, so they believed, passed along the altar-rail. This was the birth of Christianity: outside in the dark was old savage Judea, but in here the world was only a few minutes old. It was the Year One again, and I felt the old sentimental longing to believe as those, I suppose, believed who came back one by one from the rail, with lips set like closed doors around the dissolving wafer and with crossed hands. If I had said to one of them, "Teach me why you believe," what would the answer have been? I thought perhaps I knew, for once in the war—driven by fear and disgust at the sight of the dead—I had spoken to a Catholic chaplain in just that way. He didn't belong to my unit, he was a busy man—it isn't the job of a chaplain in the line to instruct or convert and he was not to blame that he could convey nothing of his faith to an outsider like myself. He lent me two books—one a penny-catechism with its catalogue of preposterous questions and answers, smug and explanatory—mystery like a butterfly killed by cyanide, stiffened and laid out with pins and paper-strips; the other a sober enough study of gospel dates. I lost them both in a few days, along with three bottles of whisky, my jeep and the corporal whose name I had not time to learn before he was killed, while I was peeing in the green canal close by. I don't suppose I'd have kept the books much longer anyway. They were not the kind of help I needed, nor was the chaplain the man to give it me. I remember asking him if he had read Morin's novels. "I haven't time to waste with him," he said abruptly.

"They were the first books," I said, "to interest me in your faith."

"You'd have done much better to read Chesterton," he said. So it was odd to find myself there at the back of the church with Morin himself. He was the first to leave and I followed him out. I was glad to go, for the sentimental attraction of a Midnight Mass was lost in the long *ennui* of the communions.

"M. Morin," I said in that low voice we assume in a church or hospital.

He looked quickly, and I thought defensively, up.

I said, "Forgive my speaking to you like this, M. Morin, but your books have given me such great pleasure." Had the man from Porlock employed the same banal phrases?

"You are English?" he asked.

"Yes."

He spoke to me then in English. "You write yourself? Forgive my asking, but I do not know your name."

"Dunlop. But I don't write. I buy and sell wine."

"A profession more worthy of respect," M. Morin said. "If you would care to drive with me—I live only ten kilometres from here—I think I could show you a wine you may not have encountered."

"Surely, it's rather late, M. Morin. And I have a driver ..."

"Send him home. After Midnight Mass I find it difficult to sleep. You would be doing me a kindness." When I hesitated he said, "As for tomorrow, that is just any day of the year, and I don't like visitors."

I tried to make a joke of it. "You mean it's my only chance?" and he replied "Yes" with seriousness. The doors of the church swung open and the congregation came slowly out into the frosty glitter, peeking at the holy water stoup with their forefingers, chatting cheerfully again as the mystery receded, greeting neighbours. A wailing child marked the lateness of the hour like a clock. M. Morin strode away and I followed him.

[3]

M. Morin drove with clumsy violence, wrenching at his gears, scraping the right-hand hedgerows as though the car were a new invention and he a courageous pioneer in its use. "So you have read some of my books?" he asked.

"A great many, when I was a schoolboy ..."

"You mean they are fit only for children?"

"I mean nothing of the sort."

"What can a child find in them?"

"I was sixteen when I began to read them. That's not a child."

"Oh well, now they are only read by the old—and the pious. Are you pious, Mr. Dunlop?"

"I'm not a Catholic."

"I'm glad to hear that. Then I shan't offend you."

"Once I thought of becoming one."

"Second thoughts are best."

"I think it was your books that made me curious."

"I will not take responsibility," he said. "I am not a theologian." We bumped over a little branch railway-track without altering speed and swerved right through a gateway much in need of repair. A light hanging in a porch shone on an open door.

"Don't you lock up," I asked him, "in these parts?"

He said, "Ten years ago—times were bad then—a hungry man was frozen to death near here on Christmas morning. He could find no one to open a door: there was a blizzard, but they were all at church. Come in," he said angrily from the porch; "are you looking round, making notes of how I live? Have you deceived me? Are you a journalist?"

If I had had my own car with me I would have driven away. "M. Morin," I said, "there are different kinds of hunger. You seem only to cater for one kind." He went ahead of me into a small study—a desk, a table, two comfortable chairs, and some bookshelves oddly bare—I could see no sign of his own books. There was a bottle of brandy on the table, ready perhaps for the stranger and the blizzard that would never again come together in this place.

"Sit down," he said, "sit down. You must forgive me if I was discourteous. I am unused to company. I will go and find the wine I spoke of. Make yourself at home." I had never seen a man less at home himself. It was as if he were camping in a house that belonged to another.

While he was away, I looked more closely at his bookshelves. He had not rebound any of his paper-backs and his shelves had the appearance of bankrupt stock: small tears and dust and the discolouration of sunlight. There was a great deal of theology, some poetry, very few novels. He came back with the wine and a plate of salami. When he had tasted the wine himself, he poured me a glass. "It will do," he said.

"It's excellent. Remarkable."

"A small vineyard twenty miles away. I will give you the address before you go. For me, on a night like this, I prefer brandy." So perhaps it was really for himself and not for the stranger, I thought, that the bottle stood ready.

"It's certainly cold."

"It was not the weather I meant."

"I have been looking at your library. You read a lot of theology?"

"Not now."

"I wonder if you would recommend ..." But I had even less success with him than with the chaplain.

"No. Not if you want to believe. If you are foolish enough to want that you must avoid theology."

"I don't understand."

He said, "A man can accept anything to do with God until scholars begin to go into the details and the implications. A man can accept the Trinity, but the arguments that follow ..."

He gave a gesture of rejection. "I would never try to determine some point in differential calculus with a two-times-two table. You end by disbelieving the calculus." He poured out two more glasses and drank his own as though it were vodka. "I used to believe in revelation, but I never believed in the capacity of the human mind."

"You used to believe?"

"Yes, Mr. Dunlop—was that the name?—*used*. If you are one of those who come seeking belief, go away. You will not find it here."

"But from your books ..."

"You will find none of them," he said, "on my shelves."

"I noticed you have some theology."

"Even disbelief," he said, with his eye on the brandy bottle, "needs bolstering." I noticed that the brandy affected him very quickly, not only his readiness to communicate with me, but even the physical appearance of his eyeballs. It was as if the little blood-cells had been waiting under the white membrane to burst at once like buds with the third glass. He said, "Can you find anything more inadequate than the scholastic arguments for the existence of God?"

"I'm afraid I don't know them."

"The arguments from an agent, from a cause?"

"No."

"They tell you that in all change there are two elements, that which is changed and that which changes it. Each agent of change is itself determined by some higher agent. Can this go on *ad infinitum?* Oh no, they say, that would not give the finality that thought demands. But does thought demand it? Why shouldn't the chain go on for ever? Man has invented the idea of infinity. In any case how trivial any argument based on what human thought demands must be. The thoughts of you and me and Monsieur Dupont. I would prefer the thoughts of an ape. Its instincts are less corrupted. Show me a gorilla praying and I might believe again."

"But surely there are other arguments?"

"Four. Each more inadequate than the other. It needs a child to say to these theologians, Why? Why not? Why not an infinite series of causes? Why should the existence of a good and a better imply the existence of a best? "This is playing with words. We invent the words and make arguments from them. The better is not a fact: it is only a word and a human judgment."

"You are arguing," I said, "against someone who can't answer you back. You see, M. Morin, I don't believe either. I'm curious, that's all."

"Ah," he said, "you've said that before—curious. Curiosity is a great trap. They used to come here in their dozens to see me. I used to get letters saying how I had converted them by this book or that. Long after I ceased to believe myself I was a carrier of belief, like a man can be a carrier of disease without being sick. Women especially." He added with disgust, "I had only to sleep with a woman to make a convert." He turned his red eyes towards me and really seemed to require an answer when he said, "What sort of Rasputin life was that?" The brandy by now had really taken a hold; I wondered how many years he had been waiting for some stranger without faith to whom he could speak with frankness.

"Did you never tell this to a priest? I always imagined in your faith ..."

"There were always too many priests," he said, "around me. The priests swarmed like flies. Near me and any woman I knew. First I was an exhibit for their faith. I was useful to them, a sign that even an intelligent man could believe. That was the period of the Dominicans, who liked the literary atmosphere and good wine. Then afterwards when the books stopped, and they smelt something—gamey—in my religion, it was the turn of the Jesuits, who never despair of what they call a man's soul."

"And why did the books stop?"

"Who knows? Did you never write verses for some girl when you were a boy?"

"Of course."

"But you didn't marry the girl, did you? The unprofessional poet writes of his feelings and when the poem is finished he finds his love dead on the page. Perhaps I wrote away my belief like the young man writes away his love. Only it took longer—twenty years and fifteen books." He held up the wine. "Another glass?"

"I would rather have some of your brandy." Unlike the wine it was a crude and common mark, and I thought again, For a beggar's sake or his own? I said, "All the same you go to Mass."

"I go to Midnight Mass on Christmas Eve," he said. "The worst of Catholics goes then—even those who do not go at Easter. It is the Mass of our childhood. And of mercy. What would they think if I were not there? I don't want to give scandal. You must realize I wouldn't speak to any one of my neighbours as I have spoken to you. I am their Catholic author, you see. Their Academician. I never wanted to help anyone believe, but God knows I wouldn't take a hand in robbing them ..."

"I was surprised at one thing when I saw you there, M. Morin."

"Yes?"

I said rashly, "You and I were the only ones who didn't take Communion."

"That is why I don't go to the church in my own village. That too would be noticed and cause scandal."

"Yes, I can see that." I stumbled heavily on (perhaps the brandy had affected me too). "Forgive me, M. Morin, but I wondered at your age what kept you from Communion. Of course now I know the reason."

"Do you?" Morin said. "Young man, I doubt it." He looked at me across his glass with impersonal enmity. He said, "You don't understand a thing I have been saying to you. What a story you would make of this if you were a journalist and yet there wouldn't be a word of truth ..."

I said stiffly, "I thought you made it perfectly clear that you had lost your faith."

"Do you think that would keep anyone from the Confessional? You are a long way from understanding the Church or the human mind, Mr. Dunlop. Why, it is one of the most common confessions of all for a priest to hear— almost as common as adultery. 'Father, I have lost my faith.' The priest, you may be sure, makes it himself often enough at the altar before he receives the Host."

I said—I was angry in return now, "Then what keeps you away? Pride? One of your Rasputin women?"

"As you so rightly thought," he said, "women are no longer a problem at my age." He looked at his watch. "Two-thirty. Perhaps I ought to drive you back."

"No," I said, "I don't want to part from you like this. It's the drink which makes us irritable. Your books are still important to me. I know I'm ignorant. I an not a Catholic and never shall be, but in the old days your books made me understand that at least it might be possible to believe. You never closed the door in my face as you are doing now. Nor did your characters, Durobier, Sagrin." I indicated the brandy bottle. "I told you just now—people are not only hungry and thirsty in that way. Because you've lost *your* faith …"

He interrupted me ferociously. "I never told you that."

"Then what have you been talking about all this time?"

"I told you I had lost my belief. That's quite a different thing. But how are you to understand?"

"You don't give me a chance."

He was obviously striving to be patient. He said, "I will put it this way. If a doctor prescribed you a drug and told you to take it every day for the rest of your life and you stopped obeying him and drank no more, and your health decayed, would you not have faith in your doctor all the more?"

"Perhaps. But I still don't understand you."

"For twenty years," Morin said, "I excommunicated myself voluntarily. I never went to Confession. I loved a woman too much to pretend to myself that I would ever leave her. You know the condition of absolution? A firm purpose of amendment. I had no such purpose. Five years ago my mistress died and my sex died with her."

"Then why couldn't you go back?"

"I was afraid. I am still afraid."

"Of what the priest would say?"

"What a strange idea you have of the Church. No, not of what the priest would say. He would say nothing. I daresay there is no greater gift you can give a priest in the confessional, Mr. Dunlop, than to return to it after many years. He feels of use again. But can't you understand? I can tell myself now that my lack of belief is a final proof that the Church is right and the faith is true. I had cut myself off for twenty years from grace and my belief withered as the priests said it would. I don't believe in God and His Son and His angels and His saints, but I know the reason why I don't believe and the reason is—the Church is true and what she taught me is true. For twenty years I have been without the sacraments and I can see the effect. The wafer must be more than wafer."

"But if you went back …?"

"If I went back and belief did not return? That is what I fear, Mr. Dunlop. As long as I keep away from the sacraments, my lack of belief is an argument for the Church. But if I returned and they failed me, then I would really be a man without faith, who had better hide himself quickly in the grave so as not to discourage others." He laughed uneasily. "Paradoxical, Mr. Dunlop?"

"That is what they said of your books."

"I know."

"Your characters carried their ideas to extreme lengths. So your critics said."

"And you think I do too?"

"Yes, M. Morin."

His eyes wouldn't meet mine. He grimaced beyond me. "At least I am not a carrier of disease any longer. You have escaped infection." He added, "Time for bed, Mr. Dunlop. Time for bed. The young need more sleep."

"I am not as young as that."

"To me you seem very young."

He drove me back to my hotel and we hardly spoke. I was thinking of the strange faith which held him even now after he had ceased to believe. I had felt very little curiosity since that moment of the war when I had spoken to the chaplain, but now I began to wonder again.

M. Morin considered he had ceased to be a carrier, and I couldn't help hoping that he was right. He had forgotten to give me the address of the vineyard, but I had forgotten to ask him for it when I said good night.

The Coming
of the Christ-Child

by

BESSIE HEAD

HE WAS BORN on a small mission station in the Eastern Cape
and he came from a long line of mission-educated men;
great-grandfathers, grandfathers and even his own father had
all been priests. Except for a brief period of public activity,
the quietude and obscurity of that life was to cling around
him all his days. Later, in the turmoil and tumult of his life
in Johannesburg, where Christmas Eve was a drunken riot,
he liked to tell friends of the way in which his parents had

welcomed the coming of the Christ-Child each Christmas
Eve:

"We would sit in silence with bowed heads; just silent like
that for a half an hour before midnight. I still like the way the
old people did it...."

One part of the history of South Africa was also the history
of Christianity because it was only the missions that represented a continuous effort to strengthen black people in their
struggle to survive, and provided them with a tenuous link
between past and future. The psychological battering the older
generations underwent was so terrible as to reduce them to a
state beyond the nonhuman. It could also be said that all the
people unconsciously chose Christianity to maintain their
compactness, their wholeness and humanity, for they were
assaulted on all sides as primitives who were two thousand
years behind the white man in civilization. They were robbed
of everything they possessed—their land and cattle—and
when they lost everything, they brought to Christianity the
same reverence they had once offered to tribe, custom and
ancestral worship. The younger generations remembered the
elders; Christianity created generations of holy people all over
the land.

And so the foundations of a new order of life were laid by
the missions, and since the ministry was a tradition in his own
family, its evolutionary pattern could be traced right from his
great-grandfather's time when the lonely outpost mission
church was also the first elementary school existing solely to
teach the Bible. From Bible schools, children began to scratch
on slates and receive a more general education, until a number
of high schools and one university college, attached to

missions, spread like a network throughout the land. He was a product of this evolutionary stream and by the time he was born his family enjoyed considerable prestige. They were affluent and lived in a comfortable house, the property of the church, which was surrounded by a large garden. Their life belonged to the community; their home life was the stormy centre of all the tragedies that had fallen on the people, who, no matter which way they turned, were defaulters and criminals in their own land. Much is known about the fearful face of white supremacy, its greed and ruthless horrors. They fell upon the people like a leaden weight and they lay there, an agonizing burden to endure.

One day there was—but then there were so many such days—a major catastrophe for the church. The police entered during the hour of worship (it was a point with all the white races of the land that no part of a black man's life was sacred and inviolable) and arrested most of the men as poll tax defaulters. The issue at that time was how people with an income of twenty shillings a year could pay a poll tax of twenty shillings a year. There was only such misery in the rural areas, grandly demarcated as the "native reserves." Land was almost non-existent and people thrust back into the reserves struggled to graze stock on small patches of the earth. The stock were worthless, scabby and diseased and almost unsaleable. Starving men with stock losses were driven into working on the mines and the Boer farms for wages just sufficient to cover their poll tax. When their labour was no longer needed in the mines they were endorsed back to the mythical rural areas. There was no such thing as the rural areas left—only hard patterns of greed of which all the people were victims. It was impressed on people that they were guilty of one supposed crime after another and in this way they were conditioned to offer themselves as a huge reservoir of cheap labour.

Thus it was that the grubby day-to-day detail of human misery unfolded before the young man's eyes. Often only five shillings stood between a man and his conviction as a defaulter of some kind, and it was his father's habit to dip deep into his own pocket or the coffers of the church to aid one of his members. That day of the mass arrest of the men in church was to linger vividly in the young man's mind. His father walked up and down for some time, wringing his hands in distress, his composure shaken to the core. Then he had attempted to compose himself and continue the disrupted service, but a cynical male voice in the congregation shouted:

"Answer this question, Father. How is it that when the white man came here, he had only the Bible and we the land. Today, he has the land and we the Bible," and a second disruption ensued from weeping women whose husbands were among those arrested.

From habit the old man dropped to his knees and buried his face in his hands. The remainder of his congregation filed out slowly with solemn faces. He knelt like that for some time, unaware that his son stood quietly near, observing him with silent, grave eyes. He was a silent, pleasant young man, who often smiled. He liked reading most and could more often than not be found with his head buried in a book. Maybe his father was praying. If so, his son's words cut so sharply into the silence that the old man jerked back his head in surprise.

"There is no God, Father," the young man said in his quiet way. "These things are done by men and it is men we should have dealings with. God is powerless to help us, should there even be such a thing."

"Do you get these ideas from books, my son?" his father asked, uncertainly. "I have not had the education you are having now because there was no University College in my days, so I have not travelled as far as you in loss of faith, even though I live in the trough of despair."

This difference in views hardly disrupted the harmonious relationship between father and son. Later, people were to revere an indefinable quality in the young politician, not realizing that he rose from the deep heart of the country, where in spite of all that was said, people were not the "humiliated, downtrodden blacks," but men like his father. Later, he was to display a courage, unequalled by any black man in the land. The romance and legends of the earlier history still quivered in the air of the rural area where he was born. Nine land wars had the tribes fought against the British. Great kings like Hintsa had conducted the wars, and in spite of the grubbiness and despair of the present, the older generations still liked to dwell on the details of his death. Hintsa had been a phenomenon, a ruler so brilliant that on his death his brains had been removed from his head so that some part of him could remain above ground to be revered and worshipped. It was a tradition of courage that his people treasured.

On graduating from university he did not choose the ministry as his career. Instead, he had one of those rare and elegant positions as Professor of Bantu Languages at the University of the Witwatersrand in Johannesburg. He was as elegant and cultured as his job and ahead of him stretched years and years of comfort and security. The black townships surrounding the city of Johannesburg absorbed genius of all kinds in astounding combinations. The poor and humble and the rich and talented lived side by side. Brilliant black men, with no outlet for their talents for management and organization, were the managers and organizers of huge crime rings around the country with vast amounts of men in their employ. They flashed about the townships in flashy American cars of the latest design and sold their stolen goods at backdoor prices to the millions of poor, honest black labourers who served the city. Johannesburg was the pulsing heart of the land; everything of significance that happened in the country first happened in Johannesburg. It was also the centre of the big labour shuttle; the gold mines stretching along the Witwatersrand, with their inexhaustible resources, needed thousands and thousands of black hands to haul those riches above ground. The city was complex, as international as the gold that flowed to all the banking houses of the world. It had also been the centre of ruthless exploitation and major political protest, and it seemed to have aged in cynicism and weariness ahead of the rest of the country. It was a war-weary and apathetic world that he entered in 1948. It was as though people said: "Ah, political protest? You name it, we've done it. What is it all for?" It took something new and fresh to stir the people out of their apathy and exhaustion.

Almost immediately he attracted a wide range of thinking men. Immediately, the details of his life attracted interest and he slipped into the general colour of the environment. But he carried almost the totality of the country with him. It wasn't so much his reading habits—there were hundreds of men there acquainted with Karl Marx and the Chinese revolution;

there were hundreds of men there who wore their intellectual brilliance as casually as they wore their clothes. It was the fillers he provided on parts of the country that were now myths in the minds of urban dwellers—the strange and desperate struggles waged by people in the rural areas.

"I've just been reading this book on some of the land struggles in China after the revolution," he'd say. "It was difficult for Mao Tse-Tung to get people to cultivate land because ancestor worship was practised there. I've seen people do the same thing in the Transkei where I was born. There was hardly any land left to cultivate but people would rather die of starvation than plow on the land where their ancestors were buried...."

Almost nightly there was an eager traffic of friends through his home. He enjoyed the circle of friends that gathered round him. He enjoyed knocking out his ideas against the ideas of other men and it was almost as though he were talking an unintelligible language. His friends no longer knew of the sacred values of the tribes—that all people had ever once wanted was a field where they may plow their crops and a settled home near the bones of their ancestors. Like the young men of his circle, he was a member of the Youth League of an organization that for forty-seven years had been solely representative of the interests of black people. They had brought people out on the streets on protests and demonstrations. People had been shot dead and imprisoned. A strange hypnotic dialogue pervaded the country. It was always subtly implied that black people were violent; yet it had become illegal in the year 1883 for black men to possess arms. They had little beyond sticks and stones with which to defend themselves. Violence was never a term applied to white men, but they had arms. Before these arms the people were cannon fodder. Who was violent?

Year after year, at convention after convention, this kindly body of the people's representatives mouthed noble sentiments.

"Gentlemen, we ought to remember that our struggle is a non-violent one. Nothing will be gained by violence. It will only harden the hearts of our oppressors against us...."

In 1957 there were more dead black bodies to count. Gopane village, eighteen miles outside the small town of Zeerust in the Transvaal, was up until that year a quiet and insignificant African village. A way of life had built up over the years—the older people clung to the traditional ways of plowing their fields and sent their children to Johannesburg, either to work or to acquire an education. In 1957 a law was passed compelling black women to carry a "pass book." Forty years ago the same law had been successfully resisted by the women who had offered themselves for imprisonment rather than carry the document. The "pass book" had long been in existence for black men and was the source of excruciating suffering. If a man walked out of his home without his "pass book" he simply disappeared from society for a stretch of six months or so. Most men knew the story. They supplied a Boer farmer for six months with free labour to harvest his potatoes. A "boss-boy" stood over the "prisoners" with a whip. They dug out potatoes with such speed that the nails on their fingers were worn to the bone. The women were later to tell a similar tale but in that year, 1957, people still thought they could protest about laws imposed on them. Obscure Gopane village was the first area in the country where the "pass book" was issued to women. The women quietly accepted them, walked home, piled them in a huge heap and burnt them. Very soon the village was surrounded by the South African police. They shot the women dead. From then onwards "pass books" were issued to all black women throughout the country without resistance.

Was it sheer terror at being faced with nameless horrors who would shoot unarmed women dead or did the leaders of the people imagine they represented a respectable status quo? There they were at the very next convention, droning on again:

"Gentlemen," said speaker number one, an elderly, staid, complacent member of the community. "Gentlemen, in spite of the tragedy of the past year, we must not forget that our struggle is essentially a non-violent one...."

He was going on like that—after all the incident had passed into history and let's attend to matters at hand—when there was a sudden interruption of the sort that had not disrupted those decorous, boring proceedings for years. Someone had stood up out of turn. Speaker number one looked down his nose in disdain. It was the young Professor of Bantu Languages. He was only in the Youth League section and of no significance.

"Gentlemen!" And to everyone's amazement the young man's voice quivered with rage. "May I interrupt the speaker! I am heartily sick of the proceedings of this organization. Our women were recently killed in a violent way and the speaker still requests of us that we follow a non-violent policy...."

"What are you suggesting that we do?" asked speaker number one, alarmed. "Are you suggesting that we resort to violence against our oppressors?"

"I wish that the truth be told!" And the younger man banged his hand on the table in exasperation. "Our forefathers lived on this land long before the white man came here and forced a policy of dispossession on us. We are hardly human to them! They only view us as objects of cheap labour! Why is the word *violence* such a terrible taboo from *our* side! Why can't we state in turn that *they* mean nothing to us and that it is our intention to get them off our backs! How long is this going to go on? It will go on and on until we say: NO MORE!" And he flung his arms wide in a gesture of desperation. "Gentlemen! I am sick of the equivocation and clever talk of this organization. If anyone agrees with me, would they please follow me," and he turned forthwith and left the convention hall.

Everything had happened so abruptly that there was a moment's pause of startled surprise. Then half the assembly stood up and walked out after the young man, and so began a new short era in the history of political struggle in South Africa. His political career lasted barely a year. George Padmore's book *Pan Africanism or Communism* was the rage in Johannesburg at that time and he and his splinter group allied themselves with its sentiments.

In spite of the tragedies of the country, that year seemed to provide a humorous interlude to the leaders of the traditional people's movement. Their whole attention was distracted into ridiculing the efforts of their new rival; they failed to recognize a creative mind in their midst. The papers that were issued in a steady stream were the work of a creative artist and not that of a hardened self-seeking politician. The problems they outlined were always new and unexpected. They began slowly from the bottom, outlining basic problems:

"We can make little progress if our people regard them-selves as inferior. For three hundred years the whites have inculcated a feeling of inferiority in us. They only address us as 'boy' and 'girl,' yet we are men and women with children of our own and homes of our own. Our people would resent it if we called them 'kwedini' or 'mfana' or 'moshemane,' all of which means 'boy.' Why then do they accept indignity, insult and humiliation from the white foreigner…?"

A counter paper was immediately issued by the people's traditional movement:

"We have some upstarts in our midst who have prom-ised to lead the people to a new dawn but they are only soft gentlemen who want to be 'Sir-ed' and 'Madam-ed.' Who has led the people in mass demonstrations? Who is the true voice of the people…?"

They arranged for stones to be cast at him as he addressed public rallies and for general heckling and disruption of the proceedings. Yet during that single year he provided people with a wide range of political education such as the traditional people's movement had not been able to offer in all their long history. His papers touched on everything from foreign invest-ment in the land which further secured the bonds of oppression to some problems of the future which were phrased as questions:

"Can we make a planned economy work within the framework of a political democracy? It has not done so in any of the countries that practise it today.…We cannot guarantee minority rights because we are fighting precisely that group-exclusiveness which those who plead for minority rights would like to perpetuate. Surely we have guaranteed the highest if we have guaranteed individual liberties…?"

The land could be peaceful for months, even years. There was a machinery at hand to crush the slightest protest. Men either fled its ravenous, insensitive brutal jaws, or, obsessed as a few men often are with making some final noble gesture or statement, they walked directly into the brutal jaws. It was always a fatal decision. No human nobility lit up the land. People were hungry for ideas, for a new direction, yet men of higher motivation were irresistibly drawn towards the machine. That machine was already gory with human blood and since it was only a machine it remained unmoved, unshaken, unbroken. Obsessed with clarifying a legality, he walked directly into the machine. The laws of the land were all illegal, he said. They were made exclusively by a white minority without consulting the black majority. It was a government of a white minority for a white minority; therefore the black majority was under no moral obligation to obey its laws. At his bidding thousands of black men throughout the land laid down their "pass books" outside the gates of the police stations.

He had a curious trial. White security police had attended all his public meetings and taken notes but there were no witnesses for the State except one illiterate black policeman. He gave a short halting statement that made people in the public gallery roar with laughter.

"I attended a political gathering addressed by this man. I heard him say: The pass book. That is our water-pipe to parliament."

There were sixty-nine dead bodies outside a Sharpeville police station. He was sentenced to three years' imprisonment for sedition. Then a special bill was passed to detain him in prison for life. He was released after nine years, but served with so many banning orders that he could barely communicate with his fellow men. Then he became ill and died.

An equivalent blanket of silence fell upon the land. The crackdown on all political opposition was so severe that hundreds quailed and fled before the monstrous machine. It was the end of the long legend of non-violent protest. But a miracle people had not expected was that from 1957 onwards the white man was being systematically expelled from Africa, as a political force, as a governing power. Only the southern lands lay in bondage. Since people had been silenced on such a massive scale, the course and direction of events was no longer theirs. It had slipped from their grasp some time ago into the hands of the men who were training for revolution.

When all was said and done and revolutions had been fought and won, perhaps only dreamers longed for a voice like the man who was as beautiful as the coming of the Christ-Child.

For Christmas

by

JUAN JOSÉ HERNÁNDEZ

IT WAS SUMMER. Mercedes was sharpening her knife on the kitchen threshold stone, while flies piled up on the blood-stained paper in which the meat had been wrapped. The smell of bleach from the white clothes hung out to dry, the smell of droppings from the chicken coop drifted in through the shutters. Mercedes turned her head to look at Lila, who wagged her tail with her eyes glued to the meat. It was difficult for the dog to walk; she would probably have her puppies before the end of the month. "Hungry again, damn thing," said Mercedes, and tossed her a piece of meat, which Lila hastily devoured.

Animals get mange and other diseases; Mercedes wasn't sympathetic towards them. Nevertheless, to justify having the dog in the house, she said that Lila was shy and clean, like a maiden. Now, she could no longer call her a maiden. "Of course, she's hungry. Silly thing, must be carrying at least eight puppies, and she's so happy. Like us: they never learn their lesson."

She poked the hot coals in the stove, put the frying pan over the flame and went out to the patio for a minute. The violent light of the noonday sun blinded her. Putting one hand to her forehead like a visor, she canvassed the trees. Observing the round shadow of an orange tree, she decided that would be the one. Jose, her husband, was going to arrive at any moment. He had left early to go job hunting, but at all the work sites he always found the same sign displayed: "No openings," and had to accept the same old odd jobs: unloading bricks from a truck, setting tiles or repairing a leaky roof. Jose would be thirsty when he got home. Victor needed to go to the store to get a cold soda-water. Mercedes crossed to the other side of the patio, the overheated tiles burning the soles of her feet. She stopped a few feet from a fig tree and shouted, "Victor!" A bird-pecked fig fell into the quince-jelly can filled with drinking water for the hens. The boy nimbly descended the fig tree and walked toward his mother.

Victor had climbed the fig tree after breakfast. Straddling one of the branches, and forming circles with both hands over one eye like a telescope, he scanned the horizon in search of pirates. The tree's foliage, swaying in the wind, was a ship in the middle of the ocean. Victor played alone, of necessity. His best friend, Mario, had been sent to the Youth Camp; he hadn't seen his friend Blacky since Mercedes discovered that he had lice and threw him out of the house, "That's all we need. In an asphalt neighbourhood, children with lice," and just in case, she shaved Victor's head clean.

Mario, in the Youth Camp, had also been shaved like an army recruit. Being there, thought Victor, must be like being punished or being sent to your room, because whenever he got into the least bit of mischief, it was sufficient warning for his mother to say, in a threatening tone, "I'll tell your father when he gets home, and he'll send you to the Camp."

However, for some time, his mother had been using a different approach to get him to obey, "Now, Victor, are you going to behave like that when your little brother arrives?" His baby brother would be born by Christmas. At first Victor was afraid they were trying to fool him; his parents often used that date to avoid fulfilling a promise: to give him a toy, or to take him to the park to the merry-go-round. If Victor got annoyed and asked for the tenth time, "When are you going to buy me a Meccano set?", his mother or father would say, "For Christmas."

But the birth of his little brother seemed certain. He remembered that last month, during lunch, his mother warned him that it might be a little girl. His father said that this wasn't a laughing matter, that he had made a bet (a case of beer) with his foreman, and that he was absolutely certain it was a little boy. "We'll call him Joaquin."

Joaquin, Mercedes's father, had died the previous summer, in the same house they now lived in. "Grandpa went to heaven," they explained to him. But although he knew they were lying to him, Victor pretended to believe them, just as he pretended to believe in Father Christmas.

Ever since then, his father spoke in a respectful tone whenever he referred to his dead grandfather. Before that, he would frequently hear his father saying, irritated: "I don't understand why Joaquin let so much land. He's a miser. He could give us just a piece at the back where we could build a decent house and live comfortably."

At that time, Victor and his parents lived in a two-room wooden shack, built on an old garbage dump that a government-contracted company had filled and parcelled for sale in lots.

Jose bought a lot close to the dirt road where a sign advertised: "A grand sub-division, The Roses, will be built here." A year later, the place was full to the brim with houses, most with slab walls and zinc roofs; others, the cheaper ones, made of thatch with a burlap drape to cover the entrance. The new neighbourhood teemed with spurge weeds and nettles; rainstorms frequently exposed cow bones and refuse buried in the garbage dump. So the name changed from The Roses neighbourhood to The Pot Luck neighbourhood.

"It won't be paradise," Victor's father said, "but who knows? A few years from now, when they pave the road, the little lot might go up in value." Mercedes raised her eyebrows skeptically, and endured the annoyances of the neighbourhood in silence. Each morning she had to stand in line with the other women to draw water with the hand pump bought with money collected from the families on the neighbouring lots. The heat made the land dry; food kept in the meat locker went rancid; and the enormous mouths of the anthills opened up everywhere. If her husband was not home on the official holidays, she would bolt the door shut in fear of the drunks passing by on their bicycles with a bottle of wine in one hand, grasping the handlebars with the other to show off their balance, which they proved by the complicated zigzag drawn by the wheels in the dirt road. Sometimes one of the men would fall off his bicycle with a thud, try to get back up, but fall again. The dogs would go sniff his clothes and lick his face; then the drunk would call them names, curse his luck and then cry, until he ended up going to sleep in the same place where he had fallen.

One day, Victor found out that his grandfather, Joaquin, was sick.

"I went to see dad," Mercedes said to her husband while she was cleaning her nail polish with a rag soaked in turpentine. "The poor man is very ill."

"Nobody lives forever," Jose answered with indifference. But when he noticed that his wife covered her eyes with her hands, he went up to her and gave her a hug. "Don't be like that. The old man has a long way to go. He's made of iron."

Then they went for a walk. It started to get dark. As dusk fell, the song of the cicadas started to become audible, harsh at first, then melodious, and finally the voices, coming together in successive ascending stages, became shrill—a single vibrating howl that stretched into the distance across the burning sky.

Alone in the house, Victor thought about his sick grandfather. He did not like him, even though the old man gave him candy. He used to come visit when his father was at work. When he heard his grandfather's voice, Victor would run and hide under the bed. He didn't like to be fondled by his trembling hands with rust-coloured blemishes. His grandfather would make him come out of his hiding-place. Although Victor would shout and kick to escape, the old man would hold him down, and he couldn't get away or avoid the kisses on his cheeks and tugging on his ears. He'd end up crying, while his grandfather would roar with laughter. "Leave him alone, dad; he's just being silly," Mercedes would snap at him. "Here's your beer."

The last afternoon he visited, instead of torturing him or reading the police news in *The Daily Gazette* out loud, Joaquin stayed in his chair, gazing as if absorbed in thought, with his mouth drawn downward, which he barely half-opened from time to time to let out a dull moan. "If you don't feel well, dad, you should stay in bed," Mercedes said when she saw that he brushed aside the beer and the plate of black olives.

A month later, they moved to his grandfather's house. Victor liked the new house, because in The Roses neighbourhood his mother didn't let him have any friends. "You can learn only bad habits from those gypsies," she told him, repeating Joaquin's words, which was what he called the children who sold oranges and fresh eggs.

His grandfather's house was big: three bedrooms with high, narrow doors that led to the balcony, a tiled patio and some fruit trees and a chicken coop in the back. Victor carefully inspected the rooms. In a trunk he found a bunch of keys, a flashlight and a railroad cap. He climbed the trees. The store-keeper's wife gave him a puppy that turned out to be female, and his mother named her Lila. He also made friends with

Mario, the laundrywoman's son. But his grandfather's health got worse during the winter. At the doctor's advice, his parents decided to take him into town to be examined by a specialist. Victor, who had stayed with some neighbours while his parents were gone, heard the adults gossiping as they drank their maté: "What a waste of money! There's no cure for the old man." When they returned, his grandfather no longer got out of bed. He stayed there with his hands crossed over his chest and his head sunk into the pillow, letting out a continuous moan. Sometimes the illness drove him crazy; then he would curse at his nurse, and with one swipe fling to the floor the boxes of injections and the bottles neatly arranged on the nightstand.

From his room, Victor could hear his grandfather's heavy breathing at night; then the breathing became a dull snoring, and his parents sent him again to spend a few days with the neighbours. That was when Mario told him that Joaquin was dying.

When he returned home, his grandfather's room had been turned into a dining room. Time passed, nobody spoke anymore about the dead man. Now the favourite topic was the birth of his brother, who would be named Joaquin. Victor would have preferred any other name; his grandfather's name frightened him.

His father came home and asked where Victor was. "He went to get a soda-water," Mercedes said. "He'll be back soon."

She served dinner and sat facing her husband. Then in a soft voice she said. "Jose, I think we should tell him. It's not fair to deceive him. He's so excited."

"What for?" Jose said, shrugging his shoulders. "These are your affairs. In a few days, Victor won't even be thinking about it any more. That's how kids are."

He continued eating as if not concerned; his jaws moved slowly and rhythmically; his face was red and his forehead soaked in sweat. Suddenly, a feeling of resentful humiliation came over Mercedes. "Why talk? When I told you that I had decided to have the midwife get rid of it, you told me that these are women things, as if I had become pregnant from the air I breathe. You're all the same. Because you bring the money home, we have to prepare your meals and jump into bed whenever you fancy it.

"You can't keep fooling Victor," she insisted. "He's too old now."

Moments before he left to get the soda-water, Victor had said, "I know where my little brother is." She looked at him surprised. Then Victor reached out his arm and rested the palm of his hand on her stomach. "He's there, inside. Mario told me."

"What does Mario know?" Mercedes quickly responded. "He has a bad mouth. That's why they sent him to the Youth Camp. The same thing will happen to you, if you keep up this nonsense."

Mario's mother could not afford to send her son to school. She used to wash clothes, but had to quit working because of chronic eczema on her hands. Then she had to resign herself to sending her son to the Camp. In order to get him admitted, she had to ask the neighbours, going house to house, to sign a statement that she was completely destitute. "You're a lucky woman," she had said to Mercedes. "You have just one son, a husband who works and a house you inherited from your father, may he rest in peace."

But the house was mortgaged. They had done it to cover the expenses from Joaquin's illness.

"The doctors were scum," Jose said to his wife soon after the old man died. "It's a good thing I didn't sell our house in The Roses. Anyway, we're going back there."

"I'll never return to that neighbourhood," Mercedes answered. "I'd rather work as a servant to help pay the mortgage. It's not for me, but for Victor. We'll need to send him to school soon."

After that, it all became even more complicated; her husband didn't find work. And also, her suspicions were confirmed; she was pregnant. "What sense is there in bringing a child into the world to give him a life of sadness?" Mercedes said to herself. She didn't want to end up like the women in The Roses who had a child every year. Children who looked like gypsies, as her dead father would say. Children sitting around in mud with their pants held up at the waist with a string. It was a miserable sight: sickly, dirty children, waiting for a bowl of warm milk to soak a piece of stale bread in; barefoot women walking through the sun-drenched streets with a towel on their head, or leaning over the body of a drunk to get him up and drag him home. A house that represented things accumulated over years and years of poverty: the shiny double bed, the only luxury on the dirt floor, the ceramic pot, the Sacred Heart made of painted plaster, the blue crystal vase with plastic lilies. And it all meant nothing if the man of the house wasn't there, the husband whom they forgave for his drunkenness, insults, beatings and even infidelity, because his presence alone justified these abuses to themselves and to the world, when they'd say: "This bracelet was a gift from my husband," or else, "I can't pay, sir, my husband left me," in a meek voice mixed with helplessness.

"Maybe Jose is right," Mercedes thought. "Victor will forget. We'll promise him something, like a tricycle, for Christmas."

Mercedes woke up startled when she felt a light tickling sensation in her feet. Because of the heat, she and her husband were sleeping at night on a mattress on the floor on the balcony. Jose also opened his eyes.

"It's nothing," said Mercedes. "It's Lila, poor thing."

The dog had rested her front paws on the mattress and was moaning beseechingly.

"I don't know what good it is to have that dog in the house," Jose said grumpily. "We should never have let Victor take her in. Dogs are filthy."

Mercedes got up and took Lila in her arms. Then she put an old sheet she used for ironing inside an empty apple crate, and laid the dog down there. Day began to break. Mercedes stayed next to the crate, her knees going numb. "There are six," she whispered, while tears ran down her cheeks. "Six, no, eight, like I thought. Damn thing. Just like us: they never learn their lesson."

A Risk for
Father Christmas

by

SIEGFRIED LENZ

THEY HAD PROMISED some fast extra cash, so I went into their office and introduced myself. The office was in a bar, behind a fogged-up glass case containing meatballs, herring fillets with greying rings of onion, fruit drops and jars of shiny pickles. Mulka was sitting at a table, next to him a gaunt secretary smoking a cigarette—everything had been arranged in the corner in a makeshift manner appropriate to fast extra cash. Mulka had spread out a large map of the town in front of him, a thick carpenter's pencil in his hand, and I watched as he drew circles over the town, vigorous right angles that he crossed out after hasty consideration—the unstinting work of a General Staff headquarters.

Mulka's office, the source of the advertisement promising fast extra cash, placed Father Christmases; all over town, wherever the celestial red-coated bringer of joy was needed, he would send one along. He provided the fluffy beards and the red, frozen, smiling masks; he provided coats, boots and a minibus to drive the Father Christmases to people's houses, to the "operational area" as Mulka would say—the joy they brought was rigidly organized.

The gaunt secretary glanced up at me, took a look at my false nose that they had sewn on after my injury, and then she typed my name and address, nibbling all the while at a cold meatball and taking a drag on her cigarette after every bite. She wearily pushed the papers containing my particulars over to Mulka, who sat brooding over the map of the town, his "operational map"; the thick carpenter's pencil rose, circled over the map and suddenly shot downwards. "Here," said Mulka, "here is your area, in Hochfeld. A good quarter, very good even. You report to Köhnke."

"What about my things?" I said.

"You will get your uniform on the bus," he said. "You can get ready in the bus as well. And try to act like a Father Christmas!"

I promised him that I would. I received my advance payment and ordered a beer, which I drank while I waited until Mulka called for me. The driver led me outside. We walked through the cold rain to the minibus, and clambered into the back, where four freezing Father Christmases were already sitting, and I was given my things—the coat, the fluffy beard, the red-and-white uniform of joy. The clothes had not yet gone cold, and it was pleasant to feel the body heat of the old Father Christmases, my predecessors, who had already dispensed their share of joy; I didn't find it difficult to put the things on. Everything fitted, the boots fitted, and the cap, only the mask didn't fit—the cardboard edges pressed too sharply into my false nose; in the end, we chose an open mask that wouldn't cover my nose.

The driver helped me with all this, eyed me up, assessing the level of joy that I conveyed, and before getting in the driver's cabin, he stuck a lit cigarette in my mouth. After a wild drive, we arrived in Hochfeld—the very good area I had been assigned to. The minibus stopped under a lantern, the door opened, and the driver motioned at me to get out.

"Here it is," he said, "number fourteen, Köhnke's house—make them merry. And when you are finished with them, wait here on the street, I am just going to drop off the other Father Christmases, then I will come and pick you up."

"Fine," I said, "in about half an hour."

He slapped me encouragingly on the shoulder; I pulled the mask straight, smoothed out the red coat and went through the front garden to the silent house where my fast extra cash was waiting for me. "Köhnke," I thought to myself, "yes, I remember a Köhnke in Demjansk."

Reluctantly, I pressed the bell and listened; small footsteps, a cheery admonishment, then the door opened, and a small woman with buns in her hair wearing a white patterned apron stood before me. For a second, her face showed a sort of happy alarm, a brief glow, but that quickly disappeared—impatiently, she dragged me inside by the sleeve and pointed to a sack lying in a small, sloping cupboard under the stairs.

"Quickly," she said, "I mustn't be outside for long. Now you must follow me. The parcels are all labelled, and you should hopefully be able to read them."

"Sure," I said, "if I have to."

"And take your time when handing out the presents. Make a few threats while you're at it as well."

"Who," I said, "whom should I threaten?"

"My husband of course, who else!"

"Will do," I said.

I swung the sack onto my shoulder and trudged up the stairs with heavy joy-bringing steps (the walking was included in the price). I stopped in front of the door behind which the woman had disappeared, cleared my throat hard, made a dark forest sound, the sound of promise, then gave a hefty knock and, upon hearing the woman shout "Come in!" from inside, I entered.

There were no children there; the tree was burning, two sparklers were fizzing and, in front of the tree, beneath the fire-spitting candles, was a heavy man in a black suit, standing there quietly with his hands folded, looking at me, relieved and full of expectation—it was Köhnke, my colonel in Demjansk.

I put the sack down on the floor, hesitated, looked in confusion at the little woman, and when she came closer, I whispered: "The children? Where are the children?"

"We don't have any children," she replied quietly, then said reluctantly: "but please begin."

Still hesitating, I opened the sack, looking helplessly from her to him—the woman nodded, he looked at me smiling, smiling and strangely relieved. Slowly, my fingers reached into the sack, and felt around until they caught hold of the string of a parcel—the parcel was for him. "Ludwig!" I called loudly. "Here!" he cried happily, and he carried the parcel to a table in both hands and unwrapped a set of pyjamas. I then took out more parcels, one after the other, calling out their names, "Ludwig" and "Hannah," and they took the presents gleefully and unwrapped them. Surreptitiously, the woman signalled to me to threaten him with my stick; I hesitated, and the woman signalled again. But then, just as I was about to start threatening, the colonel turned toward me; he approached me respectfully, with outstretched hands and trembling lips. Again the woman motioned to me to threaten him; again I could not do it.

"You have succeeded," said the colonel suddenly. "You came through. I was afraid you would not make it."

"I found your house straight away," I said.

"You have a fine nose, my son."

"It was a Christmas present, Sir. I got the nose for Christmas at the time."

"I am glad that you reached us."

"It was easy, Sir; it went very quickly."

"Every time, I am afraid that you will not make it. Every time—"

"There's no reason to be afraid," I said, "Father Christmas always reaches his destination."

"Yes," he said, "they do generally reach their destination. But still I have this fear; I have had it ever since Demjansk."

"Since Demjansk," I said.

"Back then, we were expecting him at the command post. They had already telephoned from headquarters to say that he was on his way, but still we waited and waited. We waited for such a long time that we became restless and I sent a man out to look for Father Christmas and bring him back to us."

"The man never returned," I said.

"No," he said. "The man did not return, even though they were only shooting harassing fire, and very sporadically."

"They were shooting sparklers, Sir."

"My son," he said gently. "Oh, my son. We went out and looked for them in the snow near the forest. And first we found the man. He was still alive."

"He is still alive, Sir."

"And in the snow near the forest lay Father Christmas. He lay there with his sack and his stick, and did not stir."

"A dead Father Christmas, Sir."

"He was still wearing his beard, and the red coat and the lined boots. He was lying face down. Never, never have I seen anything so sad as the dead Father Christmas."

"There is always a risk," I said, "even for those who bring joy, even for Father Christmas, there is a risk."

"My son," he said, "there should never be a risk for Father Christmas, not for him. Father Christmas should never be at risk."

"But there is always a risk," I said.

"Yes," he said, "I know. And I have always known this, ever since Demjansk, when I saw the dead Father Christmas lying near the forest—I always think of how he could not reach me. Every time I have this great fear, because I have seen many things, but nothing so terrible as the dead Father Christmas."

The colonel bowed his head; his wife, who was now very agitated, signalled to me to threaten him with the stick—but I couldn't do it. I couldn't do it, even though I should have been afraid that she would complain to Mulka about me and that Mulka could deduct something from my pay. I couldn't cope with cheerful admonition through the stick.

Quietly, I went to the door, dragging the limp sack behind me; as I carefully opened the door, the colonel looked at me, a happy but concerned look: "Take care," he whispered, "take care," and I nodded and stepped outside. I knew that his warning was sincere.

Below, the minibus was waiting for me; six freezing Father Christmases in the back, silent and freezing, exhausted from the joy they had dispensed. No one said a word as we drove to headquarters. I took off the uniform and reported to Mulka behind the glass window. He didn't look up. His pencil circled over the map of the town, the circles became slower, then the pencil shot downwards: "Here," he said, "here is a new operation for you. You can put your uniform back on now."

"Thank you," I said, "thank you very much."

"Don't you want to do it any more? Don't you want to bring any more joy?"

"To whom?" I said. "I don't know where I am going now. I need some schnapps first. The risk—the risk is too great."

Winter Dog

by

ALISTAIR MacLEOD

I AM WRITING this in December. In the period close to Christmas, and three days after the first snowfall in this region of southwestern Ontario. The snow came quietly in the night or in the early morning. When we went to bed near midnight, there was none at all. Then early in the morning we heard the children singing Christmas songs from their rooms across the hall. It was very dark and I rolled over to check the time. It was 4:30 A.M. One of them must have awakened and looked out the window to find the snow and then eagerly awakened the others. They are half crazed by the promise of Christmas, and the discovery of the snow is an unexpected giddy surprise. There was no snow promised for this area, not even yesterday.

"What are you doing?" I call, although it is obvious.

"Singing Christmas songs," they shout back with equal obviousness, "because it snowed."

"Try to be quiet," I say, "or you'll wake the baby."

"She's already awake," they say. "She's listening to our singing. She likes it. Can we go out and make a snowman?"

I roll from my bed and go to the window. The neighbouring houses are muffled in snow and silence and there are as yet no lights in any of them. The snow has stopped falling and its whitened quietness reflects the shadows of the night.

"This snow is no good for snowmen," I say. "It is too dry."

"How can snow be dry?" asks a young voice. Then an older one says, "Well, then can we go out and make the first tracks?"

They take my silence for consent and there are great sounds of rustling and giggling as they go downstairs to touch the light switches and rummage and jostle for coats and boots.

"What on earth is happening?" asks my wife from her bed. "What are they doing?"

"They are going outside to make the first tracks in the snow," I say. "It snowed quite heavily last night."

"What time is it?"

"Shortly after 4:30."

"Oh."

We ourselves have been nervous and restless for the past weeks. We have been troubled by illness and uncertainty in those we love far away on Canada's East Coast. We have already considered and rejected driving the fifteen hundred miles. Too far, too uncertain, too expensive, fickle weather, the complications of transporting Santa Claus.

Instead, we sleep uncertainly and toss in unbidden dreams. We jump when the phone rings after 10:00 P.M. and are then reassured by the distant voices.

"First of all, there is nothing wrong," they say. "Things are just the same."

Sometimes we make calls ourselves, even to the hospital in Halifax, and are surprised at the voices which answer.

"I just got here this afternoon from Newfoundland. I'm going to try to stay a week. He seems better today. He's sleeping now."

At other times we receive calls from farther west, from Edmonton and Calgary and Vancouver. People hoping to find objectivity in the most subjective of situations. Strung out in uncertainty across the time zones from British Columbia to Newfoundland.

Within our present city, people move and consider possibilities:

If he dies tonight we'll leave right away. Can you come?

We will have to drive as we'll never get air reservations at this time.

I'm not sure if my car is good enough. I'm always afraid of the mountains near Cabano.

If we were stranded in Rivière du Loup we would be worse off than being here. It would be too far for anyone to come and get us.

My car will go but I'm not so sure I can drive it all the way. My eyes are not so good anymore, especially at night in drifting snow.

Perhaps there'll be no drifting snow.

There's always drifting snow.

We'll take my car if you'll drive it. We'll have to drive straight through.

John phoned and said he'll give us his car if we want it or he'll drive—either his own car or someone else's.

He drinks too heavily, especially for long-distance driving, and at this time of year. He's been drinking ever since this news began.

He drinks because he cares. It's just the way he is.

Not everybody drinks.

Not everybody cares, and if he gives you his word, he'll never drink until he gets there. We all know that.

But so far nothing has happened. Things seem to remain the same.

Through the window and out on the white plane of the snow, the silent, laughing children now appear. They move in their muffled clothes like mummers on the whitest of stages. They dance and gesture noiselessly, flopping their arms in parodies of heavy, happy, earthbound birds. They have been warned by the eldest to be aware of the sleeping neighbours so they cavort only in pantomime, sometimes raising mittened hands to their mouths to suppress their joyous laughter. They dance and prance in the moonlight, tossing snow in one another's direction, tracing out various shapes and initials, forming lines which snake across the previously unmarked whiteness. All of it in silence, unknown and unseen and unheard to the neighbouring world. They seem unreal even to me, their father, standing at his darkened window. It is almost as if they have danced out of the world of folklore like happy elves who cavort and mimic and caper through the private hours of this whitened dark, only to vanish with the coming of the morning's light and leaving only the signs of their activities behind. I am tempted to check the recently vacated beds to confirm what perhaps I think I know.

Then out of the corner of my eye I see him. The golden collie-like dog. He appears almost as if from the wings of the stage or as a figure newly noticed in the lower corner of a winter painting. He sits quietly and watches the playful scene before him and then, as if responding to a silent invitation, bounds into its midst. The children chase him in frantic circles, falling and rolling as he doubles back and darts and dodges between their legs and through their outstretched arms. He seizes a mitt loosened from its owner's hand, and tosses it happily in the air and then snatches it back into his jaws an instant before it reaches the ground and seconds before the tumbling bodies fall on the emptiness of its expected destination. He races to the edge of the scene and lies facing them, holding the mitt tantalizingly between his paws, and then as they dash towards him, he leaps forward again, tossing and catching it before him and zig-zagging through them as the Sunday football player might return the much sought-after ball. After he has gone through and eluded them all, he looks back over his shoulder and again, like an elated athlete, tosses the mitt high in what seems like an imaginary end zone. Then he seizes it once more and lopes in a wide circle around his pursuers, eventually coming closer and closer to them until once more their stretching hands are able to actually touch his shoulders and back and haunches, although he continues always to wriggle free. He is touched but never captured, which is the nature of the game. Then he is gone. As suddenly as he came. I strain my eyes in the direction of the adjoining street, towards the house where I have often seen him, always within a yard enclosed by woven links of chain. I see the flash of his silhouette, outlined perhaps against the snow or the light cast by the street lamps or the moon. It arcs upwards and seems to hang for an instant high above the top of the fence and then it descends on the other side. He lands on his shoulder in a fluff of snow and with a half roll regains his feet and vanishes within the shadow of his owner's house.

"What are you looking at?" asks my wife.

"That golden collie-like dog from the other street was just playing with the children in the snow."

"But he's always in that fenced-in yard."

"I guess not always. He jumped the fence just now and went back in. I guess the owners and the rest of us think he's fenced in but he knows he's not. He probably comes out every night and leads an exciting life. I hope they don't see his tracks or they'll probably begin to chain him."

"What are the children doing?"

"They look tired now from chasing the dog. They'll probably soon be back in. I think I'll go downstairs and wait for them and make myself a cup of coffee."

"Okay."

I look once more towards the fenced-in yard but the dog is nowhere to be seen.

I first saw such a dog when I was twelve and he came as a pup of about two months in a crate to the railroad station which was about eight miles from where we lived. Someone must have phoned or dropped in to say: "Your dog's at the station."

He had come to Cape Breton in response to a letter and a cheque which my father had sent to Morrisburg, Ontario. We had seen the ads for "cattle collie dogs" in the *Family Herald,* which was the farm newspaper of the time, and we were in need of a good young working dog.

His crate was clean and neat and there was still a supply of dog biscuits with him and a can in the corner to hold water. The baggage handlers had looked after him well on the trip east, and he appeared in good spirits. He had a white collar and chest and four rather large white paws and a small white blaze on his forehead. The rest of him was a fluffy, golden brown, although his eyebrows and the tips of his ears as well as the end of his tail were darker, tingeing almost to black. When he grew to his full size the blackish shadings became really black, and although he had the long, heavy coat of a collie, it was in certain areas more grey than gold. He was also taller than the average collie and with a deeper chest. He seemed to be at least part German Shepherd.

It was winter when he came and we kept him in the house where he slept behind the stove in a box lined with an old coat. Our other dogs slept mostly in the stables or outside in the lees of woodpiles or under porches or curled up on the banking of the house. We seemed to care more for him because he was smaller and it was winter and he was somehow like a visitor; and also because more was expected of him and also perhaps because we had paid money for him and thought about his coming for some time—like a "planned" child. Skeptical neighbours and relatives who thought the idea of paying money for a dog was rather exotic or frivolous would ask: "Is that your Ontario dog" or "Do you think your Ontario dog will be any good?"

He turned out to be no good at all and no one knew why. Perhaps it was because of the suspected German Shepherd blood. But he could not "get the hang of it." Although we worked him and trained him as we had other dogs, he seemed always to bring panic instead of order and to make things worse instead of better. He became a "head dog," which meant that instead of working behind the cattle he lunged at their heads, impeding them from any forward motion and causing them to turn in endless, meaningless bewildered circles. On the few occasions when he did go behind them, he was "rough," which meant that instead of being a floating, nipping, suggestive presence, he actually bit them and caused them to gallop, which was another sin. Sometimes in the summer the milk cows suffering from his misunderstood pursuit would jam pell mell into the stable, tossing their wide horns in fear, and with their great sides heaving and perspiring while down their legs and tails the wasted milk ran in rivulets mingling with the blood caused by his slashing wounds. He was, it was said, "worse than nothing."

Gradually everyone despaired, although he continued to grow grey and golden and was, as everyone agreed, a "beautiful-looking dog."

He was also tremendously strong and in the winter months I would hitch him to a sleigh which he pulled easily and willingly on almost any kind of surface. When he was harnessed I used to put a collar around his neck and attach a light line to it so that I might have some minimum control over him, but it was hardly ever needed. He would pull home the Christmas tree or the bag of flour or the deer which was shot far back in the woods; and when we visited our winter snares he would pull home the gunnysacks which contained the partridges and rabbits which we gathered.

He would also pull us, especially on the flat windswept stretches of land beside the sea. There the snow was never really deep and the water that oozed from a series of freshwater springs and ponds contributed to a glaze of ice and crisply crusted snow which the sleigh runners seemed to sing over without ever breaking through. He would begin with an easy lope and then increase his swiftness until both he and the sleigh seemed to touch the surface at only irregular intervals. He would stretch out then with his ears flattened against his head and his shoulders bunching and contracting in the rhythm of his speed. Behind him on the sleigh we would cling tenaciously to the wooden slats as the particles of ice and snow dislodged by his nails hurtled towards our faces. We would avert our heads and close our eyes and the wind stung so sharply that the difference between freezing and burning could not be known. He would do that until late in the afternoon when it was time to return home and begin our chores.

On the sunny winter Sunday that I am thinking of, I planned to visit my snares. There seemed no other children around that afternoon and the adults were expecting relatives. I harnessed the dog to the sleigh, opened the door of the house and shouted that I was going to look at my snares. We began to climb the hill behind the house on our way to the woods when we looked back and out towards the sea. The "big ice," which was what we called the major pack of drift ice, was in solidly against the shore and stretched out beyond the range of vision. It had not been "in" yesterday, although for the past weeks we had seen it moving offshore, sometimes close and sometimes distant, depending on the winds and tides. The coming of the big ice marked the official beginning of the coldest part of winter. It was mostly drift ice from the Arctic and Labrador, although some of it was fresh-water ice from the estuary of the St. Lawrence. It drifted down with the dropping temperatures, bringing its own mysterious coldness and stretching for hundreds of miles in craters and pans, sometimes in grotesque shapes and sometimes in dazzling architectural forms. It was blue and white and sometimes grey and at other times a dazzling emerald green.

The dog and I changed our direction towards the sea, to find what the ice might yield. Our land had always been beside the sea and we had always gone towards it to find newness and the extraordinary; and over the years we, as others along the coast, had found quite a lot, although never the pirate chests of gold which were supposed to abound or the reasons for the mysterious lights that our elders still spoke of and persisted in seeing. But kegs of rum had washed up, and sometimes bloated horses and various fishing paraphernalia and valuable timber and furniture from foundered ships. The door of my room was apparently the galley door from a ship called the *Judith Franklin* which was wrecked during the early winter in which my great-grandfather was building his house. My grandfather told of how they had heard the cries and seen the lights as the ship neared the rocks and of how they had run down in the dark and tossed lines to the people while tying themselves to trees on the shore. All were saved, including women clinging to small children. The next day the builders of the new house went down to the shore and salvaged what they could from the wreckage of the vanquished ship. A sort of symbolic marriage of the new and the old: doors and shelving, stairways, hatches, wooden chests and trunks and various glass figurines and lanterns which were miraculously never broken.

People came too. The dead as well as the living. Bodies of men swept overboard and reported lost at sea and the bodies of men still crouched within the shelter of their boats' broken bows. And sometimes in late winter young sealers who had quit their vessels would walk across the ice and come to our doors. They were usually very young—some still in their teens—and had signed on for jobs they could not or no longer wished to handle. They were often disoriented and did not know where they were, only that they had seen land and had decided to walk towards it. They were often frostbitten and with little money and uncertain as to how they might get to Halifax. The dog and I walked towards the ice upon the sea.

Sometimes it was hard to "get on" the ice, which meant that at the point where the pack met the shore there might be open water or irregularities caused by the indentations of the coast-line or the workings of the tides and currents, but for us on that day there was no difficulty at all. We were "on" easily and effortlessly and enthused in our new adventure. For the first mile there was nothing but the vastness of the white expanse. We came to a clear stretch where the ice was as smooth and unruffled as that of an indoor arena and I knelt on the sleigh while the dog loped easily along. Gradually the ice changed to an uneven terrain of pressure ridges and hummocks, making it impossible to ride farther; and then suddenly, upon round-ing a hummock, I saw the perfect seal. At first I thought it was alive, as did the dog who stopped so suddenly in his tracks that the sleigh almost collided with his legs. The hackles on the back of his neck rose and he growled in the dangerous way he was beginning to develop. But the seal was dead, yet facing us in a frozen perfection that was difficult to believe. There was a light powder of snow over its darker coat and a delicate rime of frost still formed the outline of its whiskers. Its eyes were wide open and it stared straight ahead towards the land. Even now in memory it seems more real than reality—as if it were transformed by frozen art into something more arresting than life itself. The way the sudden seal in the museum exhibit freezes your eyes with the touch of truth. Immediately I wanted to take it home.

It was frozen solidly in a base of ice so I began to look for something that might serve as a pry. I let the dog out of his harness and hung the sleigh and harness on top of the hummock to mark the place and began my search. Some distance away I found a pole about twelve feet long. It is always surprising to find such things on the ice field but they are, often amazingly, there, almost in the same way that you might find a pole floating in the summer ocean. Unpredictable but possible. I took the pole back and began my work. The dog went off on explorations of his own.

Although it was firmly frozen, the task did not seem impossible and by inserting the end of the pole under first one side and then the other and working from the front to the back, it was possible to cause a gradual loosening. I remember thinking how very warm it was because I was working hard and perspiring heavily. When the dog came back he was uneasy, and I realized it was starting to snow a bit but I was almost done. He sniffed with disinterest at the seal and began to whine a bit, which was something he did not often do. Finally, after another quarter of an hour, I was able to roll my trophy onto the sleigh and with the dog in harness we set off. We had gone perhaps two hundred yards when the seal slid free. I took the dog and the sleigh back and once again managed to roll the seal on. This time I took the line from the dog's collar and tied the seal to the sleigh, reasoning that the dog would go home anyway and there would be no need to guide him. My fingers were numb as I tried to fasten the awkward knots and the dog began to whine and rear. When I gave the command he bolted forward and I clung at the back of the sleigh to the seal. The snow was heavier now and blowing in my face but we were moving rapidly and when we came to the stretch of arena-like ice we skimmed across it almost like an iceboat, the profile of the frozen seal at the front of the sleigh like those figures at the prows of Viking ships. At the very end of the smooth stretch, we went through. From my position at the end of the sleigh I felt him drop almost before I saw him, and rolled backwards seconds before the sleigh and seal followed him into the blackness of the water. He went under once carried by his own momentum but surfaced almost immediately with his head up and his paws scrambling at the icy, jagged edge of the hole; but when the weight and momentum of the sleigh and its burden struck, he went down again, this time out of sight.

I realized we had struck a "seam" and that the stretch of smooth ice had been deceivingly and temporarily joined to the rougher ice near the shore and now was in the process of breaking away. I saw the widening line before me and jumped to the other side just as his head miraculously came up once more. I lay on my stomach and grabbed his collar in both my hands and then in a moment of panic did not know what to do. I could feel myself sliding towards him and the darkness of the water and was aware of the weight that pulled me forward and down. I was also aware of his razor-sharp claws flailing violently before my face and knew that I might lose my eyes. And I was aware that his own eyes were bulging from their sockets and that he might think I was trying to choke him and might lunge and slash my face with his teeth in desperation. I knew all of this but somehow did nothing about it; it seemed almost simpler to hang on and be drawn into the darkness of the gently slopping water, seeming to slop gently in spite of all the agitation. Then suddenly he was free, scrambling over my shoulder and dragging the sleigh behind him. The seal surfaced again, buoyed up perhaps by the physics of its frozen body or the nature of its fur. Still looking more genuine than it could have in life, its snout and head broke the open water and it seemed to look at us curiously for an instant before it vanished permanently beneath the ice. The loose and badly tied knots had apparently not held when the sleigh was in a near-vertical position and we were saved by the ineptitude of my own numbed fingers. We had been spared for a future time.

He lay gasping and choking for a moment, coughing up the icy salt water, and then almost immediately his coat began to freeze. I realized then how cold I was myself and that even in the moments I had been lying on the ice, my clothes had begun to adhere to it. My earlier heated perspiration was now a cold rime upon my body and I imagined it outlining me there, beneath my clothes, in a sketch of frosty white. I got on the sleigh once more and crouched low as he began to race towards home. His coat was freezing fast, and as he ran the individual ice-coated hairs began to clack together like rhythmical castanets attuned to the motion of his body. It was snowing quite heavily in our faces now and it seemed to be approaching dusk, although I doubted if it were so on the land which I could now no longer see. I realized all the obvious things I should have considered earlier. That if the snow was blowing in our faces, the wind was off the land, and if it was off the land, it was blowing the ice pack back out to sea. That was probably one reason why the seam had opened. And also that the ice had only been "in" one night and had not had a chance to "set." I realized other things as well. That it was the time of the late afternoon when the tide was falling. That no one knew where we were. That I had said we were going to look at snares, which was not where we had gone at all. And I remembered now that I had received no answer even to that misinformation, so perhaps I had not even been heard. And also if there was drifting snow like this on land, our tracks would by now have been obliterated.

We came to a rough section of ice: huge slabs on their sides and others piled one on top of the other as if they were in some strange form of storage. It was no longer possible to ride the sleigh but as I stood up I lifted it and hung on to it as a means of holding on to the dog. The line usually attached to his collar had sunk with the vanished seal. My knees were stiff when I stood up; and deprived of the windbreak effect which the dog had provided, I felt the snow driving full into my face, particularly my eyes. It did not merely impede my vision, the way distant snow flurries might, but actually entered my eyes, causing them to water and freeze nearly shut. I was aware of the weight of ice on my eyelashes and could see them as they gradually lowered and became heavier. I did not remember ice like this when I got on, although I did not find that terribly surprising. I pressed the soles of my numbed feet firmly down upon it to try and feel if it was moving out, but it was impossible to tell because there was no fixed point of reference. Almost the sensation one gets on a conveyor belt at airports or on escalators; although you are standing still you recognize motion, but should you shut your eyes and be deprived of sight, even that recognition may become ambiguously uncertain.

The dog began to whine and to walk around me in circles, binding my legs with the traces of the harness as I continued to grasp the sleigh. Finally I decided to let him go as there seemed no way to hold him and there was nothing else to do. I unhitched the traces and doubled them up as best I could and tucked them under the backpad of his harness so they would not drag behind him and become snagged on any obstacles. I did not take off my mitts to do so as I was afraid I would not be able to get them back on. He vanished into the snow almost immediately.

The sleigh had been a gift from an uncle, so I hung on to it and carried it with both hands before me like an ineffectual shield against the wind and snow. I lowered my head as much as I could and turned it sideways so the wind would beat against my head instead of directly into my face. Sometimes I would turn and walk backwards for a few steps. Although I knew it was not the wisest thing to do, it seemed at times the only way to breathe. And then I began to feel the water sloshing about my feet.

Sometimes when the tides or currents ran heavily and the ice began to separate, the water that was beneath it would well up and wash over it almost as if it were reflooding it. Sometimes you could see the hard ice clearly beneath the water but at other times a sort of floating slush was formed mingling with snow and "slob" ice which was not yet solid. It was thick and dense and soupy and it was impossible to see what lay beneath it. Experienced men on the ice sometimes carried a slender pole so they could test the consistency of the footing which might or might not lie before them, but I was obviously not one of them, although I had a momentary twinge for the pole I had used to dislodge the seal. Still, there was nothing to do but go forward.

When I went through, the first sensation was almost of relief and relaxation for the water initially made me feel much warmer than I had been on the surface. It was the most dangerous of false sensations for I knew my clothes were becoming heavier by the second. I clung to the sleigh somewhat as a raft and lunged forward with it in a kind of up-and-down swimming motion, hoping that it might strike some sort of solidity before my arms became so weighted and sodden that I could no longer lift them. I cried out then for the first time into the driving snow.

He came almost immediately, although I could see he was afraid and the slobbing slush was up to his knees. Still, he seemed to be on some kind of solid footing for he was not swimming. I splashed towards him and when almost there, desperately threw the sleigh before me and lunged for the edge of what seemed like his footing, but it only gave way as if my hands were closing on icy insubstantial porridge. He moved forward then, although I still could not tell if what supported him would be of any use to me. Finally I grasped the breast strap of his harness. He began to back up then, and as I said, he was tremendously strong. The harness began to slide forward on his shoulders but he continued to pull as I continued to grasp and then I could feel my elbows on what seemed like solid ice and I was able to hook them on the edge and draw myself, dripping and soaking, like another seal out of the black water and onto the whiteness of the slushy ice. Almost at once my clothes began to freeze. My elbows and knees began to creak when I bent them as if I were a robot from the realm of science fiction and then I could see myself clothed in transparent ice as if I had been coated with shellac or finished with clear varnish.

As the fall into the winter sea had at first seemed ironically warm, so now my garments of ice seemed a protection against the biting wind, but I knew it was a deceptive sensation and that I did not have much time before me. The dog faced into the wind and I followed him. This time he stayed in sight, and at times even turned back to wait for me. He was cautious but certain and gradually the slush disappeared, and although we were still in water, the ice was hard and clear beneath it. The frozen heaviness of my clothes began to weigh on me and I could feel myself, ironically, perspiring within my suit of icy armour. I was very tired, which I knew was another dangerous sensation. And then I saw the land. It was very close and a sudden surprise. Almost like coming upon a stalled and unexpected automobile in a highway's winter storm. It was only yards away, and although there was no longer any ice actually touching the shore, there were several pans of it floating in the region between. The dog jumped from one to the other and I followed him, still clutching the sleigh, and missing only the last pan which floated close to the rocky shore. The water came only to my waist and I was able to touch the bottom and splash noisily on land. We had been spared again for a future time and I was never to know whether he had reached the shore himself and come back or whether he had heard my call against the wind.

We began to run towards home and the land lightened and there were touches of evening sun. The wind still blew but no snow was falling. Yet when I looked back, the ice and the ocean were invisible in the swirling squalls. It was like looking at another far and distant country on the screen of a snowy television.

I became obsessed, now that I could afford the luxury, with not being found disobedient or considered a fool. The visitors' vehicles were still in the yard so I imagined most of the family to be in the parlour or living room, and I circled the house and entered through the kitchen, taking the dog with me. I was able to get upstairs unnoticed and get my clothes changed and when I came down I mingled with everybody and tried to appear as normal as I could. My own family was caught up with the visitors and only general comments came my way. The dog, who could not change his clothes, lay under the table with his head on his paws and he was also largely unnoticed. Later as the ice melted from his coat, a puddle formed around him, which I casually mopped up. Still later someone said, "I wonder where that dog has been, his coat is soaking wet." I was never to tell anyone of the afternoon's experience or that he had saved my life.

Two winters later I was sitting at a neighbour's kitchen table when I looked out the window and saw the dog as he was shot.

He had followed my father and also me and had been sitting rather regally on a little hill beside the house and I suppose had presented an ideal target. But he had moved at just the right or wrong time and instead of killing him the high-powered bullet smashed into his shoulder. He jumped into the air and turned his snapping teeth upon the wound, trying to bite the cause of the pain he could not see. And then he turned towards home, unsteady but still strong on his three remaining legs. No doubt he felt, as we all do, that if he could get home he might be saved, but he did not make it, as we knew he could not, because of the amount of blood in the snow and the wavering pattern of his three-legged tracks. Yet he was, as I said, tremendously strong and he managed almost three-quarters of a mile. The house he sought must have been within his vision when he died for we could see it quite clearly when we came to his body by the roadside. His eyes were open and his tongue was clenched between his teeth and the little blood he had left dropped red and black on the winter snow. He was not to be saved for a future time anymore.

I learned later that my father had asked the neighbour to shoot him and that we had led him into a kind of ambush. Perhaps my father did so because the neighbour was younger and had a better gun or was a better shot. Perhaps because my father did not want to be involved. It was obvious he had not planned on things turning out so messy.

The dog had become increasingly powerful and protective, to the extent that people were afraid to come into the yard. And he had also bitten two of the neighbour's children and caused them to be frightened of passing our house on their journeys to and from school. And perhaps there was also the feeling in the community that he was getting more than his share of the breeding: that he travelled farther than other dogs on his nightly forays and that he fought off and injured the other smaller dogs who might compete with him for female favours. Perhaps there was fear that his dominance and undesirable characteristics did not bode well for future generations.

This has been the writing down of a memory triggered by the sight of a golden dog at play in the silent snow with my own excited children. After they came in and had their hot chocolate, the wind began to blow; and by the time I left for work, there was no evidence of their early-morning revels or any dog tracks leading to the chain-link fence. The "enclosed" dog looked impassively at me as I brushed the snow from the buried windshield. What does he know? he seemed to say.

The snow continues to drift and to persist as another uncertainty added to those we already have. Should we be forced to drive tonight, it will be a long, tough journey into the wind and the driving snow which is pounding across Ontario and Quebec and New Brunswick and against the granite coast of Nova Scotia. Should we be drawn by death, we might well meet our own. Still, it is only because I am alive that I can even consider such possibilities. Had I not been saved by the golden dog, I would not have these tight concerns or children playing in the snow or of course these memories. It is because of him that I have been able to come this far in time.

It is too bad that I could not have saved him as well and my feelings did him little good as I looked upon his bloodied body there beside the road. It was too late and out of my control and even if I had known the possibilities of the future it would not have been easy.

He was with us only for a while and brought his own changes, and yet he still persists. He persists in my memory and in my life and he persists physically as well. He is there in this winter storm. There in the golden-grey dogs with their black-tipped ears and tails, sleeping in the stables or in the lees of woodpiles or under porches or curled beside the houses which face towards the sea.

The Turkey Season

by

ALICE MUNRO

WHEN I WAS FOURTEEN I got a job at the Turkey Barn for the Christmas season. I was still too young to get a job working in a store or as a part-time waitress; I was also too nervous.

I was a turkey gutter. The other people who worked at the Turkey Barn were Lily and Marjorie and Gladys, who were also gutters; Irene and Henry, who were pluckers; Herb Abbott, the foreman, who superintended the whole operation and filled in wherever he was needed. Morgan

Elliott was the owner and boss. He and his son, Morgy, did the killing.

Morgy I knew from school. I thought him stupid and despicable and was uneasy about having to consider him in a new and possibly superior guise, as the boss's son. But his father treated him so roughly, yelling and swearing at him, that he seemed no more than the lowest of the workers. The other person related to the boss was Gladys. She was his sister, and in her case there did seem to be some privilege of position. She worked slowly and went home if she was not feeling well, and was not friendly to Lily and Marjorie, although she was, a little, to me. She had come back to live with Morgan and his family after working for many years in Toronto, in a bank. This was not the sort of job she was used to. Lily and Marjorie, talking about her when she wasn't there, said she had had a nervous breakdown. They said Morgan made her work in the Turkey Barn to pay for her keep. They also said, with no worry about the contradiction, that she had taken the job because she was after a man, and that the man was Herb Abbott.

All I could see when I closed my eyes, the first few nights after working there, was turkeys. I saw them hanging upside down, plucked and stiffened, pale and cold, with the heads and necks limp, the eyes and nostrils clotted with dark blood; the remaining bits of feathers—those dark and bloody, too— seemed to form a crown. I saw them not with aversion but with a sense of endless work to be done.

Herb Abbott showed me what to do. You put the turkey down on the table and cut its head off with a cleaver. Then you took the loose skin around the neck and stripped it back to reveal the crop, nestled in the cleft between the gullet and the windpipe.

"Feel the gravel," said Herb encouragingly. He made me close my fingers around the crop. Then he showed me how to work my hand down behind it to cut it out, and the gullet and windpipe as well. He used shears to cut the vertebrae.

"Scrunch, scrunch," he said soothingly. "Now, put your hand in."

I did. It was deathly cold in there, in the turkey's dark insides.

"Watch out for bone splinters."

Working cautiously in the dark, I had to pull the connecting tissues loose.

"Ups-a-daisy." Herb turned the bird over and flexed each leg. "Knees up, Mother Brown. Now." He took a heavy knife and placed it directly on the knee knuckle joints and cut off the shank.

"Have a look at the worms."

Pearly-white strings, pulled out of the shank, were creeping about on their own.

"That's just the tendons shrinking. Now comes the nice part!"

He slit the bird at its bottom end, letting out a rotten smell.

"Are you educated?"

I did not know what to say.

"What's that smell?"

"Hydrogen sulfide."

"Educated," said Herb, sighing. "All right. Work your fingers around and get the guts loose. Easy. Easy. Keep your fingers together. Keep the palm inwards. Feel the ribs with the back of your hand. Feel the guts fit into your palm. Feel that? Keep going. Break the strings—as many as you can. Keep going. Feel a hard lump? That's the gizzard. Feel a soft lump? That's the heart. O.K.? O.K. Get your fingers around the gizzard. Easy. Start pulling this way. That's right. That's right. Start to pull her out."

It was not easy at all. I wasn't even sure what I had was the gizzard. My hand was full of cold pulp.

"Pull," he said, and I brought out a glistening, liverish mass.

"Got it. There's the lights. You know what they are? Lungs. There's the heart. There's the gizzard. There's the gall. Now, you don't ever want to break that gall inside or it will taste the entire turkey." Tactfully, he scraped out what I had missed, including the testicles, which were like a pair of white grapes.

"Nice pair of earrings," Herb said.

Herb Abbott was a tall, firm, plump man. His hair was dark and thin, combined straight back from a widow's peak, and his eyes seemed to be slightly slanted, so that he looked like a pale Chinese or like pictures of the Devil, except that he was smooth-faced and benign. Whatever he did around the Turkey Barn—gutting, as he was now, or loading the truck, or hanging the carcasses—was done with efficient, economical movements, quickly and buoyantly. "Notice about Herb—he always walks like he had a boat moving underneath him," Marjorie said, and it was true. Herb worked on the lake boats, during the season, as a cook. Then he worked for Morgan until after Christmas. The rest of the time he helped around the poolroom, making hamburgers, sweeping up, stopping fights before they got started. That was where he lived; he had a room above the poolroom on the main street.

In all the operations at the Turkey Barn it seemed to be Herb who had the efficiency and honour of the business continually on his mind; it was he who kept everything under control. Seeing him in the yard talking to Morgan, who was a thick, short man, red in the face, an unpredictable bully, you would be sure that it was Herb who was the boss and Morgan the hired help. But it was not so.

If I had not had Herb to show me, I don't think I could have learned turkey gutting at all. I was clumsy with my hands and had been shamed for it so often that the least show of impatience on the part of the person instructing me could have brought on a dithering paralysis. I could not stand to be watched by anybody but Herb. Particularly, I couldn't stand to be watched by Lily and Marjorie, two middle-aged sisters, who were very fast and thorough and competitive gutters. They sang at their work and talked abusively and intimately to the turkey carcasses.

"Don't you nick me, you old bugger!"

"Aren't you the old crap factory!"

I had never heard women talk like that.

Gladys was not a fast gutter, though she must have been thorough; Herb would have talked to her otherwise. She never sang and certainly she never swore. I thought her rather old, though she was not as old as Lily and Marjorie; she must have been over thirty. She seemed offended by everything that went on and had the air of keeping plenty of bitter judgments to herself. I never tried to talk to her, but she spoke to me one day in the cold little washroom off the gutting shed. She was putting pancake makeup on her face. The colour of the makeup was so distinct from the colour of her skin that it was as if she were slapping orange paint over a whitewashed, bumpy wall.

She asked me if my hair was naturally curly.

I said yes.

"You don't have to get a permanent?"

"No."

"You're lucky. I have to do mine up every night. The chemicals in my system won't allow me to get a permanent."

There are different ways women have of talking about their looks. Some women make it clear that what they do to keep themselves up is for the sake of sex, for men. Others, like Gladys, make the job out to be a kind of housekeeping, whose very difficulties they pride themselves on. Gladys was genteel. I could see her in the bank, in a navy-blue dress with the kind of detachable white collar you can wash at night. She would be grumpy and correct.

Another time, she spoke to me about her periods, which were profuse and painful. She wanted to know about mine. There was an uneasy, prudish, agitated expression on her face. I was saved by Irene, who was using the toilet and called out, "Do like me, and you'll be rid of all your problems for a while." Irene was only a few years older than I was, but she was recently—tardily—married, and heavily pregnant.

Gladys ignored her, running cold water on her hands. The hands of all of us were red and sore-looking from the work. "I can't use that soap. If I use it, I break out in a rash," Gladys said. "If I bring my own soap in here, I can't afford to have other people using it, because I pay a lot for it—it's a special anti-allergy soap."

I think the idea that Lily and Marjorie promoted—that

Gladys was after Herb Abbott—sprang from their belief that single people ought to be teased and embarrassed whenever possible, and from their interest in Herb, which led to the feeling that somebody ought to be after him. They wondered about him. What they wondered was: How can a man want so little? No wife, no family, no house. The details of his daily life, the small preferences, were of interest. Where had he been brought up? (Here and there and all over.) How far had he gone in school? (Far enough.) Where was his girlfriend? (Never tell.) Did he drink coffee or tea if he got the choice? (Coffee.)

When they talked about Gladys's being after him they must have really wanted to talk about sex—what he wanted and what he got. They must have felt a voluptuous curiosity about him, as I did. He aroused this feeling by being circumspect and not making the jokes some men did, and at the same time by not being squeamish or gentlemanly. Some men, showing me the testicles from the turkey, would have acted as if the very existence of testicles were somehow a bad joke on me, something a girl could be taunted about; another sort of man would have been embarrassed and would have thought he had to protect me from embarrassment. A man who didn't seem to feel one way or the other was an oddity—as much to older women, probably, as to me. But what was so welcome to me may have been disturbing to them. They wanted to jolt him. They even wanted Gladys to jolt him, if she could.

There wasn't any idea then—at least in Logan, Ontario, in the late forties—about homosexuality's going beyond very narrow confines. Women, certainly, believed in its rarity and in definite boundaries. There were homosexuals in town, and we knew who they were: an elegant, light-voiced, wavy-haired paperhanger who called himself an interior decorator; the minister's widow's fat, spoiled only son, who went so far as to enter baking contests and had crocheted a tablecloth; a hypochondriacal church organist and music teacher who kept the choir and his pupils in line with screaming tantrums. Once the label was fixed, there was a good deal of tolerance for these people, and their talents for decorating, for crocheting, and for music were appreciated—especially by women. "The poor fellow," they said. "He doesn't do any harm." They really seemed to believe—the women did—that it was the penchant for baking or music that was the determining factor, and that it was this activity that made the man what he was—not any other detours he might take, or wish to take. A desire to play the violin would be taken as more a deviation from manliness than would a wish to shun women. Indeed, the idea was that any manly man would wish to shun women but most of them were caught off guard, and for good.

I don't want to go into the question of whether Herb was homosexual or not, because the definition is of no use to me. I think that probably he was, but maybe he was not. (Even considering what happened later, I think that.) He is not a puzzle so arbitrarily solved.

THE OTHER PLUCKER, who worked with Irene, was Henry Streets, a neighbour of ours. There was nothing remarkable about him except that he was eighty-six years old and still, as he said of himself, a devil for work. He had whiskey in his thermos, and drank it from time to time through the day. It was Henry who had said to me, in our kitchen, "You ought to get yourself a job at the Turkey Barn. They need another gutter." Then my father said at once, "Not her, Henry. She's got ten thumbs," and Henry said he was just joking—it was dirty work. But I was already determined to try it—I had a great need to be successful in a job like this. I was almost in the condition of a grownup person who is ashamed of never having learned to read, so much did I feel my ineptness at manual work. Work, to everybody I knew, meant doing things I was no good at doing, and work was what people prided themselves on and measured each other by. (It goes without saying that the things I was good at, like schoolwork, were suspect or held in plain contempt.) So it was a surprise and then a triumph for me not to get fired, and to be able to turn out clean turkeys at a rate that was not disgraceful. I don't know if I really understood how much Herb Abbott was responsible for this, but he would sometimes say, "Good girl," or pat my waist and say, "You're getting to be a good gutter—you'll go a long ways in the world," and when I felt his quick, kind touch through the heavy sweater and bloody smock I wore, I felt my face glow and I wanted to lean back against him as he stood behind me. I wanted to rest my head against his wide, fleshy shoulder. When I went to sleep at night, lying on my side, I would rub my cheek against the pillow and think of that as Herb's shoulder.

I was interested in how he talked to Gladys, how he looked at her or noticed her. This interest was not jealous. I think I wanted something to happen with them. I quivered in curious expectation, as Lily and Marjorie did. We all wanted to see the flicker of sexuality in him, hear it in his voice, not because we thought it would make him seem more like other men but because we knew that with him it would be entirely different. He was kinder and more patient than most women, and as stern and remote, in some ways, as any man. We wanted to see how he could be moved.

If Gladys wanted this, too, she didn't give any signs of it. It is impossible for me to tell with women like her whether they are as thick and deadly as they seem, not wanting anything much but opportunities for irritation and contempt, or if they are all choked up with gloomy fires and useless passions.

Marjorie and Lily talked about marriage. They did not have much good to say about it, in spite of their feeling that it was a state nobody should be allowed to stay out of. Marjorie said that shortly after her marriage she had gone into the wood-shed with the intention of swallowing Paris green.

"I'd have done it," she said. "But the man came along in the grocery truck and I had to go out and buy the groceries. This was when we lived on the farm."

Her husband was cruel to her in those days, but later he suffered an accident—he rolled the tractor and was so badly hurt he would be an invalid all his life. They moved to town, and Marjorie was the boss now.

"He starts to sulk the other night and say he don't want his supper. Well, I just picked up his wrist and held it. He was scared I was going to twist his arm. He could see I'd do it. So I say, 'You *what*?' And he says, 'I'll eat it.'"

They talked about their father. He was a man of the old school. He had a noose in the woodshed (not the Paris green woodshed—this would be an earlier one, on another farm), and when they got on his nerves he used to line them up and threaten to hang them. Lily, who was the younger, would shake till she fell down. This same father had arranged to marry Marjorie off to a crony of his when she was just sixteen. That was the husband who had driven her to the Paris green. Their father did it because he wanted to be sure she wouldn't get into trouble.

"Hot blood," Lily said.

I was horrified, and asked, "Why didn't you run away?"

"His word was law," Marjorie said.

They said that was what was the matter with kids nowadays—it was the kids that ruled the roost. A father's word should be law. They brought up their own kids strictly, and none had turned out bad yet. When Marjorie's son wet the bed she threatened to cut off his dingy with the butcher knife. That cured him.

They said ninety per cent of the young girls nowadays drank, and swore, and took it lying down. They did not have daughters, but if they did and caught them at anything like that they would beat them raw. Irene, they said, used to go to the hockey games with her ski pants slit and nothing under them, for convenience in the snowdrifts afterward. Terrible.

I wanted to point out some contradictions. Marjorie and Lily themselves drank and swore, and what was so wonderful about the strong will of a father who would insure you a lifetime of unhappiness? (What I did not see was that Marjorie and Lily were not unhappy altogether—could not be, because of their sense of consequence, their pride and style.) I could be enraged then at the lack of logic in most adults' talk—the way they held to their pronouncements no matter what evidence might be presented to them. How could these women's hands be so gifted, so delicate and clever—for I knew they would be as good at dozens of other jobs as they were at gutting; they would be good at quilting and darning and painting and papering and kneading dough and setting out seedlings—and their thinking so slapdash, clumsy, infuriating?

Lily said she never let her husband come near her if he had been drinking. Marjorie said since the time she nearly died with a hemorrhage she never let her husband come near her, period. Lily said quickly that it was only when he'd been drinking that he tried anything. I could see that it was a matter of pride not to let your husband come near you, but I couldn't quite believe that "come near" meant "have sex." The idea of Marjorie and Lily being sought out for such purposes seemed grotesque. They had bad teeth, their stomachs sagged, their faces were dull and spotty. I decided to take "come near" literally.

THE TWO WEEKS BEFORE Christmas was a frantic time at the Turkey Barn. I began to go in for an hour before school as well as after school and on weekends. In the morning, when I walked to work, the street lights would still be on and the morning stars shining. There was the Turkey Barn, on the edge of a white field, with a row of big pine trees behind it, and always, no matter how cold and still it was, these trees were lifting their branches and sighing and straining. It seems unlikely that on my way to the Turkey Barn, for an hour of gutting turkeys, I should have experienced such a sense of promise and at the same time of perfect, impenetrable mystery in the universe, but I did. Herb had something to do with that, and so did the cold snap—the series of hard, clear mornings. The truth is, such feelings weren't hard to come by then. I would get them but not know how they were to be connected with anything in real life.

One morning at the Turkey Barn there was a new gutter. This was a boy eighteen or nineteen years old, a stranger named Brian. It seemed he was a relative, or perhaps just a friend, of Herb Abbott's. He was staying with Herb. He had worked on a lake boat last summer. He said he had got sick of it, though, and quit.

What he said was, "Yeah, fuckin' boats, I got sick of that."

Language at the Turkey Barn was coarse and free, but this was one word never heard there. And Brian's use of it seemed not careless but flaunting, mixing insult and provocation. Perhaps it was his general style that made it so. He had amazing good looks: taffy hair, bright-blue eyes, ruddy skin, well-shaped body—the sort of good looks nobody disagrees about for a moment. But a single, relentless notion had got such a hold on him that he could not keep from turning all his assets into parody. His mouth was wet-looking and slightly open most of the time, his eyes were half shut, his expression a hopeful leer, his movements indolent, exaggerated, inviting. Perhaps if he had been put on a stage with a microphone and a guitar and let grunt and howl and wriggle and excite, he would have seemed a true celebrant. Lacking a stage, he was unconvincing. After a while he seemed just like somebody with a bad case of hiccups—his insistent sexuality was that monotonous and meaningless.

If he had toned down a bit, Marjorie and Lily would probably have enjoyed him. They could have kept up a game of telling him to shut his filthy mouth and keep his hands to himself. As it was, they said they were sick of him, and meant it. Once, Marjorie took up her gutting knife. "Keep your distance," she said. "I mean from me and my sister and that kid."

She did not tell him to keep his distance from Gladys, because Gladys wasn't there at the time and Marjorie would probably not have felt like protecting her anyway. But it was Gladys Brian particularly liked to bother. She would throw down her knife and go into the washroom and stay there ten minutes and come out with a stony face. She didn't say she was sick anymore and go home, the way she used to. Marjorie said Morgan was mad at Gladys for sponging and she couldn't get away with it any longer.

Gladys said to me, "I can't stand that kind of thing. I can't stand people mentioning that kind of thing and that kind of—gestures. It makes me sick to my stomach."

I believed her. She was terribly white. But why, in that case, did she not complain to Morgan? Perhaps relations between them were too uneasy, perhaps she could not bring herself to repeat or describe such things. Why did none of us complain—if not to Morgan, at least to Herb? I never thought of it. Brian seemed just something to put up with, like the freezing cold in the gutting shed and the smell of blood and waste. When Marjorie and Lily did threaten to complain, it was about Brian's laziness.

He was not a good gutter. He said his hands were too big. So Herb took him off gutting, told him he was to sweep and clean up, make packages of giblets, and help load the truck. This meant that he did not have to be in any one place or doing any one job at a given time, so much of the time he did nothing. He would start sweeping up, leave that and mop the tables, leave that and have a cigarette, lounge against the table bothering us until Herb called him to help load. Herb was very busy now and spent a lot of time making deliveries, so it was possible he did not know the extent of Brian's idleness.

"I don't know why Herb don't fire you," Marjorie said. "I guess the answer is he don't want you hanging around sponging on him, with no place to go."

"I know where to go," said Brian.

"Keep your sloppy mouth shut," said Marjorie. "I pity Herb. Getting saddled."

ON THE LAST SCHOOL DAY before Christmas we got out early in the afternoon. I went home and changed my clothes and came into work at about three o'clock. Nobody was working. Everybody was in the gutting shed, where Morgan Elliott was swinging a cleaver over the gutting table and yelling. I couldn't make out what the yelling was about, and thought someone must have made a terrible mistake in his work; perhaps it had been me. Then I saw Brian on the other side of the table, looking very sulky and mean, and standing well back. The sexual leer was not altogether gone from his face, but it was flattened out and mixed with a look of impotent bad temper and some fear. That's it, I thought; Brian is getting fired for being so sloppy and lazy. Even when I made out Morgan saying "pervert" and "filthy" and "maniac," I still thought that was what was happening. Marjorie and Lily, and even brassy Irene, were standing around with downcast, rather pious looks, such as children get when somebody is suffering a terrible bawling out at school. Only old Henry seemed able to keep a cautious grin on his face. Gladys was not to be seen.

Herb was standing closer to Morgan than anybody else. He was not interfering but was keeping an eye on the cleaver. Morgy was blubbering, though he didn't seem to be in any immediate danger.

Morgan was yelling at Brian to get out. "And out of this town—I mean it—and don't you wait till tomorrow if you still want your arse in one piece! Out!" he shouted, and the cleaver swung dramatically towards the door. Brian started in that direction but, whether he meant to or not, he made a swaggering, taunting motion of the buttocks. This made Morgan break into a roar and run after him, swinging the cleaver in a stagy way. Brian ran, and Morgan ran after him, and Irene screamed and grabbed her stomach. Morgan was too heavy to run any distance and probably could not have thrown the cleaver very far, either. Herb watched from the doorway. Soon Morgan came back and flung the cleaver down on the table.

"All back to work! No more gawking around here! You don't get paid for gawking! What are you getting under way at?" he said, with a hard look at Irene.

"Nothing," Irene said meekly.

"If you're getting under way get out of here."

"I'm not."

"All right, then!"

We got to work. Herb took off his blood-smeared smock and put on his jacket and went off, probably to see that Brian got ready to go on the suppertime bus. He did not say a word. Morgan and his son went out to the yard, and Irene and Henry went back to the adjoining shed, where they did the plucking, working knee-deep in the feathers Brian was supposed to keep swept up.

"Where's Gladys?" I said softly.

"Recuperating," said Marjorie. She, too, spoke in a quieter voice than usual, and "recuperating" was not the sort of word she and Lily normally used. It was a word to be used about Gladys, with a mocking intent.

They didn't want to talk about what had happened, because they were afraid Morgan might come in and catch them at it and fire them. Good workers as they were, they were afraid of that. Besides, they hadn't seen anything. They must have been annoyed that they hadn't. All I ever found out was that Brian had either done something or shown something to Gladys as she came out of the washroom and she had started screaming and having hysterics.

Now she'll likely be laid up with another nervous breakdown, they said. And he'll be on his way out of town. And good riddance, they said, to both of them.

I have a picture of the Turkey Barn crew taken on Christmas Eve. It was taken with a flash camera that was someone's Christmas extravagance. I think it was Irene's. But Herb Abbott must have been the one who took the picture. He was the one who could be trusted to know or to learn immediately how to manage anything new, and flash cameras were fairly new at the time. The picture was taken about ten o'clock on Christmas Eve, after Herb and Morgy had come back from making the last delivery and we had washed off the gutting table and swept and mopped the cement floor. We had taken off our bloody smocks and heavy sweaters and gone into the little room called the lunchroom, where there was a table and a heater. We still wore our working clothes: overalls and shirts. The men wore caps and the women kerchiefs, tied in the wartime style. I am stout and cheerful and comradely in the picture, transformed into someone I don't ever remember being or pretending to be. I look years older than fourteen. Irene is the only one who has taken off her kerchief, freeing her long red hair. She peers out from it with a meek, sluttish, inviting look, which would match her reputation but is not like any look of hers I remember. Yes, it must have been her camera; she is posing for it, with that look, more deliberately than anyone else is. Marjorie and Lily are smiling, true to form, but their smiles are sour and reckless. With their hair hidden, and such figures as they have bundled up, they look like a couple of tough and jovial but testy workmen. Their kerchiefs look misplaced; caps would be better. Henry is in high spirits, glad to be part of the work force, grinning and looking twenty years younger than his age. Then Morgy, with his hangdog look, not trusting the occasion's bounty, and Morgan very flushed and bosslike and satisfied. He has just given each of us our bonus turkey. Each of these turkeys has a leg or a wing missing, or a malformation of some kind, so none of them are saleable at the full price. But Morgan has been at pains to tell us that you often get the best meat off the gimpy ones, and he has shown us that he's taking one home himself.

We are all holding mugs or large, thick china cups, which contain not the usual tea but rye whiskey. Morgan and Henry have been drinking since suppertime. Marjorie and Lily say they only want a little, and only take it at all because it's Christmas Eve and they are dead on their feet. Irene says she's dead on her feet as well but that doesn't mean she only wants a little. Herb has poured quite generously not just for her but for Lily and Marjorie, too, and they do not object. He has measured mine and Morgy's out at the same time, very stingily, and poured in Coca-Cola. This is the first drink I have ever had, and as a result I will believe for years that rye-and-Coca-Cola is a standard sort of drink and will always ask for it, until I notice that few other people drink it and that it makes me sick. I didn't get sick that Christmas Eve, though; Herb had not given me enough. Except for an odd taste, and my own feeling of consequence, it was like drinking Coca-Cola.

I don't need Herb in the picture to remember what he looked like. That is, if he looked like himself, as he did all the time at the Turkey Barn and the few times I saw him on the street—as he did all the times in my life when I saw him except one.

The time he looked somewhat unlike himself was when Morgan was cursing out Brian and, later, when Brian had run off down the road. What was this different look? I've tried to remember, because I studied it hard at the time. It wasn't much different. His face looked softer and heavier then, and if you had to describe the expression on it you would have to say it was an expression of shame. But what would he be ashamed of? Ashamed of Brian, for the way he had behaved? Surely that would be late in the day; when had Brian ever behaved otherwise? Ashamed of Morgan, for carrying on so ferociously and theatrically? Or of himself, because he was famous for nipping fights and displays of this sort in the bud and hadn't been able to do it here? Would he be ashamed that he hadn't stood up for Brian? Would he have expected himself to do that, to stand up for Brian?

All this was what I wondered at the time. Later, when I knew more, at least about sex, I decided that Brian was Herb's lover, and that Gladys really was trying to get attention from Herb, and that that was why Brian had humiliated her—with or without Herb's connivance and consent. Isn't it true that people like Herb—dignified, secretive, honourable people—will often choose somebody like Brian, will waste their helpless love on some vicious, silly person who is not even evil, or a monster, but just some importunate nuisance? I decided that Herb, with all his gentleness and carefulness, was avenging himself on us all—not just on Gladys but on us all—with Brian, and that what he was feeling when I studied his face must have been a savage and gleeful scorn. But embarrassment as well—embarrassment for Brian and for himself and for Gladys, and to some degree for all of us. Shame for all of us—that is what I thought then.

Later still, I backed off from this explanation. I got to a stage of backing off from the things I couldn't really know. It's enough for me now just to think of Herb's face with that peculiar, stricken look; to think of Brian monkeying in the shade of Herb's dignity; to think of my own mystified concentration on Herb, my need to catch him out, if I could ever get the chance, and then move in and stay close to him. How attractive, how delectable, the prospect of intimacy is, with the very person who will never grant it. I can still feel the pull of a man like that, of his promising and refusing. I would still like to know things. Never mind facts. Never mind theories, either.

When I finished my drink I wanted to say something to Herb. I stood beside him and waited for a moment when he was not listening to or talking with anyone else and when the increasingly rowdy conversation of the others would cover what I had to say.

"I'm sorry your friend had to go away."

"That's all right."

Herb spoke kindly and with amusement, and so shut me off from any further right to look at or speak about his life. He knew what I was up to. He must have known it before, with lots of women. He knew how to deal with it.

Lily had a little more whiskey in her mug and told how she and her best girlfriend (dead now, of liver trouble) had dressed up as men one time and gone into the men's side of the beer parlour, the side where it said "Men Only," because they wanted to see what it was like. They sat in a corner drinking beer and keeping their eyes and ears open, and nobody looked twice or thought a thing about them, but soon a problem arose.

"Where were we going to go? If we went around to the other side and anybody seen us going into the ladies', they would scream bloody murder. And if we went into the men's somebody'd be sure to notice we didn't do it the right way. Meanwhile the beer was going through us like a bugger!"

"What you don't do when you're young!" Marjorie said.

Several people gave me and Morgy advice. They told us to enjoy ourselves while we could. They told us to stay out of trouble. They said they had all been young once. Herb said we were a good crew and had done a good job but he didn't want to get in bad with any of the women's husbands by keeping them there too late. Marjorie and Lily expressed indifference to their husbands, but Irene announced that she loved hers and that it was not true that he had been dragged back from

Detroit to marry her, no matter what people said. Henry said it was a good life if you didn't weaken. Morgan said he wished us all the most sincere Merry Christmas.

When we came out of the Turkey Barn it was snowing. Lily said it was like a Christmas card, and so it was, with the snow whirling around the street lights in town and around the coloured lights people had put up outside their doorways. Morgan was giving Henry and Irene a ride home in the truck, acknowledging age and pregnancy and Christmas. Morgy took a shortcut through the field, and Herb walked off by himself, head down and hands in his pockets, rolling slightly, as if he were on the deck of a lake boat. Marjorie and Lily linked arms with me as if we were old comrades.

"Let's sing," Lily said. "What'll we sing?"

"'We Three Kings'?" said Marjorie. "'We Three Turkey Gutters'?"

"'I'm Dreaming of a White Christmas.'"

"Why dream? You got it!"

So we sang.

Christmas

by

VLADIMIR NABOKOV

I

AFTER WALKING BACK from the village to his manor across the
dimming snows, Sleptsov sat down in a corner, on a plush-
covered chair which he never remembered using before. It was
the kind of thing that happens after some great calamity. Not
your brother but a chance acquaintance, a vague country
neighbour to whom you never paid much attention, with

whom in normal times you exchange scarcely a word, is the one who comforts you wisely and gently, and hands you your dropped hat after the funeral service is over, and you are reeling from grief, your teeth chattering, your eyes blinded by tears. The same can be said of inanimate objects. Any room, even the coziest and the most absurdly small, in the little-used wing of a great country house has an unlived-in corner. And it was such a corner in which Sleptsov sat.

The wing was connected by a wooden gallery, now encumbered with our huge north Russian snowdrifts, to the master house, used only in summer. There was no need to awaken it, to heat it: the master had come from Petersburg for only a couple of days and had settled in the annex, where it was a simple matter to get the stoves of white Dutch tile going.

The master sat in his corner, on that plush chair, as in a doctor's waiting room. The room floated in darkness; the dense blue of early evening filtered through the crystal feathers of frost on the windowpane. Ivan, the quiet, portly valet, who had recently shaved off his moustache and now looked like his late father, the family butler, brought in a kerosene lamp, all trimmed and brimming with light. He set it on a small table, and noiselessly caged it within its pink silk shade. For an instant a tilted mirror reflected his lit ear and cropped grey hair. Then he withdrew and the door gave a subdued creak.

Sleptsov raised his hand from his knee and slowly examined it. A drop of candle wax had stuck and hardened in the thin fold of skin between two fingers. He spread his fingers and the little white scale cracked.

The following morning, after a night spent in nonsensical, fragmentary dreams totally unrelated to his grief, as Sleptsov stepped out into the cold veranda, a floorboard emitted a merry pistol crack underfoot, and the reflections of the many-coloured panes formed paradisal lozenges on the white-washed cushionless window seats. The outer door resisted at first, then opened with a luscious crunch, and the dazzling frost hit his face. The reddish sand providently sprinkled on the ice coating the porch steps resembled cinnamon, and thick icicles shot with greenish blue hung from the eaves. The snowdrifts reached all the way to the windows of the annex, tightly gripping the snug little wooden structure in their frosty clutches. The creamy white mounds of what were flower beds in summer swelled slightly above the level snow in front of the porch, and farther off loomed the radiance of the park, where every black branchlet was rimmed with silver, and the firs seemed to draw in their green paws under their bright plump load.

Wearing high felt boots and a short fur-lined coat with a karakul collar, Sleptsov strode off slowly along a straight path, the only one cleared of snow, into that blinding distant landscape. He was amazed to be still alive, and able to perceive the brilliance of the snow and feel his front teeth ache from the cold. He even noticed that a snow-covered bush resembled a fountain and that a dog had left a series of saffron marks on the slope of a snowdrift, which had burned through its crust. A little farther, the supports of a foot-bridge stuck out of the snow, and there Sleptsov stopped.

Bitterly, angrily, he pushed the thick, fluffy covering off the parapet. He vividly recalled how this bridge looked in summer. There was his son walking along the slippery planks, flecked with aments, and deftly plucking off with his net a butterfly that had settled on the railing. Now the boy sees his father. Forever-lost laughter plays on his face, under the turned-down brim of a straw hat burned dark by the sun; his hand toys with the chainlet of the leather purse attached to his belt, his dear, smooth, suntanned legs in their serge shorts and soaked sandals assume their usual cheerful widespread stance. Just recently, in Petersburg, after having babbled in his delirium about school, about his bicycle, about some great Oriental moth, he died, and yesterday Sleptsov had taken the coffin—weighed down, it seemed, with an entire lifetime—to the country, into the family vault near the village church.

It was quiet as it can only be on a bright, frosty day. Sleptsov raised his leg high, stepped off the path and, leaving blue pits behind him in the snow, made his way among the trunks of amazingly white trees to the spot where the park dropped off toward the river. Far below, ice blocks sparkled near a hole cut in the smooth expanse of white and, on the opposite bank, very straight columns of pink smoke stood above the snowy roofs of log cabins. Sleptsov took off his karakul cap and leaned against a tree trunk. Somewhere far away peasants were chopping wood—every blow bounced resonantly skyward—and beyond the light silver mist of trees, high above the squat isbas, the sun caught the equanimous radiance of the cross on the church.

3

That was where he headed after lunch, in an old sleigh with a high straight back. The cod of the black stallion clacked strongly in the frosty air, the white plumes of low branches glided overhead, and the ruts in front gave off a silvery blue sheen. When he arrived he sat for an hour or so by the grave, resting a heavy, woolen-gloved hand on the iron of the railing that burned his hand through the wool. He came home with a slight sense of disappointment, as if there, in the burial vault, he had been even further removed from his son than here, where the countless summer tracks of his rapid sandals were preserved beneath the snow.

In the evening, overcome by a fit of intense sadness, he had the main house unlocked. When the door swung open with a weighty wail, and a whiff of special, unwintery coolness came from the sonorous iron-barred vestibule, Sleptsov took the lamp with its tin reflector from the watchman's hand and entered the house alone. The parquet floors crackled eerily under his step. Room after room filled with yellow light, and the shrouded furniture seemed unfamiliar; instead of a tinkling chandelier, a soundless bag hung from the ceiling; and Sleptsov's enormous shadow, slowly extending one arm, floated across the wall and over the grey squares of curtained paintings.

He went into the room which had been his son's study in summer, set the lamp on the window ledge, and, breaking his fingernails as he did so, opened the folding shutters, even though all was darkness outside. In the blue glass the yellow flame of the slightly smoky lamp appeared, and his large, bearded face showed momentarily.

He sat down at the bare desk and sternly, from under bent brows, examined the pale wallpaper with its garlands of bluish roses; a narrow officelike cabinet, with sliding drawers from top to bottom; the couch and armchairs under slipcovers; and suddenly, dropping his head onto the desk, he started to shake, passionately, noisily, pressing first his lips, then his wet cheek, to the cold, dusty wood and clutching at its far corners.

In the desk he found a notebook, spreading boards, supplies of black pins, and an English biscuit tin that contained a large exotic cocoon which had cost three rubles. It was papery to the touch and seemed made of a brown folded leaf. His son had remembered it during his sickness, regretting that he had left it behind, but consoling himself with the thought that the chrysalid inside was probably dead. He also found a torn net: a tarlatan bag on a collapsible hoop (and the muslin still smelled of summer and sun-hot grass).

Then, bending lower and lower and sobbing with his whole body, he began pulling out one by one the glass-topped drawers of the cabinet. In the dim lamplight the even files of specimens shone silklike under the glass. Here, in this room, on that very desk, his son had spread the wings of his captures. He would first pin the carefully killed insect in the cork-bottomed groove of the setting board, between the adjustable strips of wood, and fasten down flat with pinned strips of paper the still fresh, soft wings. They had now dried long ago and been transferred to the cabinet—those spectacular Swallowtails, those dazzling Coppers and Blues, and the various Fritillaries, some mounted in a supine position to display the mother-of-pearl undersides. His son used to pronounce their Latin names with a moan of triumph or in an arch aside of disdain. And the moths, the moths, the first Aspen Hawk of five summers ago!

4

The night was smoke-blue and moonlit; thin clouds were scattered about the sky but did not touch the delicate, icy moon. The trees, masses of grey frost, cast dark shadows on the drifts, which scintillated here and there with metallic sparks. In the plush-upholstered, well-heated room of the annex Ivan had placed a two-foot fir tree in a clay pot on the table, and was just attaching a candle to its cruciform tip when Sleptsov returned from the main house, chilled, red-eyed, with grey dust smears on his cheek, carrying a wooden case under his arm. Seeing the Christmas tree on the table, he asked absently: "What's that?"

Relieving him of the case, Ivan answered in a low, mellow voice:

"There's a holiday coming up tomorrow."

"No, take it away," said Sleptsov with a frown, while thinking, Can this be Christmas Eve? How could I have forgotten?

Ivan gently insisted: "It's nice and green. Let it stand for a while."

"Please take it away," repeated Sleptsov, and bent over the case he had brought. In it he had gathered his son's belongings—the folding butterfly net, the biscuit tin with the pear-shaped cocoon, the spreading board, the pins in their lacquered box, the blue notebook. Half of the first page had been torn out, and its remaining fragment contained part of a French dictation. There followed daily entries, names of captured butterflies, and other notes:

"Walked across the bog as far as Borovichi, ... "

"Raining today. Played checkers with Father, then read Goncharov's Frigate, *a deadly bore."*

"Marvellous hot day. Rode my bike in the evening. A midge got in my eye. Deliberately rode by her dacha twice, but didn't see her ... "

Sleptsov raised his head, swallowed something hot and huge. Of whom was his son writing?

"Rode my bike as usual," he read on, *"Our eyes nearly met. My darling, my love ... "*

"This is unthinkable," whispered Sleptsov. "I'll never know...."

He bent over again, avidly deciphering the childish handwriting that slanted up then curved down in the margin.

"Saw a fresh specimen of the Camberwell Beauty today. That means autumn is here. Rain in the evening. She has probably left, and we didn't even get acquainted. Farewell, my darling. I feel terribly sad...."

"He never said anything to me...." Sleptsov tried to remember, rubbing his forehead with his palm.

On the last page there was an ink drawing: the hind view of an elephant—two thick pillars, the corners of two ears, and a tiny tail.

Sleptsov got up. He shook his head, restraining yet another onrush of hideous sobs.

"I–can't–bear–it–any–longer," he drawled between groans, repeating even more slowly, "I—can't—bear—it—any—longer...."

"It's Christmas tomorrow," came the abrupt reminder, "and I'm going to die. Of course. It's so simple. This very night ..."

He pulled out a handkerchief and dried his eyes, his beard, his cheeks. Dark streaks remained on the handkerchief.

"... death," Sleptsov said softly, as if concluding a long sentence.

The clock ticked. Frost patterns overlapped on the blue glass of the window. The open notebook shone radiantly on the table; next to it the light went through the muslin of the butterfly net, and glistened on a corner of the open tin. Sleptsov pressed his eyes shut, and had a fleeting sensation that earthly life lay before him, totally bared and comprehensible—and ghastly in its sadness, humiliatingly pointless, sterile, devoid of miracles....

At that instant there was a sudden snap—a thin sound like that of an overstretched rubber band breaking. Sleptsov opened his eyes. The cocoon in the biscuit tin had burst at its tip, and a black, wrinkled creature the size of a mouse was crawling up the wall above the table. It stopped, holding on to the surface with six black furry feet, and started palpitating strangely. It had emerged from the chrysalid because a man overcome with grief had transferred a tin box to his warm room, and the warmth had penetrated its taut leaf-and-silk envelope; it had awaited this moment so long, had collected its strength so tensely, and now, having broken out, it was slowly and miraculously expanding. Gradually the wrinkled tissues, the velvety fringes, unfurled; the fan-pleated veins grew firmer as they filled with air. It became a winged thing imperceptibly, as a maturing face imperceptibly becomes beautiful. And its wings—still feeble, still moist—kept growing and unfolding, and now they were developed to the limit set for them by God, and there, on the wall, instead of a little lump of life, instead of a dark mouse, was a great *Attacus* moth like those that fly, birdlike, around lamps in the Indian dusk.

And then those thick black wings, with a glazy eyespot on each and a purplish bloom dusting their hooked foretips, took a full breath under the impulse of tender, ravishing, almost human happiness.

The Night Before Christmas

by

THEODORE ODRACH

THE INFORMER was a wartime underground weekly edited by
Julian Lyciuk and compiled in the attic of a small, secluded
house on the fringe of the forest. In the far right hand corner
of the attic, on a crude wooden table stood a Telefunken short-
wave radio. Beside it from morning till night, with pen and
paper in hand, recording the latest news, sat Motria. She was
young and very pretty with wavy brown hair, high cheekbones, and large, melancholy, blue eyes. The daughter of an

Orthodox priest from the Pinsk Marshes, she had married an Insurgent Army commander who had been killed in 1942 by the Bolsheviks in a battle near Sarny. Her five-year-old son, Danilo, whom she missed terribly, lived with her grandmother in a village of prominent size on the banks of the Pripyat River. Along with thousands of Ukrainian women she possessed a deep desire to fight for the freedom of her country, and as a result had joined the national underground movement for independence.

In an adjoining room opposite a large window overlooking a stand of conifers, sat Oksana. She was a tall, gangly teenager, a student from a local school who rarely spoke. Little was known about her life except she was of peasant stock from a small hamlet somewhere in the Carpathian Mountains. She was a diligent worker and spent her days sitting at her desk typing out edited material given to her by Julian.

While editing *The Informer*, Julian resided in a remote settlement near Svinarin. Each morning at the crack of dawn, after wakening, he would cut across an extensive oat field and follow a thin trail of trampled brushwood to the little house in the forest. There the housekeeper would greet him with a pot of hot tea and a breakfast of rye bred and scrambled eggs. Barely having swallowed his food, he would dart upstairs and begin flipping through the large pile of statements recorded throughout the night by Motria. The news came in from three directions: Moscow, Berlin, London. Because it was often vague and contradictory, Julian came to use only a small portion of the information, the remainder of which was burned in a tile stove in the kitchen downstairs.

One morning when he had just set foot in the attic and

begun discarding the unnecessary papers, Motria glanced up at him, her eyes weary and red-rimmed.

"Is this why I spend long hours up here listening to the Telefunken, recording the news, so you can hurl it into the stove?"

"Motria," Julian tried his best to settle her. "Not everything ends up in the stove. We need accurate information for our readers and the most reliable, as you know, comes from London. But we still have to be aware of news from other places. Take a close look at the map." He pointed to a large map pinned to the wall behind her. "The black marks give us a good indication of where the Front is located."

Rubbing her eyes and suppressing a deep yawn, she lowered her head between her shoulders and with some reluctance went back to work.

Alone with news from the radio, *The Informer* also received information from various sectors of the Ukrainian Insurgent Army and a host of anonymous correspondents. All the material received was examined thoroughly by Julian, typed up, then sent off by courier to a printing outpost somewhere in the forest. Although Julian did not know of its precise location, he knew of its troubled history.

On the thirteenth of March, 1943, during the time of German occupation, an acquaintance of his, PT, had secretly dismantled his presses in Kovel. Up until that time the Germans had forced him to print propaganda material for their soldiers stationed in the area as well as material to be sent to the Third Reich. However, PT also covertly produced material for the Ukrainian underground movement—pamphlets, notices and newsletters. When a warning arrived via messenger that the Germans had discovered their clandestine activities and were planning to quash the operation and place the workers before a firing squad, supported by the Insurgent Army, four horse-drawn sleighs appeared in the middle of the night. Along with his colleagues, PT quickly loaded up the presses and drove out of town in the direction of Svinarinsky Forest. Young insurgents lined the streets at intervals to guard the way. In the heart of the forest, under the protection of the Insurgent Army, the presses now operated freely. Although *The Informer* was published weekly, Julian never came to meet with PT.

One winter morning of the same year, as day broke over the horizon Julian looked out his window. A row of icicles overhanging the pane glistened invitingly in the dim light, and in the yard a high north wind swirled flakes of snow up into the air. He wanted to sit back a moment, to absorb the tranquility and beauty of the surrounding countryside, to forget the war raging all around. But this morning he was running late. With great haste he pulled on his boots, buttoned up his sheepskin overcoat and wrapped a thick woollen scarf around his head. Stepping outside, the bright snow crunched beneath his feet and the frost collected instantly on his brows and lashes. His cheeks were numb and he kept his lips sealed to prevent the cold from entering his mouth. As he crossed the field, the great wall of the Svinarinsky Forest appeared before him. When he finally reached the little house and opened the attic door, he was startled to find Motria bent over her desk crying. Hearing him enter, she quickly dried her eyes, and said, "Don't be alarmed. There's nothing wrong, really. Today is Christmas Eve and I miss my son terribly."

It had not occurred to Julian that it was the Christmas season, let alone Christmas Eve. Glancing about he noticed the attic had been cleaned and tidied. A small table was covered with a red and black embroidered cloth, in the middle of which stood a plate filled with honey cookies and a large bowl of *kutia*. From Oksana's room flowed the wonderful scent of burning pine needles. During the night the two women had made preparations for the evening's festivities. When Julian offered to go into the woods and chop down a tree, a look of anguish passed over Motria's face. Resting her arms on the table and lowering her eyes, Julian understood instantly that a decorated tree would only remind her of her boy, whom she had not seen for several months. Instead, the three resumed working and continued to do so until the appearance of the first star.

When dusk fell over the forest and a small faint star finally emerged, upon hearing a rumbling sound, Oksana hastened to the window and yelled excitedly: "Guests have arrived!"

Footsteps could be heard down below, then they rapidly ascended the staircase. Before long four men dressed in heavy grey overcoats and high leather boots stepped onto the threshold. Julian immediately recognized his good friend, Lieutenant Sosonka. He was a middle-aged man, tall, with an elongated face and a thick grey moustache. Under his arm he held two parcels tied with red ribbon: one was for Motria, the other for Oksana.

Smiling warmly, he extended his arm first to Motria. "This is for you," he said. "A little something to insulate you from the cold." He then turned to Oksana. "And this is for you. I noticed yours were getting somewhat worn. Merry Christmas to you all!"

Tearing apart the parcels the two women's eyes lit up. Oksana slipped on a pair of black leather boots lined with sheepskin and Motria bundled herself up in a lovely brown fur-lined coat.

"And you, my good friend," Sosonka patted Julian on the shoulders, "I haven't forgotten about you."

From his pocket he produced a small pouch filled with home-grown tobacco and two books of rolling papers.

"You couldn't have brought a finer gift. Thank you."

Sosonka and his men took off their overcoats and sat down on a wooden bench opposite the decked table; from the kitchen the housekeeper, to honour the Christmas Eve fast, brought up a pot of hot mint tea and a pitcher of water. As she poured, a bright smile came to her face. "It's nice to see we'll be having company for dinner. For three days I've laboured over the twelve traditional courses. As you know supplies are scarce." Pausing briefly to comb her hair from her face, she added, rather boastfully, "I don't know how I did it, but I came up with all the food. We will have a true celebration. The bread just came out of the oven, it's still steaming."

The soldiers exchanged glances. Finally Lieutenant Sosonka rose to his feet and shaking his head, started, "Unfortunately, we have orders from headquarters to bring Motria, Oksana and Julian to the Insurgent Army camp tonight. It's getting dark outside. Time is running out. We must hurry."

"But my dinner!" In tears, the housekeeper threw up her arms.

Two horse-drawn sleighs were waiting in the yard. Oksana and the lieutenant sat in the front of the first sleigh and Julian and Motria settled behind them. The three soldiers followed at a close distance.

Up above, the sky extended in a massive stretch of royal blue. The stars sparkled in great profusion and the round silver moon cast an array of shadows. The horses trudged through the deep snow and the runners of the sleighs floated silently on top, as if suspended in mid air. Motria looked upward at the frost-covered trees and murmured:

"The night before Christmas makes me think back to when I was a child: my mother in the kitchen preparing borscht, my father wrapping presents in the living room, the sheaf of wheat in the corner, the excitement of St Nicholas. Oh, how it all vanishes so quickly."

As the sleighs passed by snow-laden shrubs and under broad overhanging branches, the cold air began to cut at Julian's face. He dropped his head and started to doze. Before long he entered a deep sleep and began to dream:

A narrow spiralling path of trampled snow appeared before him and on either side, a dark, dense forest. He was walking along this path and the gripping frost almost paralyzed him. But he kept moving. The forest was silent. Then a branch crackled and a downy white rabbit came jumping from behind a stump; there were intersecting rabbit tracks everywhere. Julian was far from civilization and could no longer hear the Christmas carols being sung in the streets. For some reason he was in a great hurry; at his waist he wore an axe. A bright full moon forced its way through the twisted branches and poured down upon his shoulders. Feeling warmed he loosened the top button of his overcoat. He then encountered a broad meandering river that was iced over; its surface was like glass and glistened under the moon's rays. Walking along the embankment he peered down, intrigued by its transparency. When he came upon a solitary rosehip bush he stopped suddenly to listen. An unexpected wind howled through the trees, then seemed to push him toward the river. He began to move downstream. Tonight was Christmas Eve and there was magic everywhere. The sound of gunfire had long since stopped: the Bolsheviks had picked up their forces and retreated to the east, the Germans to the west. Again there was peace on earth. The news excited him, yet he remained wary. The truth he decided was in the river. He undid the axe at his waist and began to hack at the ice. In a short time water came gushing out and to his great horror in the middle of the ice-hole was a speckled trout, belly-up. Shuddering, he jumped back, then ran upstream screaming.

"Wake up! Wake up!" Julian could feel someone grab him by the arm. "You must have been having a nightmare. You were jumping around so much you almost went over the side."

The horses made their way deeper into the forest. Somewhere in the far-off distance bomb explosions shook the ground, and above the canopy of trees projectors set fire to the sky. Motria hung her head between her shoulders, closed her eyes, and plugged her ears with the tips of her fingers. On either side of the path tall, magnificent trees stood proud and unmoving. The path grew narrower and narrower, twisting and turning randomly. The horses now pulled the sleighs as if by instinct, weaving in and around large boulders and towering firs and aspens. Snow fell lightly from the sky. Finally the path disappeared altogether, but the horses, snorting and switching their tails, plodded onward.

Suddenly in the distance a pale light glimmered. The horses kicked up their hooves and released a series of high-pitched, almost screeching neighs. As the sleighs approached the light, two box-like buildings appeared before them. They were constructed of old wooden planks with broad doorways and shingled roof tops. The previous summer a group of Insurgent Army men had by night dismantled these buildings and transported them via horse and wagon from the village Ozutich. Originally they had been constructed by the German army to house their soldiers, but when Bolshevik troops launched an attack and the German forces fled, these buildings were left empty. Now in the heart of the forest they were home to the Ukrainian Insurgent Army.

When Julian, Motria and Oksana entered a large hall in the first building, they were astounded to see long rows of tables neatly covered with white tablecloths and set with colourfully patterned dinnerware. On either side sat fresh-faced young men in uniform and along the far wall, laid out on the floor was an impressive collection of weapons: German machine guns, rifles, Soviet-made knives and so on. From the kitchen out back the aroma of frying mushrooms quickly penetrated the room, next came the smell of baked bread. By the head table next to a lavishly decorated Christmas tree was an icon of the Virgin Mary framed with a hand-stitched cloth and beside it stood a sheaf of wheat. When Lieutenant Sosonka entered the room the young men jumped to their feet and saluted. A procession of cooks emerged almost immediately from the kitchen carrying large bowls of *kutia,* followed by steaming borscht, platters of baked stuffed fish, cabbage rolls and *varenyky.* From a back table an elderly man dressed in civilian attire rose to his feet and began to sing: "Christ is born on Christmas Day …" His deep, ardent voice flooded the room and he was soon accompanied by the surrounding insurgents. Just before the chorus was sung a second time, Oksana drowned out the male voices with her powerful operatic soprano. Tears welled up in Motria's eyes and she sat silently twisting her hands together; she was profoundly moved, but could not bring herself to utter a sound.

As dinner was about to commence, Lieutenant Sosonka stepped up to the Christmas tree and raised his hands for attention:

"Comrades," he began, "as you know, our enemies have inordinate strengths, and now according to the latest news the Reds are beginning to overpower the Germans." He paused briefly, then taking a deep breath as if to fortify himself, added, "But no one will defeat us because tonight Christ is here by our side."

The insurgents applauded heavily. Lieutenant Sosonka recited a prayer.

Just as the candles were lit and the borscht served, a young messenger in shabby peasant clothes suddenly came barging into the dining hall. Sweat had formed on his brow and he panted heavily. Running up to Lieutenant Sosonka and almost tripping over a chair, he handed him a sealed envelope. Tearing it open, the lieutenant's face flushed an instant deep red. A tense silence followed. All eyes fell upon him. He then rose to his feet and looked at his men.

"The Reds are creeping up to the outskirts of Ozutich. Men, take up your weapons!"

The insurgents jumped up from behind the tables and went for their arms. They strapped rifles to their backs, fastened machine guns to their shoulders, and loaded belts with bullets and hand grenades. Some insurgents who had been celebrating Christmas Eve in the neighbouring building, or guarding the camp's periphery, were already assembling outside. Before long five hundred men stood at attention in several long rows. Lieutenant Sosonka shouted out, "Forward!" And in single file the young men started toward the forest, in the direction of Ozutich.

Julian, Motria and Oksana stood in silence and watched as the procession disappeared into the night; the clanking of metal could be heard for the longest time. The bright moon disappeared behind a clump of clouds and the hundreds of tracks made in the snow were left invisible.

Lines of agony and despair surfaced on Motria's face and her lips quivered. She crossed herself three times and closing her eyes, repeated again and again.

"May God help them."

Translated by Erma Odrach

The Loudest Voice

by

GRACE PALEY

THERE IS A CERTAIN PLACE where dumb-waiters boom, doors slam, dishes crash; every window is a mother's mouth bidding the street shut up, go skate somewhere else, come home. My voice is the loudest.

There, my own mother is still as full of breathing as me and the grocer stands up to speak to her. "Mrs. Abramowitz," he says, "people should not be afraid of their children."

"Ah, Mr. Bialik," my mother replies, "if you say to her or

her father 'Ssh,' they say, 'In the grave it will be quiet.'"

"From Coney Island to the cemetery," says my papa. "It's the same subway; it's the same fare."

I am right next to the pickle barrel. My pinky is making tiny whirlpools in the brine. I stop a moment to announce: "Campbell's Tomato Soup. Campbell's Vegetable Beef Soup. Campbell's S-c-otch Broth ..."

"Be quiet," the grocer says, "the labels are coming off."

"Please, Shirley, be a little quiet," my mother begs me.

In that place the whole street groans: Be quiet! Be quiet! but steals from the happy chorus of my inside self not a tittle or a jot.

There, too, but just around the corner, is a red brick building that has been old for many years. Every morning the children stand before it in double lines which must be straight. They are not insulted. They are waiting anyway.

I am usually among them. I am, in fact, the first, since I begin with "A."

One cold morning the monitor tapped me on the shoulder. "Go to Room 409, Shirley Abramowitz," he said. I did as I was told. I went in a hurry up a down staircase to Room 409, which contained sixth-graders. I had to wait at the desk without wiggling until Mr. Hilton, their teacher, had time to speak.

After five minutes he said, "Shirley?"

"What?" I whispered.

He said, "My! My! Shirley Abramowitz! They told me you had a particularly loud, clear voice and read with lots of expression. Could that be true?"

"Oh yes," I whispered.

"In that case, don't be silly; I might very well be your teacher someday. Speak up, speak up."

"Yes," I shouted.

"More like it," he said. "Now, Shirley, can you put a ribbon in your hair or a bobby pin? It's too messy."

"Yes!" I bawled.

"Now, now, calm down." He turned to the class. "Children, not a sound. Open at page 39. Read till 52. When you finish, start again." He looked me over once more. "Now, Shirley, you know, I suppose, that Christmas is coming. We are preparing a beautiful play. Most of the parts have been given out. But I still need a child with a strong voice, lots of stamina. Do you know what stamina is? You do? Smart kid. You know, I heard you read 'The Lord is my shepherd' in Assembly yesterday. I was very impressed. Wonderful delivery. Mrs. Jordan, your teacher, speaks highly of you. Now listen to me, Shirley Abramowitz, if you want to take the part and be in the play, repeat after me, 'I swear to work harder than I ever did before.'"

I looked to heaven and said at once, "Oh, I swear." I kissed my pinky and looked at God.

"That is an actor's life, my dear," he explained. "Like a soldier's, never tardy or disobedient to his general, the director. Everything," he said, "absolutely everything will depend on you."

That afternoon, all over the building, children scraped and scrubbed the turkeys and the sheaves of corn off the school-room windows. Goodbye Thanksgiving. The next morning a monitor brought red paper and green paper from the office. We made new shapes and hung them on the walls and glued them to the doors.

The teachers became happier and happier. Their heads were ringing like the bells of childhood. My best friend Evie was prone to evil, but she did not get a single demerit for whispering. We learned "Holy Night" without an error. "How wonderful!" said Miss Glacé, the student teacher. "To think that some of you don't even speak the language!" We learned "Deck the Halls" and "Hark! The Herald Angels".... They weren't ashamed and we weren't embarrassed.

Oh, but when my mother heard about it all, she said to my father: "Misha, you don't know what's going on there. Cramer is the head of the Tickets Committee."

"Who?" asked my father. "Cramer? Oh yes, an active woman."

"Active? Active has to have a reason. Listen," she said sadly, "I'm surprised to see my neighbours making tra-la-la for Christmas."

My father couldn't think of what to say to that. Then he decided: "You're in America! Clara, you wanted to come here. In Palestine the Arabs would be eating you alive. Europe you had pogroms. Argentina is full of Indians. Here you got Christmas.... Some joke, ha?"

"Very funny, Misha. What is becoming of you? If we came to a new country a long time ago to run away from tyrants, and instead we fall into a creeping pogrom, that our children learn a lot of lies, so what's the joke? Ach, Misha, your idealism is going away."

"So is your sense of humour."

"That I never had, but idealism you had a lot of."

"I'm the same Misha Abramovitch, I didn't change an iota. Ask anyone."

"Only ask me," says my mama, may she rest in peace, "I got the answer."

Meanwhile the neighbours had to think of what to say too.

Marty's father said: "You know, he has a very important part, my boy."

"Mine also," said Mr. Sauerfeld.

"Not my boy!" said Mrs. Klieg. "I said to him no. The answer is no. When I say no! I mean no!"

The rabbi's wife said, "It's disgusting!" But no one listened to her. Under the narrow sky of God's great wisdom she wore a strawberry-blond wig.

Every day was noisy and full of experience. I was Right-hand Man. Mr. Hilton said: "How could I get along without you, Shirley?"

He said: "Your mother and father ought to get down on their knees every night and thank God for giving them a child like you."

He also said: "You're absolutely a pleasure to work with, my dear, dear child."

Sometimes he said: "For God's sakes, what did I do with the script? Shirley! Shirley! Find it."

Then I answered quietly: "Here it is, Mr. Hilton."

Once in a while, when he was very tired, he would cry out: "Shirley, I'm just tired of screaming at those kids. Will you tell Ira Pushkov not to come in till Lester points to that star the second time?"

Then I roared: "Ira Pushkov, what's the matter with you? Dope! Mr. Hilton told you five times already, don't come in till Lester points to that star the second time."

"Ach, Clara," my father asked, "what does she do there till six o'clock she can't even put the plates on the table?"

"Christmas," said my mother coldly.

"Ho! Ho!" my father said. "Christmas. What's the harm? After all, history teaches everyone. We learn from reading this is a holiday from pagan times also, candles, lights, even Chanukah. So we learn it's not altogether Christian. So if they think it's a private holiday, they're only ignorant, not patriotic. What belongs to history, belongs to all men. You want to go back to the Middle Ages? Is it better to shave your head with a secondhand razor? Does it hurt Shirley to learn to speak up? It does not. So maybe someday she won't live between the kitchen and the shop. She's not a fool."

I thank you, Papa, for your kindness. It is true about me to this day. I am foolish but I am not a fool.

That night my father kissed me and said with great interest in my career, "Shirley, tomorrow's your big day. Congrats."

"Save it," my mother said. Then she shut all the windows in order to prevent tonsillitis.

In the morning it snowed. On the street corner a tree had been decorated for us by a kind city administration. In order to miss its chilly shadow our neighbours walked three blocks east to buy a loaf of bread. The butcher pulled down black window shades to keep the coloured lights from shining on his chickens. Oh, not me. On the way to school, with both my hands I tossed it a kiss of tolerance. Poor thing, it was a stranger in Egypt.

I walked straight into the auditorium past the staring children. "Go ahead, Shirley!" said the monitors. Four boys, big for their age, had already started work as prop-men and stagehands.

Mr. Hilton was very nervous. He was not even happy. Whatever he started to say ended in a sideward look of sadness. He sat slumped in the middle of the first row and asked me to help Miss Glacé. I did this, although she thought my voice too resonant and said, "Show-off!"

Parents began to arrive long before we were ready. They wanted to make a good impression. From among the yards of drapes I peeked out at the audience. I saw my embarrassed mother.

Ira, Lester, and Meyer were pasted to their beards by Miss Glacé. She almost forgot to thread the star on its wire, but I reminded her. I coughed a few times to clear my throat. Miss Glacé looked around and saw that everyone was in costume and on line waiting to play his part. She whispered, "All right ..." Then:

Jackie Sauerfeld, the prettiest boy in first grade, parted the curtains with his skinny elbow and in a high voice sang out:

"Parents dear
We are here
To make a Christmas play in time.
It we give
In narrative
And illustrate with pantomime."

He disappeared.

My voice burst immediately from the wings to the great shock of Ira, Lester, and Meyer, who were waiting for it but were surprised all the same.

"I remember, I remember, the house where I was born ..."

Miss Glacé yanked the curtain open and there it was, the house—an old hayloft, where Celia Kornbluh lay in the straw with Cindy Lou, her favourite doll. Ira, Lester, and Meyer moved slowly from the wings toward her, sometimes pointing to a moving star and sometimes ahead to Cindy Lou.

It was a long story and it was a sad story. I carefully pronounced all the words about my lonesome childhood, while little Eddie Braunstein wandered upstage and down with his shepherd's stick, looking for sheep. I brought up lonesomeness again, and not being understood at all except by some women everybody hated. Eddie was too small for that and Marty Groff took his place, wearing his father's prayer shawl. I announced twelve friends, and half the boys in the fourth grade gathered round Marty, who stood on an orange crate while my voice harangued. Sorrowful and loud, I declaimed about love and God and Man, but because of the terrible deceit of Abie Stock we came suddenly to a famous moment. Marty, whose remembering tongue I was, waited at the foot of the cross. He stared desperately at the audience. I groaned, "My God, my God, why hast thou forsaken me?" The soldiers who were sheiks grabbed poor Marty to pin him up to die, but he wrenched free, turned again to the audience, and spread his arms aloft to show despair and the end. I murmured at the top of my voice, "The rest is silence, but as everyone in this room, in this city—in this world—now knows, I shall have life eternal."

That night Mrs. Kornbluh visited our kitchen for a glass of tea.

"How's the virgin?" asked my father with a look of concern.

"For a man with a daughter, you got a fresh mouth, Abramovitch."

"Here," said my father kindly, "have some lemon, it'll sweeten your disposition."

They debated a little in Yiddish, then fell in a puddle of Russian and Polish. What I understood next was my father, who said, "Still and all, it was certainly a beautiful affair, you have to admit, introducing us to the beliefs of a different culture."

"Well, yes," said Mrs. Kornbluh. "The only thing ... you know Charlie Turner—that cute boy in Celia's class—a couple others? They got very small parts or no part at all. In very bad taste, it seemed to me. After all, it's their religion."

"Ach," explained my mother, "what could Mr. Hilton do? They got very small voices; after all, why should they holler? The English language they know from the beginning by heart. They're blond like angels. You think it's so important they should get in the play? Christmas ... the whole piece of goods ... they own it."

I listened and listened until I couldn't listen any more. Too sleepy, I climbed out of bed and kneeled. I made a little church of my hands and said, "Hear, O Israel ..." Then I called out in Yiddish, "Please, good night, good night. Ssh." My father said, "Ssh yourself," and slammed the kitchen door.

I was happy. I fell asleep at once. I had prayed for everybody: my talking family, cousins far away, passersby, and all the lonesome Christians. I expected to be heard. My voice was certainly the loudest.

Saint Nikolaus

by

SERGIO RAMÍREZ

THE MOMENT Frau Schleting came towards him, arms
outstretched, to get him to dance, he knew it was the start of
the disaster he had feared all evening but now was powerless
to avert.

If only he could have taken his hundred-mark fee and left
as soon as he had finished his job, by now he would have been
back in the dank loneliness of his room, smoking his last
Krone before wrapping himself in the quilt that was falling

apart at the seams, to go to sleep with no greater fear than that the dull routine of his days would go on unchanged.

The first complication had been the sheer size of the pile of presents. He had spent close to an hour helping the boy unwrap the parcels, and they had still done fewer than half. The child's fascination had given way to disinterest, and he was dozing in the middle of a profusion of toys, wrapping paper, boxes and ribbons when Herr Schleting carried him off to bed.

But that hadn't really been the cause—he might even so have got his money and left the house, walked down into the U-Bahn at Viktorie-Louise-Platz, and have been in his room before it had begun to snow. Yes, he muttered to himself as he listened to the measured but inexorable tread of footsteps coming up the stairs: it was Frau Schleting who had brought on the disaster.

A hundred marks would ease a lot of his worries, he had said to himself the night before when Petrus, the barman in Los Nopales, had suggested the kind of job that anyone in his position would have been glad to accept: there were still a few vacancies for Santa Clauses to go and entertain rich children in their homes on Christmas Eve. Petrus's girlfriend worked in the Kantstrasse employment agency and could arrange everything.

That morning, when he arrived at the agency, she had whispered a warning that this wasn't really a job for foreigners, still less for people who looked Latin American or Turkish: they always preferred white, ruddy-cheeked men. But since she was on his side, she wouldn't mention that at all to them, and gave him the address and telephone number: Barbarossastrasse

19/II, in Wilmersdorf: Herr and Frau Schleting. Ring before-hand to sort out the details.

By noon, he still didn't have a Santa Claus costume, and realized he was going to have to ask Krista if she'd lend him the fifty marks he needed to hire the suit and put down a deposit. When he went to look for her at her work in the tiny basement stationer's shop of the Europa Centre, she had answered in her habitual gruff voice, hoarse from cigarette smoking and thickened still further by her feigned anger, that yes she would lend him the money, but that this was the very last favour she would ever do him.

Fifteen years earlier, when he had arrived in Berlin from Maracaibo to study electrical engineering at the Technical University, thanks to his father's snobbish desire to see his son a graduate engineer from Germany, one of his first misfor-tunes had been to meet Krista, then working as a cashier in the Goethe Institute.

He never mentioned Krista in the long letters he wrote his father attempting to explain his repeated failures as a student, but if he had to put the blame on anyone, it would have been her, not because she really was the culprit, but simply because she had been a part of his life here from the very beginning. And when eventually he gave up attending the university, and with his father's death had begun to scratch a living as a waiter or a stand-in musician in pizzerias and Latino restaurants, Krista was still around, sitting all alone at her table, slowly sipping her beer (even though lately they scarcely exchanged a word) and slowly wasting away in her pursuit of him.

The tiny costume rental shop in Karl Marxstrasse, in Neuköln, had only one Santa Claus outfit left, which didn't fit him. In recent years he had acquired a paunch just like his father's, the suit was far too tight, even though he imagined Santa Clauses ought to be decidedly rotund, which he certainly wasn't. The red flannel trouser legs left a wide expanse of calf exposed, and worse still, the boots weren't included in the outfit, so he would have to turn up in his worn-out winter shoes.

But finally, hours earlier on this Christmas Eve, he had donned the costume and walked down the stairs of the nondescript, grey building identical to so many others along the Manitusstrasse in the outlying workers' district of Kreuzberg, overrun these days by Turkish immigrants, who crowded the streets gesticulating like characters in silent movies and set up their stalls on the pavements or under the bridges.

His footsteps echoed like hammer blows down the endless wooden staircase. As he stepped out into the yard, in whose lofty walls only an occasional lighted window shone, gusts of icy wind stung his face beneath the shiny strands of the false beard. Side by side in the darkness of the yard, the frozen rubbish bins resembled a row of tombstones.

Trying hard to conceal the red suit under his overcoat, he had walked along the Maybach Ufer as stealthily as a burglar, but the cold made his hand shake so much that the tinkling of his bell gave him away in spite of himself to the rare passersby who scurried along the street and rushed into the dark doorways. He left behind the black waters of the canal with its reflections of the street lamps in the night still free of snow, and made his way down into the Kottbusser Tör U-Bahn.

The station platform was deserted apart from a tiny, smartly dressed old lady, who at first stared at him in amazement, then smiled pleasantly to show she had understood. He walked past her to the furthest of the brightly lit, empty yellow cars that had just pulled up in front of them with a drawn-out gentle sigh.

The train moved off in the direction of Nollendorf-Platz, where he had to change. As so often before, the giants on the station advertisements flashed in front of him. He knew that, though in the end the passengers were swallowed up by the darkness of the tunnels, they remained up there in their multi-coloured Valhalla, their confident smiles like disdainful sneers, a constant reminder of how insignificant was his passage through the stations on his daily journeys in those same yellow trains, set against their happy, triumphant permanence high on the walls. Once again he was dazzled by the vision of a girl with magnificent hair smoking a cigarette, the same girl who through the days of summer, when a clinging smell of dog shit filled the Berlin air, stared defiantly out at the world as she hung from the rigging of a white yacht. Now, as he slipped into the tunnel, she had on a pair of skis and was looking haughtily out from a perfect, snowy landscape, so bursting with happiness her eyes were gleaming mercilessly: *gut gelaunt geniessen*.

He felt for the packet of Krone inside the Santa Claus jacket that reeked of mothballs. A cough followed in the lonely train car, his chronic racking cough from all those icy winters. He was down to his last three cigarettes. He felt for them simply to reassure himself they still existed, that they hadn't already become part of his past, because until the night before he had been getting a packet of Krone every day in Los Nopales out of the money he earned playing the drums for the Caribbean group that appeared there.

Los Nopales was a dive in Carmenstrasse frequented by students. In spite of its name, the only thing Mexican about it was a dusty wide-brimmed sombrero pinned to a Mexican blanket over the bar. The previous evening the police had closed the place down for reasons of hygiene, and Petrus, as he was paying him off, had handed him a final packet of Krone together with a few marks. There's no chance of you lot working as Santa Clauses, Petrus had joked to the Caribbean musicians as they snapped shut their instrument cases in the gloom and made their way out through the kitchen door. The blacks had all shaken their heads, highly amused.

The shops in the Viktorie-Louise-Platz loomed in the darkness, their neon lights extinguished on this silent Christmas Eve. As he crossed the rough cobbles of the square trying to find Barbarossastrasse, he could feel both his toes poking out of the holes in the thick pair of socks. A wave of anger swept over him at the scratchy false beard, at his nagging cough, at this absolute certainty that he would never return to Maracaibo. His father's death, which meant an end to the stream of letters that had brought him good humour, enthusiasm, a never-failing cheque and an unswerving optimism that one day he would be an engineer despite the passing of the years, also meant that all his connections with his family had ceased, apart from an occasional letter from his two sisters, who were married to genuine engineers. They wrote to him, with a mixture of affection and scorn, as "the German," in a distant echo of his father's former cheerfulness.

Then when he had rung the doorbell, he met Herr Schleting, impeccably dressed in a black dinner suit, the very image of one of those mature, dignified giants who advertised

Jägermeister brandy: *Der Deutsche mit dem freundlichen Akzent*. Over his shoulder he could see, not a wretched evil smelling hole like his own, with books piled in heaps in the corners, rolls of useless plans, and tourist posters of Venezuela as the only decoration, but instead a supernaturally lit living room, just like those of the billboard giants, a seemingly endless mansion whose spaciousness was extended infinitely by mirrors, white walls, crimson curtains, marble fireplaces, and crystal chandeliers, statuettes, flower vases, standard lamps, a vast expanse of carpet: and all this set out as exquisitely as in the Möbel Grünewald ad: *die altmodische Neumode*.

Cautious and diffident, Herr Schleting had smiled and ushered him in with a curt nod of the head. Precisely as they had agreed over the telephone, the little boy was waiting for him seated on the red velvet armchair next to the massive fireplace that had more the air of an altar. Quiet but expectant, wearing a blue corduroy suit, the child must have been given instructions not to budge from the huge pile of blue, red, and gold boxes, which towered almost as high as the glittering Christmas tree.

Herr Schleting had exclaimed, with festive solemnity: "Santa Claus! Santa Claus!" and stepped back so that he could begin; but he stood hesitating on the doorstep in stunned bewilderment, not knowing how to start, confronted by the apparition of the boy on his distant throne in the centre of this huge advertising poster.

He couldn't recall how or why he had started to laugh strenuously and fling his arms up and down like the toy Santa Clauses in the stores, as the occasion demanded, with every gesture sneaking a look at Herr Schleting, who still stood, smiling imperturbably, in the open doorway. He swaggered over to the boy, at last remembering to ring his bell, and hearing his own deep-throated false laughter as if the sound took a long while to emerge from his throat, where it was a struggle as to whether his wheezing cough or the guffaws would win out.

It was some time later that Frau Schleting had made her appearance. By then he had already started to help the boy unwrap his presents, throwing in the occasional chortle, when suddenly he heard the strains of "Stille Nacht, Heilige Nacht" blaring out. It was then that he had seen her, dancing alone as if in a dream, waving a bottle of Mumm in one hand, a glass high over her head in the other, as she swayed to the rhythm. She was oblivious to Santa Claus's triumphant arrival and to the ceremony of the presents. Just as in the Mumm advertisements, she was dressed in a long, white lace gown, low-cut at the back, her neck and wrists bedecked with jewels: *Mumm, reicher Genuss entspringt der Natur.*

Herr Schleting had gone discreetly over to turn the music down, then returned to his vantage point for the opening of the presents, but Frau Schleting insisted on turning it up again, and went on dancing, bottle in hand. Finally it was Herr Schleting who gave up and allowed her to continue with her Christmas cheer.

When the boy had become drowsy, Herr Schleting motioned politely for him to stop. He asked him to take a seat for a moment while he put his son to bed. All this time Frau Schleting carried on spinning around the room without paying him the slightest attention. She drank from her glass of Mumm, and by now was clapping to the beat of a Bavarian brass band that had replaced the carol.

On his return, Herr Schleting had asked him sombrely if he would care for anything to drink and he, spluttering through the troublesome strands of the false beard, had answered automatically that he'd like a beer, not really sure he wanted a drink at all, but feeling that a beer would be the most modest and respectful thing to ask for in all that glittering luxury.

Herr Schleting pulled the green bottle from his sleeve like a magician and ceremoniously poured the Kronbacher out into a long-stemmed glass, much weightier in his hand than it had appeared. Somewhere beyond the glass where the golden beer shone, *mit Felsquellwasser gebraut,* was a greeny-blue pond sketched hazily behind a bank of reeds that swayed gently in the breeze.

Herr Schleting stood, his arms folded in front of him, looking on with the detached air of a scientist as he waited for him to finish his drink. He was swallowing it down as quickly as he could, convinced that as soon as he stood up Herr Schleting would whisk a gold-edged leather wallet from his dinner jacket pocket and hand him a brand-new, crisp, hundred-mark note.

With what in all likelihood were intended as his parting words, Herr Schleting had then asked him—pronouncing each word slowly and distinctly as people do when trying to be polite to foreigners, where exactly he came from. How extraordinary! he had said with a hollow laugh, he hadn't spotted his accent at all on the telephone: as if rather than being a compliment to his German, this made it even more amazing and comical, like the Santa Claus hood jammed on the mop of his already greying Afro hair.

It was at this point that Frau Schleting, who had apparently only just realized he was there, came over. That was the start of the disaster. "My Spanish Santa Claus! Oh, *que viva España*!" she shouted gaily. From somewhere high above him—she was an uncommonly tall woman—she offered him her slender, bejewelled hand, gripping him vigorously in the handshake, but then letting herself fall on to the sofa so suddenly that for a moment he was scared she might crash on top of him. She swept back her hair and, nibbling at the rim of her glass, stared at him with passionate eyes.

He had no idea how to respond, beyond folding his white-gloved hands over his stomach that bulged in the tight red jacket, and shooting a worried look in the direction of Herr Schleting. The latter, doubtless out of a sense of propriety, preferred to pretend he hadn't seen a thing, the only sign of any impatience on his part being the way he drummed the heel of his patent leather shoe on the thick-piled carpet.

Then, with what was an apparently careless gesture, Frau Schleting had started to run a fingernail up and down his trouser leg, mirroring the movement with her lips round the rim of the glass. He glanced again at Herr Schleting, who this time pursed his lips and shook his head in annoyance.

He had stood up to say goodbye, get his money and leave, but was forcibly held back. She clawed at his arm and made him sit down again, ensnaring him with burning glances. This time, when he collapsed disheartened on to the sofa, there was no need to look over imploringly at Herr Schleting. He at last had begun to rebuke his wife, in his quiet, steely voice: she was not behaving as she should, it was unworthy of her to give a false impression to foreigners like that—stressing the word *foreigners* to emphasize how unthinkable her conduct was; even though the festivities excused a certain amount of goodwill, he begged her to regain her composure. All this accompanied by a tiny stretched smile, yet another demonstration of his unfailing politeness.

It had started to snow. The snow fell silently past the windows; as always, it filled him with wonder and delight, although this didn't in any way lessen his embarrassment at the mess he was in. He was the only one who noticed the snow. Suddenly, Frau Schleting proposed a toast to Christmas and to Spain. Without waiting for her husband to agree, she filled their glasses, the champagne overflowing onto table and carpet.

Bound by the strictures of his courtesy, Herr Schleting stood up and drank. He too was forced to toast, swallowing the champagne as quickly as he had the beer. This merely meant that she filled his glass again, splashing wine down the front of his costume; and each time he emptied it, anxious to be off, she refilled it, serving herself at the same time.

Herr Schleting, who some time before had placed his own glass well out of reach, now slapped his knees as he made to rise. He wished to thank Mister ... who must have other appointments to keep, other homes to visit that night, and so it must be time to say farewell. At this Herr Schleting rose to his feet and with the same elegant, unruffled gesture as he had ushered him in, made to show him the door.

How many glasses of Mumm had Frau Schleting plied him with? He hadn't the faintest idea. He had already tossed aside his red hood, so that now it was his bushy Afro hair that Frau Schleting was ogling, chattering all the time about Spain. He lounged back on the sofa, no longer protesting as she continued to fill his glass, guffawing as he tried to explain that he had nothing to do with Spain, and uninvited holding forth about

Venezuela—the plains, *Alma Llanera,* the mountains, the people from his home town Maracaibo, the forest of oil derricks on the lake, the heat, and how you could fry an egg at noon on the pavement in Maracaibo. He was even telling jokes about dictators and Pérez Jiménez, but these didn't even raise the flicker of a smile on Herr Schleting's face.

It was still snowing outside, but by now he hated the idea of this dirty, freezing snow, the slippery surface of the salted pavements, the stale smell of soot in the U-Bahn entrance at Viktorie-Louise-Platz, the dismal lights in the tunnels and the muffled roar of the trains, hated the thought of the eternal smirking giants in their vigil on the walls this Christmas midnight. "Here's to you," he had called out, drinking now in his best carefree manner, spreadeagled on the sofa. He unbuttoned the Santa Claus jacket to feel for a Krone, and his red and grey checked lumberjack shirt spilled out. He asked Herr Schleting for a light.

Never for a second had Herr Schleting appeared taken aback by his impertinence. He merely straightened his bow tie and paced up and down, his arms still folded across his chest. Frau Schleting was stretched out on the sofa, and lay there toying with her empty glass. She had slipped off her shoes, and was tickling him with her toes. Suddenly though, she stirred, leapt up and asked him if he knew how to dance "Que Viva España!"

To which he had replied laughing that he knew nothing about *pasodobles,* that was for fairies: no, he would teach her to dance *joropos, cumbias, guarachas, mambos.* She would have none of that—what she wanted was to dance "Que Viva España" with her Spanish Santa Claus.

Sometime about then Herr Schleting had slipped into the dining room. From there, as he used his lighter to light the candles, he reminded his wife that their traditional Christmas dinner was waiting on the table. He said this in the same even tone, as though there were only the two of them present and nothing untoward had happened. Her only answer was to repeat that she wanted to dance "Que Viva España" with her Spanish Santa Claus. She staggered over to a pile of records to look for it. He was snorting with laughter—no, she'd got it all wrong, he wasn't Spanish, where on earth had she got that idea? Herr Schleting, as his wife began to shout *Olé! Olé!* warned in the same soft-spoken cool voice that nobody was going to play "Que Viva España!" nobody was going to dance "Que Viva España!"

"Que Viva España!" burst from the stereo. It was when she swayed over to him, snapping her fingers to the rhythm like a flamenco dancer, that he had realized the disaster was inevitable.

Inevitable when, in spite of being perfectly aware that Herr Schleting had suddenly disappeared from the dining room, he was fool enough to start dancing with her, and let her pull him close and breathe her yeasty breath into his false beard— *uno, dos, uno, dos, olé!*—while she stroked the back of his neck with a bony, bejewelled hand. Even more inevitable when she tried to pull off his beard to kiss him properly, still beating out the *pasodoble* rhythm and frogmarching him in between the furniture.

All at once the lights went out, and the room was lit solely by the scarlet and emerald decorations of the giant Christmas tree. Not only did Frau Schleting fail to sense the danger, but the darkness seemed to excite her still further. She shouted again at the top of her voice: *que viva España!* locking him in her embrace. The explosions drowned her shout, and fragments of the huge gilt-framed mirror shattered onto the side tables and armchairs. Herr Schleting was standing in a cloud of gunsmoke, calmly cradling a double-barrelled shotgun. He caught a glimpse of the green hunter's cap with its countless badges. Frau Schleting, blissfully unaware of the explosions, went on dancing crazily, all alone. He himself was frantically scrabbling on all fours to find his red hood and the false beard—which Frau Schleting had eventually succeeded in pulling off—because he had to return all the items of the costume. As he crawled over to the door two more loud bangs rang out, followed by another two as he fled headlong down the stairs.

Now, back in the damp loneliness of his room in Manitusstrasse he is sitting on the bed smoking his very last Krone. The red flashes from the patrol cars down in the yard spiral up towards his window, lending the frosty windowpanes an oven-like glow. He can hear the hollow sound of the policemen's footsteps as they climb to arrest him for being a foreigner who has disturbed the peace of a German home. The Santa Claus costume is draped over the same armchair in which he has sat for so many years poring over engineering textbooks without ever understanding a thing. Filled with the bitterness and frustration he'll take back with him to Maracaibo, he knows in an instant that he'll be dubbed, with pitying sarcasm: *the German*. For ever.

Translated by Nick Caistor

God Is Nowhere;
God Is Now Here

by

ITOH SEIKOH

IT WAS at Xmas.

A relative had died, and I had gone home to my parents' house.

There I was, back in my old room again. I went rooting through my things, pulling out this and that. It worked out that I spent a long time doing it.

My brain was numb from the cheap grain alcohol that had been served, round after round, at the funeral, but something my uncle said had stuck in my mind. My uncle lived in the next town, and he had been his usual mean and obnoxious self. There was something about the *way* he had spoken to me. It wouldn't let go of me, and that was probably why I had thrown myself into this business with such vengeance.

I had worked through the night, being careful not to disturb my parents, who were snoring away downstairs. It was five in the morning before I reached the inner recesses of the closet, and crawling on my knees, I unearthed such artifacts as a bent spoon and a miniature flashlight bulb that we had used in shop class.

And out of the deepest alluvium of old memories I excavated a magnifying glass.

No need to subject it to X rays for dating: I could identify without question the day and age when it had lived on this earth. Namely, Showa 45. That was 1970. I was in the fourth grade.

THE LENS CAME into my possession one day shortly before Xmas that year.

My memory is quite clear about it: there were four of us in our gang—Shin, Maru, Mitsugu, and myself. The city was alive with a holiday mood. But we were angry with the world and feeling peculiarly hyper.

We had just gotten caught and reported for setting off a rocket firecracker. We had fired it through the open window of an apartment building.

As if it were not enough to have the homeroom teacher show up, even the principal came. They dragged us off to the apartment and made us apologize to the young couple who lived there.

I remember the walk home afterward. The evening sky bore down on us and seemed ready to crush us with its weight. But we were angry and determined not to give in. Shin, who was the ringleader of our gang, tried to cheer us up.

"We can be proud of ourselves. We were tough and took our punishment, didn't we? But that couple—they're wimps who wouldn't think twice about having a fight in broad daylight right in front of everybody. You think they have any pride?"

"You said it, Shin. They deserved what we did to them," Maru chimed in. His shoulders were thrown back in anger, but there was something too heavy, and uncommonly forced, about the sound of his voice. Especially for a fourth-grader.

He was not alone in this. All of us were trying too hard to pretend we were adults.

We recognized only the strong, and held the weak in unmitigated contempt. That was the morality we had adopted for ourselves. And we had come to believe that we, and we alone, were capable of maintaining this code.

Naturally, we reserved our greatest scorn for the likes of a woman who shrieked her head off over a little firecracker thrown in her apartment window. And for the teacher, or the principal, whose sole reaction to the incident was to apologize, oblivious to whether it was the woman, or her slightly soiled apron, to which they bowed repeatedly.

Nonetheless, we were filled with pain, and pain to the bursting point. We kept walking with no direction in mind. No one tried to go home.

I was the first to notice the little boy.

A very small boy.

He was riding a pink pig hunkered down at the entrance to the park. One of the boy's hands was extended in our direction. He sat perfectly still. He appeared to be made of the same concrete as the pig.

"Look at that, will you? Real weird."

I had opened my mouth without thinking of the consequences.

The boy looked like a baby doll. He had a very white complexion, and his forehead protruded oddly from a mass of soft curls that covered his head. Moreover, he held a plastic magnifying glass in his right hand that he extended toward us. He was looking at us through the lens.

"Hey, Mitsugu. Let's give him a scare."

Shin was talking. Mitsugu was the smallest of the four of us. He was the one who always had to play messenger boy for Shin.

"What's with you, kid?"

But the little boy did not reply in spite of Mitsugu's attempts to provoke him. Nor was there any change in the vague smile on the boy's face.

He simply continued to hold up the magnifying glass, and struggling ineptly to keep one eye shut, tried to focus on Mitsugu.

Maru laughed at Mitsugu when Mitsugu flinched and turned away.

"You looked like a POW with a gun pointed at your head."

But Maru fell into a silent funk when he realized the lens had been turned on him too.

"Think he's a first-grader?"

Shin was talking to me. Now the little boy was focusing the lens on Shin.

"I didn't ask *you,* idiot."

Shin was shouting. Things were getting serious. I wanted to warn the little boy how cruel Shin could be when he got mad.

"Never seen him before. He's too big to be in the Midori Day School. Probably not a transfer from another school, either."

I tried to speak as matter-of-factly as possible. Just so Shin wouldn't get any crazy ideas.

It was already too late.

Shin clawed at the back of his darkly complected neck. He was concocting some sort of plan. The makings of a lynching, no doubt.

The little boy perceived nothing. He continued to smile.

I was afraid. But in Shin's presence, there was no way I might admit to anything even vaguely suggestive of fear. Do that, and Shin would lynch *me.* I kept my eyes directed to the ground and said nothing. Maru and Mitsugu did the same.

The area behind the metal works was already dark. There was only the light from the houses on the other side of the wall to see by as Shin went about his business. He had pulled a plastic bag out of a trash can in the park, and into it he patiently emptied a container of toluene. We stood there watching passively, even as we choked on the fumes.

The lynching began.

Mitsugu's hands were shaking. The little boy had been stretched out face up on the sheet of cardboard. It was Mitsugu's job to lower the plastic bag and hold it directly over the boy's face.

The little boy did not resist. To the contrary, he made a point of bravely extending his right arm and holding the magnifying glass higher. He studied our faces one by one. He even smiled at us.

"Take a look at this jerk, will you. He can't even figure out what is about to happen to him."

Shin was talking as he got to his feet.

"If you don't like it, say so! That's the way it is with you wimps. And look at that asinine grin on his face. That's why it's so easy for us to do him in. We're the strong ones."

But Shin's knees were shaking, and I was struggling desperately to fight back the fear I felt as I stood there holding down the little boy's left arm. I suspect Maru, who had been told to hold the boy's legs, was on the verge of crying, too. Although the boy offered no resistance, Maru had spread-eagled himself over the boy's legs so that I couldn't see his face.

"Dumb wimp. Say something."

Shin had pushed Mitsugu aside, along with the bag of toluene he held in his hand, and jumped on top of the boy.

"You're going to die, idiot. Get the picture? You want us to save you, right? Then, say something!"

THE LITTLE BOY'S LARGE EYES were like empty cavities. Nonetheless, he raised his right hand so that he could study Shin's face with the magnifying glass.

"You don't want to die, huh?"

We stood there staring at the boy, hoping that his thin lips would move and he would say something. But he did no more than let the corners of his mouth curl into a faint smile.

"So you *do* want to die, after all?"

How can I forget the look on the little boy's face just then? It defied description. Neither was it a reply to Shin's question, nor was it a matter of wanting, or not wanting, to die. He just smiled. It was as simple as that. Moreover, the smile meant nothing—neither a belief that his life would be spared nor a seeking of release by abandoning all hope. He merely turned and gave us a smile.

I lifted the magnifying glass in the cold air and let the lens come back to life after a lapse of seventeen years. I looked out the window.

THE LENS did not reflect the landscape, reversing it as in a looking glass.

It had remained unchanged: it was the same as it was when the little boy possessed it.

It was still a reject—a dud—that will never know the perfection of being in focus. The only worlds to be grasped in its silent reflection will remain forever vague and indistinct.

Translated by William J. Tyler

The Leaf-Sweeper

by

MURIEL SPARK

BEHIND THE TOWN HALL there is a wooded parkland which, towards the end of November, begins to draw a thin blue cloud right into itself; and as a rule the park floats in this haze until mid-February. I pass every day, and see Johnnie Geddes in the heart of this mist, sweeping up the leaves. Now and again he stops, and jerking his long head erect, looks indignantly at the pile of leaves, as if it ought not to be there; then he sweeps on. This business of leaf-sweeping he learnt during the years he spent in the asylum; it was the job they always gave him to do; and when he was discharged the town council gave him the leaves to sweep. But the indignant movement of the head comes naturally to him, for this has been one of his habits since he was the most promising and buoyant and vociferous graduate of his year. He looks much older than he is, for it is not quite twenty years ago that Johnnie founded the Society for the Abolition of Christmas.

Johnnie was living with his aunt then. I was at school, and in the Christmas holidays Miss Geddes gave me her nephew's pamphlet, *How to Grow Rich at Christmas*. It sounded very likely, but it turned out that you grow rich at Christmas by doing away with Christmas, and so pondered Johnnie's pamphlet no further.

But it was only his first attempt. He had, within the next three years, founded his society of Abolitionists. His new book, *Abolish Christmas or We Die,* was in great demand at the public library, and my turn for it came at last. Johnnie was really convincing, this time, and most people were completely won over until after they had closed the book. I got an old copy for sixpence the other day, and despite the lapse of time it still proves conclusively that Christmas is a national crime. Johnnie demonstrates that every human-unit in the kingdom faces inevitable starvation within a period inversely proportional to that in which one in every six industrial-productivity units, if you see what he means, stop producing toys to fill the stockings of the educational-intake units. He cites appalling statistics to show that 1.024 per cent of the time squandered each Christmas in reckless shopping and thoughtless church-going brings the nation closer to its doom by five years. A few readers protested, but Johnnie was able to demolish their muddled arguments, and meanwhile the Society for the Abolition of Christmas increased. But Johnnie was troubled. Not only did Christmas rage throughout the kingdom as usual that year, but he had private information that many of the Society's members had broken the Oath of Abstention.

He decided, then, to strike at the very roots of Christmas. Johnnie gave up his job on the Drainage Supply Board; he gave up all his prospects, and, financed by a few supporters, retreated for two years to study the roots of Christmas. Then, all jubilant, Johnnie produced his next and last book, in which he established, either that Christmas was an invention of the Early Fathers to propitiate the pagans, or it was invented by the pagans to placate the Early Fathers, I forget which. Against the advice of his friends, Johnnie entitled it *Christmas and Christianity*. It sold eighteen copies. Johnnie never really recovered from this; and it happened, about that time, that the girl he was engaged to, an ardent Abolitionist, sent him a pullover she had knitted, for Christmas; he sent it back, enclosing a copy of the Society's rules, and she sent back the ring. But in any case, during Johnnie's absence, the Society had been undermined by a moderate faction. These moderates finally became more moderate, and the whole thing broke up.

Soon after this, I left the district, and it was some years before I saw Johnnie again. One Sunday afternoon in summer, I was idling among the crowds who were gathered to hear the speakers at Hyde Park. One little crowd surrounded a man who bore a banner marked "Crusade against Christmas"; his voice was frightening; it carried an unusually long way. This was Johnnie. A man in the crowd told me Johnnie was there every Sunday, very violent about Christmas, and that he would soon be taken up for insulting language. As I saw in the papers, he was soon taken up for insulting language. And a few months later I heard that poor Johnnie was in a mental home, because he had Christmas on the brain and couldn't stop shouting about it.

After that I forgot all about him until three years ago, in December, I went to live near the town where Johnnie had spent his youth. On the afternoon of Christmas Eve I was walking with a friend, noticing what had changed in my absence, and what hadn't. We passed a long, large house, once famous for its armoury, and I saw that the iron gates were wide open.

"They used to be kept shut," I said.

"That's an asylum now," said my friend; "they let the mild cases work in the grounds, and leave the gates open to give them a feeling of freedom."

"But," said my friend, "they lock everything inside. Door after door. The lift as well; they keep it locked."

While my friend was chattering, I stood in the gateway and looked in. Just beyond the gate was a great bare elm-tree. There I saw a man in brown corduroys, sweeping up the leaves. Poor soul, he was shouting about Christmas.

"That's Johnnie Geddes," I said. "Has he been here all these years?"

"Yes," said my friend as we walked on. "I believe he gets worse at this time of year."

"Does his aunt see him?"

"Yes. And she sees nobody else."

We were, in fact, approaching the house where Miss Geddes lived. I suggested we call on her. I had known her well.

"No fear," said my friend.

I decided to go in, all the same, and my friend walked on to the town.

Miss Geddes had changed, more than the landscape. She had been a solemn, calm woman, and now she moved about quickly, and gave short agitated smiles. She took me to her sitting-room, and as she opened the door she called to someone inside,

"Johnnie, see who's come to see us!"

A man, dressed in a dark suit, was standing on a chair, fixing holly behind a picture. He jumped down.

"Happy Christmas," he said. "A Happy and a Merry Christmas, indeed. I do hope," he said, "you're going to stay for tea, as we've got a delightful Christmas cake, and at this season of goodwill I would be cheered indeed if you could see how charmingly it's decorated; it has 'Happy Christmas' in red icing, and then there's a robin, and—"

"Johnnie," said Miss Geddes, "you're forgetting the carols."

"The carols," he said. He lifted a gramophone record from a pile and put it on. It was "The Holly and the Ivy."

"It's 'The Holly and the Ivy,'" said Miss Geddes. "Can't we have something else? We had that all morning."

"It is sublime," he said, beaming from his chair, and holding up his hand for silence.

While Miss Geddes went to fetch the tea, and he sat absorbed in his carol, I watched him. He was so like Johnnie, that if I hadn't seen poor Johnnie a few moments before, sweeping up the asylum leaves, I would have thought he really was Johnnie. Miss Geddes returned with the tray, and while he rose to put on another record, he said something that startled me.

"I saw you in the crowd that Sunday when I was speaking at Hyde Park."

"What a memory you have!" said Miss Geddes.

"It must be ten years ago," he said.

"My nephew has altered his opinion of Christmas," she explained. "He always comes home for Christmas now, and don't we have a jolly time, Johnnie?"

"Rather!" he said. "Oh, let me cut the cake."

He was very excited about the cake. With a flourish he dug a large knife into the side. The knife slipped, and I saw it run deep into his finger. Miss Geddes did not move. He wrenched his cut finger away, and went on slicing the cake.

"Isn't it bleeding?" I said.

He held up his hand. I could see the deep cut, but there was no blood.

Deliberately, and perhaps desperately, I turned to Miss Geddes.

"That house up the road," I said, "I see it's a mental home now. I passed it this afternoon."

"Johnnie," said Miss Geddes, as one who knows the game is up, "go and fetch the mince pies."

He went, whistling a carol.

"You passed the asylum," said Miss Geddes wearily.

"Yes," I said.

"And you saw Johnnie sweeping up the leaves."

"Yes."

We could still hear the whistling of the carol.

"Who is *he*?" I said.

"That's Johnnie's ghost," she said. "He comes home every Christmas. But," she said, "I don't like him. I can't bear him any longer, and I'm going away tomorrow. I don't want Johnnie's ghost, I want Johnnie in flesh and blood."

I shuddered, thinking of the cut finger that could not bleed. And I left, before Johnnie's ghost returned with the mince pies.

Next day, as I had arranged to join a family who lived in the town, I started walking over about noon. Because of the light mist, I didn't see at first who it was approaching. It was a man, waving his arm to me. It turned out to be Johnnie's ghost.

"Happy Christmas. What do you think," said Johnnie's ghost, "my aunt has gone to London. Fancy, on Christmas Day, and I thought she was at church, and here I am without anyone to spend a jolly Christmas with, and, of course, I forgive her, as it's the season of goodwill, but I'm glad to see you, because now I can come with you, wherever it is you're going, and we can all have a Happy …"

"Go away," I said, and walked on.

It sounds hard. But perhaps you don't know how repulsive and loathsome is the ghost of a living man. The ghosts of the dead may be all right, but the ghost of mad Johnnie gave me the creeps.

"Clear off," I said.

He continued walking beside me. "As it's the time of goodwill, I make allowances for your tone," he said. "But I'm coming."

We had reached the asylum gates, and there, in the grounds, I saw Johnnie sweeping the leaves. I suppose it was his way of going on strike, working on Christmas Day. He was making a noise about Christmas.

On a sudden impulse I said to Johnnie's ghost, "You want company?"

"Certainly," he replied. "It's the season of …"

"Then you shall have it," I said.

I stood in the gateway. "Oh, Johnnie," I called.

He looked up.

"I've brought your ghost to see you, Johnnie."

"Well, well," said Johnnie, advancing to meet his ghost. "Just imagine it!"

"Happy Christmas," said Johnnie's ghost.

"Oh, really?" said Johnnie.

I left them to it. And when I looked back, wondering if they would come to blows, I saw that Johnnie's ghost was sweeping the leaves as well. They seemed to be arguing at the same time. But it was still misty, and really, I can't say whether, when I looked a second time, there were two men or one man sweeping the leaves.

Johnnie began to improve in the New Year. At least, he stopped shouting about Christmas, and then he never mentioned it at all; in a few months, when he had almost stopped saying anything, they discharged him.

The town council gave him the leaves of the park to sweep. He seldom speaks, and recognizes nobody. I see him every day at the late end of the year, working within the mist. Sometimes, if there is a sudden gust, he jerks his head up to watch a few leaves falling behind him, as if amazed that they are undeniably there, although, by rights, the falling of leaves should be stopped.

Mother Christmas

by

MICHEL TOURNIER

WOULD THE VILLAGE of Pouldreuzic enjoy a time of peace? For
years, it had been torn apart by conflict: supporters of the
clergy against the Radicals, the denominational school run by
the Brothers against the local state school, the parish priest
against the schoolmaster. The hostilities, which changed
colours with the seasons, took on a legendary brilliance as the
year-end festivities arrived. For practical reasons, midnight
mass took place on December 24 at six in the evening. At the

same time, the schoolmaster, dressed up as Father Christmas, would give out toys to the pupils at the state school. Under his ministrations, Father Christmas became a pagan, radical, anti-clerical hero against whom the parish priest would brandish the baby Jesus in his living nativity scene (renowned throughout the canton) just as one throws holy water in the Devil's face.

Would a truce indeed come to Pouldreuzic? You see, the schoolmaster had retired and had been replaced by a schoolmistress who was new to the area. Everyone was watching her to see which side she was on. Madame Oiselin, a mother of two—including a three-month old baby—was divorced, which seemed to be proof of her secular credentials. But the clergy's supporters immediately won out on the first Sunday, as the new schoolmistress made a conspicuous appearance at church.

It seemed that the die had been cast. There would no longer be a sacrilegious Christmas tree during "midnight" mass, and the parish priest would retain sole control over the land. Everyone was therefore greatly surprised when Madame Oiselin announced to her charges that there would be no change to the tradition and that Father Christmas would give out his gifts at the usual time. What was she up to? And who would play the role of Father Christmas? The postman and the village constable, who came to everyone's mind due to their socialist leanings, maintained that they were unaware of any plan. When it was learned that Madame Oiselin would be lending her baby to the parish priest to play the baby Jesus in his living nativity scene, the villagers' astonishment reached its peak.

In the beginning, all went well. The little Oiselin child slept soundly as the faithful filed by the nativity scene, their eyes sharp with curiosity. The ox and donkey—a live ox and a live donkey—seemed moved by this secular baby who had been so miraculously transformed into the Saviour.

Unfortunately, the baby started fussing as the gospel reading began and his screams exploded just as the priest ascended the pulpit. No one had ever heard a baby's voice that loud. In vain, the young girl playing the Virgin Mary rocked him against her meagre bosom. Scarlet with anger, stamping his feet and waving his arms, the little brat made the church's vaulted ceiling ring with his furious cries. The priest could not get a word in edgewise.

Finally, he called over one of the choirboys and whispered an order in his ear. Without removing his surplice, the young boy left, the sound of his clogs fading away in the distance.

A few minutes later, the clericalist half of the village, all gathered together in the nave, saw an incredible sight that would go down in legend in the region of Pont-L'Abbé. Father Christmas himself broke into the church and rushed up to the manger. Then, he pushed aside his big, white cotton-wool beard, unbuttoned his red jacket and offered a generous breast to the suddenly calm baby Jesus.

Translated by Wendy Greene

Another Christmas

by
WILLIAM TREVOR

YOU ALWAYS LOOKED BACK, she thought. You looked back at other years, other Christmas cards arriving, the children younger. There was the year Patrick had cried, disliking the holly she was decorating the living-room with. There was the year Bridget had got a speck of coke in her eye on Christmas Eve and had to be taken to the hospital at Hammersmith in the middle of the night. There was the first year of their marriage, when she and Dermot were still in Waterford. And ever since they'd come to London there was the presence on Christmas Day of their landlord, Mr. Joyce, a man whom they had watched becoming elderly.

She was middle-aged now, with touches of grey in her fluffy jet-black hair, a woman known for her cheerfulness, running a bit to fat. Her husband was the opposite: thin and seeming ascetic, with more than a hint of the priest in him, a good man. "Will we get married, Norah?" he'd said one night in the Tara Ballroom in Waterford, November 6th, 1953. The proposal had astonished her: it was his brother Ned, bulky and fresh-faced, a different kettle of fish altogether, whom she'd been expecting to make it.

Patiently he held a chair for her while she strung paper-chains across the room, from one picture-rail to another. He warned her to be careful about attaching anything to the electric light. He still held the chair while she put sprigs of holly behind the pictures. He was cautious by nature and alarmed by little things, particularly anxious in case she fell off chairs. He'd never mount a chair himself, to put up decorations or anything else: he'd be useless at it in his opinion and it was his opinion that mattered. He'd never been able to do a thing about the house but it didn't matter because since the boys had grown up they'd attended to whatever she couldn't manage herself. You wouldn't dream of remarking on it: he was the way he was, considerate and thoughtful in what he did do, teetotal, clever, full of fondness for herself and for the family they'd reared, full of respect for her also.

"Isn't it remarkable how quick it comes round, Norah?" he said while he held the chair. "Isn't it no time since last year?"

"No time at all."

"Though a lot happened in the year, Norah."

"An awful lot happened."

Two of the pictures she decorated were scenes of Waterford: the quays and a man driving sheep past the Bank of Ireland. Her mother had given them to her, taking them down from the hall of the farm-house.

There was a picture of the Virgin and Child, and other, smaller pictures. She placed her last sprig of holly, a piece with berries on it, above the Virgin's halo.

"I'll make a cup of tea," she said, descending from the chair and smiling at him.

"A cup of tea'd be great, Norah."

The living-room, containing three brown armchairs and a table with upright chairs around it, and a sideboard with a television set on it, was crowded by this furniture and seemed even smaller than it was because of the decorations that had been added. On the mantelpiece, above a built-in gas fire, Christmas cards were arrayed on either side of an ornate green clock.

The house was in a terrace in Fulham. It had always been too small for the family, but now that Patrick and Brendan no longer lived there things were easier. Patrick had married a girl called Pearl six months ago, almost as soon as his period of training with the Midland Bank had ended. Brendan was training in Liverpool, with a firm of computer manufacturers. The three remaining children were still at school, Bridget at the nearby convent, Cathal and Tom at the Sacred Heart Primary. When Patrick and Brendan had moved out the room they'd always shared had become Bridget's. Until then Bridget had slept in her parents' room and she'd have to return there this Christmas because Brendan would be back for three nights. Patrick and Pearl would just come for Christmas Day. They'd be going to Pearl's people, in Croydon, on Boxing Day—St Stephen's Day, as Norah and Dermot always called it, in the Irish manner.

"It'll be great, having them all," he said. "A family again, Norah."

"And Pearl."

"She's part of us now, Norah."

"Will you have biscuits with your tea? I have a packet of Nice."

He said he would, thanking her. He was a meter-reader with North Thames Gas, a position he had held for twenty-one years, ever since he'd emigrated. In Waterford he'd worked as a clerk in the Customs, not earning very much and not much caring for the stuffy, smoke-laden office he shared with half-a-dozen other clerks. He had come to England because Norah had thought it was a good idea, because she'd always wanted to work in a London shop. She'd been given a job in Dickins & Jones, in the household linens' department, and he'd been taken on as a meter-reader, cycling from door to door, remembering the different houses and where the meters were situated in each, being agreeable to householders: all of it suited him from the start. He devoted time to thought while he rode about, and in particular to religious matters.

In her small kitchen she made the tea and carried it on a tray into the living-room. She'd been late this year with the decorations. She always liked to get them up a week in advance because they set the mood, making everyone feel right for Christmas. She'd been busy with stuff for a stall Father Malley had asked her to run for his Christmas Sale. A fashion stall he'd called it, but not quite knowing what he meant she'd just asked people for any old clothes they had, jumble really. Because of the time it had taken she hadn't had a minute to see to the decorations until this afternoon, two days before Christmas Eve. But that, as it turned out, had been all for the best. Bridget and Cathal and Tom had gone up to Putney to the pictures, Dermot didn't work on a Monday afternoon: it was convenient that they'd have an hour or two alone together because there was the matter of Mr. Joyce to bring up. Not that she wanted to bring it up, but it couldn't be just left there.

"The cup that cheers," he said, breaking a biscuit in half. Deliberately she put off raising the subject she had in mind. She watched him nibbling the biscuit and then dropping three heaped spoons of sugar into his tea and stirring it. He loved tea. The first time he'd taken her out, to the Savoy Cinema in Waterford, they'd had tea afterwards in the cinema café and they'd talked about the film and about people they knew. He'd come to live in Waterford from the country, from the farm his brother had inherited, quite close to her father's farm. He reckoned he'd settled, he told her that night: Waterford wasn't sensational, but it suited him in a lot of ways. If he hadn't married her he'd still be there, working eight hours a day in the Customs and not caring for it, yet managing to get by because he had his religion to assist him.

"Did we get a card from Father Jack yet?" he inquired, referring to a distant cousin, a priest in Chicago.

"Not yet. But it's always on the late side, Father Jack's. It was February last year."

She sipped her tea, sitting in one of the other brown armchairs, on the other side of the gas fire. It was pleasant being there alone with him in the decorated room, the green clock ticking on the mantelpiece, the Christmas cards, dusk gathering outside. She smiled and laughed, taking another biscuit while he lit a cigarette. "Isn't this great?" she said. "A bit of peace for ourselves?"

Solemnly he nodded.

"Peace comes dropping slow," he said, and she knew he was quoting from some book or other. Quite often he said things she didn't understand. "Peace and goodwill," he added, and she understood that all right.

He tapped the ash from his cigarette into an ashtray which was kept for his use, beside the gas fire. All his movements were slow. He was a slow thinker, even though he was clever. He arrived at a conclusion, having thought long and carefully; he balanced everything in his mind. "We must think about that, Norah," he said that day, twenty-two years ago, when she'd suggested that they should move to England. A week later he'd said that if she really wanted to he'd agree.

They talked about Bridget and Cathal and Tom. When they came in from the cinema they'd only just have time to change their clothes before setting out again for the Christmas party at Bridget's convent.

"It's a big day for them. Let them lie in in the morning, Norah."

"They could lie in for ever," she said, laughing in case there might seem to be harshness in this recommendation. With Christmas excitement running high, the less she heard from them the better.

"Did you get Cathal the gadgets he wanted?"

"Chemistry stuff. A set in a box."

"You're great the way you manage, Norah."

She denied that. She poured more tea for both of them. She said, as casually as she could:

"Mr. Joyce won't come. I'm not counting him in for Christmas Day."

"He hasn't failed us yet, Norah."

"He won't come this year." She smiled through the gloom at him. "I think we'd best warn the children about it."

"Where would he go if he didn't come here? Where'd he get his dinner?"

"Lyons used to be open in the old days."

"He'd never do that."

"The Bulrush Café has a turkey dinner advertised. There's a lot of people go in for that now. If you have a mother doing a job she maybe hasn't the time for the cooking. They go out to a hotel or a café, three or four pounds a head—"

"Mr. Joyce wouldn't go to a café. No one could go into a café on their own on Christmas Day."

"He won't come here, dear."

It had to be said: it was no good just pretending, laying a place for the old man on an assumption that had no basis to it. Mr. Joyce would not come because Mr. Joyce, last August, had ceased to visit them. Every Friday night he used to come, for a cup of tea and a chat, to watch the nine o'clock news with them. Every Christmas Day he'd brought carefully chosen presents for the children, and chocolates and nuts and cigarettes. He'd given Patrick and Pearl a radio as a wedding present.

"I think he'll come all right. I think maybe he hasn't been too well. God help him, it's a great age, Norah."

"He hasn't been ill, Dermot."

Every Friday Mr. Joyce had sat there in the third of the brown armchairs, watching the television, his bald head inclined so that his good ear was closer to the screen. He was tallish, rather bent now, frail and bony, with a modest white moustache. In his time he'd been a builder, which was how he had come to own property in Fulham, a self-made man who'd never married. That evening in August he had been quite as usual. Bridget had kissed him good-night because for as long as she could remember she'd always done that when he came on Friday evenings. He'd asked Cathal how he was getting on with his afternoon paper round.

There had never been any difficulties over the house. They considered that he was fair in his dealings with them; they were his tenants and his friends. When the Irish bombed English people to death in Birmingham and Guildford he did not cease to arrive every Friday evening and on Christmas Day. The bombings were discussed after the News, the Tower of London bomb, the bomb in the bus, and all the others. "Maniacs," Mr. Joyce said and nobody contradicted him.

"He would never forget the children, Norah. Not at Christmastime."

His voice addressed her from the shadows. She felt the warmth of the gas fire reflected in her face and knew if she looked in a mirror she'd see that she was quite flushed. Dermot's face never reddened. Even though he was nervy, he never displayed emotion. On all occasions his face retained its paleness, his eyes acquired no glimmer of passion. No wife could have a better husband, yet in the matter of Mr. Joyce he was so wrong it almost frightened her.

"Is it tomorrow I call in for the turkey?" he said.

She nodded, hoping he'd ask her if anything was the matter because as a rule she never just nodded in reply to a question. But he didn't say anything. He stubbed his cigarette out. He asked if there was another cup of tea in the pot.

"Dermot, would you take something round to Mr. Joyce?"

"A message, is it?"

"I have a tartan tie for him."

"Wouldn't you give it to him on the day, Norah? Like you always do." He spoke softly, still insisting. She shook her head.

It was all her fault. If she hadn't said they should go to England, if she hadn't wanted to work in a London shop, they wouldn't be caught in the trap they'd made for themselves. Their children spoke with London accents. Patrick and Brendan worked for English firms and would make their homes in England. Patrick had married an English girl. They were Catholics and they had Irish names, yet home for them was not Waterford.

"Could you make it up with Mr. Joyce, Dermot? Could you go round with the tie and say you were sorry?"

"Sorry?"

"You know what I mean." In spite of herself her voice had acquired a trace of impatience, an edginess that was unusual in it. She did not ever speak to him like that. It was the way she occasionally spoke to the children.

"What would I say I was sorry for, Norah?"

"For what you said that night." She smiled, calming her agitation. He lit another cigarette, the flame of the match briefly illuminating his face. Nothing had changed in his face. He said:

"I don't think Mr. Joyce and I had any disagreement, Norah."

"I know, Dermot. You didn't mean anything—"

"There was no disagreement, girl."

There had been no disagreement, but on that evening in August something else had happened. On the nine o'clock news there had been a report of another outrage and afterwards, when Dermot had turned the television off, there'd been the familiar comment on it. He couldn't understand the mentality of people like that, Mr. Joyce said yet again, killing just anyone, destroying life for no reason. Dermot had shaken his head over it, she herself had said it was uncivilized. Then Dermot had added that they mustn't of course forget what the Catholics in the North had suffered. The bombs were a crime but it didn't do to forget that the crime would not be there if generations of Catholics in the North had not been treated as animals. There'd been a silence then, a difficult kind of silence which she'd broken herself. All that was in the past, she'd said hastily, in a rush, nothing in the past or the present or anywhere else could justify the killing of innocent people. Even so, Dermot had added, it didn't do to avoid the truth. Mr. Joyce had not said anything.

"I'd say there was no need to go round with the tie, Norah. I'd say he'd make the effort on Christmas Day."

"Of course he won't." Her voice was raised, with more than impatience in it now. But her anger was controlled. "Of course he won't come."

"It's a time for goodwill, Norah. Another Christmas: to remind us."

He spoke slowly, the words prompted by some interpretation of God's voice in answer to a prayer. She recognized that in his deliberate tone.

"It isn't just another Christmas. It's an awful kind of Christmas. It's a Christmas to be ashamed, and you're making it worse, Dermot." Her lips were trembling in a way that was uncomfortable. If she tried to calm herself she'd become jittery instead, she might even begin to cry. Mr. Joyce had been generous and tactful, she said loudly. It made no difference to Mr. Joyce that they were Irish people, that their children went to school with the children of I.R.A. men. Yet his generosity and his tact had been thrown back in his face. Everyone knew that the Catholics in the North had suffered, that generations of injustice had been twisted into the shape of a cause. But you couldn't say it to an old man who had hardly been outside Fulham in his life. You couldn't say it because when you did it sounded like an excuse for murder.

"You have to state the truth, Norah. It's there to be told."

"I never yet cared for a North of Ireland person, Catholic or Protestant. Let them fight it out and not bother us."

"You shouldn't say that, Norah."

"It's more of your truth for you."

He didn't reply. There was the gleam of his face for a moment as he drew on his cigarette. In all their married life they had never had a quarrel that was in any way serious, yet she felt herself now in the presence of a seriousness that was too much for her. She had told him that whenever a new bombing took place she prayed it might be the work of the Angry Brigade, or any group that wasn't Irish. She'd told him that in shops she'd begun to feel embarrassed because of her Waterford accent. He'd said she must have courage, and she realized now that he had drawn on courage himself when he'd made the remark to Mr. Joyce. He would have prayed and considered before making it. He would have seen it in the end as his Catholic duty.

"He thinks you don't condemn people being killed." She spoke quietly even though she felt a wildness inside her. She felt she should be out on the streets, shouting in her Waterford accent, violently stating that the bombers were more despicable with every breath they drew, that hatred and death were all they deserved. She saw herself on Fulham Broadway, haranguing the passers-by, her greying hair blown in the wind, her voice more passionate than it had ever been before. But none of it was the kind of thing she could do because she was not that kind of woman. She hadn't the courage, any more than she had the courage to urge her anger to explode in their living-room. For all the years of her marriage there had never been the need of such courage before: she was aware of that, but found no consolation in it.

"I think he's maybe seen it by now," he said. "How one thing leads to another."

She felt insulted by the words. She willed herself the strength to shout, to pour out a torrent of fury at him, but the strength did not come. Standing up, she stumbled in the gloom and felt a piece of holly under the sole of her shoe. She turned the light on.

"I'll pray that Mr. Joyce will come," he said.

She looked at him, pale and thin, with his priestly face. For the first time since he had asked her to marry him in the Tara Ballroom she did not love him. He was cleverer than she was, yet he seemed half blind. He was good, yet he seemed hard in his goodness, as though he'd be better without it. Up to the very last moment on Christmas Day there would be the pretence that their landlord might arrive, that God would answer a prayer because His truth had been honoured. She considered it hypocrisy, unable to help herself in that opinion.

He talked but she did not listen. He spoke of keeping faith with their own, of being a Catholic. Crime begot crime, he said, God wanted it to be known that one evil led to another. She continued to look at him while he spoke, pretending to listen but wondering instead if in twelve months' time, when another Christmas came, he would still be cycling from house to house to read gas meters. Or would people have objected, requesting a meter-reader who was not Irish? An objection to a man with an Irish accent was down-to-earth and ordinary. It didn't belong in the same grand category as crime begetting crime or God wanting something to be known, or in the category of truth and conscience. In the present circumstances the objection would be understandable and fair. It seemed even right that it should be made, for it was a man with an Irish accent in whom the worst had been brought out by the troubles that had come, who was guilty of a cruelty no one would have believed him capable of. Their harmless elderly landlord might die in the course of that same year, a friendship he had valued lost, his last Christmas lonely. Grand though it might seem in one way, all of it was petty.

Once, as a girl, she might have cried, but her contented marriage had caused her to lose that habit. She cleared up the tea things, reflecting that the bombers would be pleased if they could note the victory they'd scored in a living-room in Fulham. And on Christmas Day, when a family sat down to a conventional meal, the victory would be greater. There would be crackers and chatter and excitement, the Queen and the Pope would deliver speeches. Dermot would discuss these Christmas messages with Patrick and Brendan, as he'd discussed them in the past with Mr. Joyce. He would be as kind as ever. He would console Bridget and Cathal and Tom by saying that Mr. Joyce hadn't been up to the journey. And whenever she looked at him she would remember the Christmases of the past. She would feel ashamed of him, and of herself.

O'Brien's
First Christmas

by

JEANETTE WINTERSON

ANYONE WHO LOOKED up could see it: TWENTY-SEVEN SHOP-
PING DAYS TO CHRISTMAS, in red letters, followed by a storm
of dancing Santas, then a whirlwind of angels, trumpets
rampant.

The department store was very large. If you were to lay its
merchandise end to end, starting with a silk stocking and
closing on a plastic baby Jesus, you would have belted the
world. The opulence of the store defeated all shoppers. Even

in the hectic twenty-seven days to Christmas, even including the extended opening hours, there was no exodus of goods that could make the slightest impression on the well stocked shelves.

O'Brien, who worked in the Pet Department, had watched women stacking their baskets with hand and body lotion in an attractive reindeer wrap. Customers who looked quite normal were falling in delight upon pyramids of fondant creams packed in Bethlehem-by-Night boxes. It made no difference. Whatever they demolished returned. This phenomenon, as far as O'Brien could calculate, meant that two-thirds of the spending world would be eating sticky stuff or spreading it over themselves on December 25th.

She poured out a measure of hand and body lotion and broke open a fondant cream. The filling was the same in both. Somewhere, in a town no one visited, stood a factory dedicated to the manufacture of pale yellow sticky stuff waiting to be dispatched in labelless vats to profiteers who traded exclusively in Christmas.

O'Brien didn't like Christmas. Every year she prayed for an ordinary miracle to take her away from the swelling round of ageing aunts who knitted her socks and asked about her young man. She didn't have a young man. She lived alone and worked in the Pet Department for company. At a staff discount of 35 percent it made sense for her to have a pet of her own, but her landlady, a Christian Scientist, did not approve of what she called "Stray Molecules."

"Hair," she said, "carries germs, and what is hairier than an animal?"

So O'Brien faced another Christmas alone.

In the store shoppers enjoyed the kind of solidarity we read about in the war years. There was none of the vulgar pushing and shoving usually associated with peak time buying. People made way for one another in the queues and chatted about the weather and the impending snowfall.

"Snow for Christmas," said one. "That's how it should be." It was right and nice. Enough presents, enough money, clean flame-effect log fires courtesy of the Gas Board. Snow for the children.

O'Brien flicked through the Lonely Hearts. There were extra pages of them at Christmas, just as there was extra everything else. How could it be that column after column of sane, loving, slim men and women, without obvious perversions, were spending Christmas alone? Were the happy families in the department store a beguiling minority?

She had once answered a Lonely Hearts advertisement and eaten dinner with a small young man who mended organ pipes. He had suggested they get married that night by special licence. O'Brien had declined on the grounds that a whirlwind romance would tire her out after so little practice. It seemed rather like going to advanced aerobics when you couldn't manage five minutes on the exercise bicycle. She had asked him why he was in such a hurry.

"I have a heart condition."

So it was like aerobics after all.

After that she had joined a camera club, where a number of men had been keen to help her in the darkroom, but all of them had square hairy hands that reminded her of joke shop gorilla paws.

"Don't set your sights too high," her aunts warned.

But she did. She set them in the constellations, in the roaring lion, and the flanks of the bull. In December, when the stars were bright, she saw herself in another life, happy.

"You've got to have a dream," she told the Newfoundland pup destined to become a Christmas present. "I don't know what I want. I'm just drifting."

She'd heard that men knew what they wanted, so she asked Clive, the Floor Manager.

"I'd like to run my own branch of McDonald's. A really big one with full breakfasts and party seating."

O'Brien tried, but she couldn't get excited. It was the same with vacuum cleaners; she could use the power but where was the glamour?

WHEN SHE RETURNED to her lodgings that evening her land-lady was solemnly nailing a holly wreath to the front door.

"This is not for myself, you understand, it is for my tenants. Next I will hang paper chains in the hall." O'Brien's landlady always spoke very slowly because she had been a Hungarian Countess. A Countess does not rush her words.

O'Brien, still in her red duffle coat, found herself holding on to one end of a paper chain, while her landlady creaked up the aluminum steps, six tacks between her teeth.

"Soon be Christmas," said O'Brien. "I'm making a New Year's resolution to change my life, otherwise, what's the point?"

"Life has no point," said her landlady. "You would be better to get married or start an evening class. For the last seven years I have busied myself with brass rubbings."

The hall was cold. The paper chain was too short. O'Brien didn't want advice. She made her excuses and mounted the stairs. Her landlady, perhaps stung by a pang of sympathy, offered her a can of sardines for supper.

"They are not in tomato sauce but olive oil."

O'Brien though, had other plans.

Inside her room she began to make a list of the things people thought of as their future: Marriage, children, a career, travel, a home, enough money, lots of money. Christmas time brought these things sharply into focus. If you had them, any of them, you could feel especially pleased with life over the twelve days of feasting and family. If you didn't have them, you felt the lack more keenly. You felt like an outsider. Odd that a festival to celebrate the most austere of births should become the season of conspicuous consumption. O'Brien didn't know much about theology but she knew there had been a muck-up somewhere.

As she looked at the list, she began to realize that an off the peg future, however nicely designed, wouldn't be the life she sensed when she looked up at the stars. Immediately she felt guilty. Who was she to imagine she could find something better than other people's best?

"What's wrong with settling down and getting married?" she said out loud.

"Nothing," said her landlady, appearing around the door without knocking. "It's normal. We should all try to be normal," and she put down the sardines on O'Brien's kitchenette, and left.

"Nothing wrong," thought O'Brien, "but what is right for me?"

She lay awake through the night, listening to the radio beaming out songs and bonhomie for Christmas. She wanted to stay under the blankets forever, being warm and watching the bar of the electric fire. She remembered a story she had read as a child about a princess invited to a ball. Her father offered her more than two hundred gowns to choose from but none of them fitted and they were too difficult to alter. At last she went in her silk shift with her hair down, and still she was more beautiful than anyone.

"Be yourself," said O'Brien, not altogether sure what she meant.

AT THE STILL POINT of the night O'Brien awoke with a sense that she was no longer alone in the room. She was right. At the bottom of her bed sat a young woman wearing an organza tutu.

O'Brien didn't bother to panic. She was used to her neighbour's friends blundering into the wrong room.

"Vicky is next door," she said. "Do you want the light on?"

"I'm the Christmas fairy," said the woman. "Do you want to make a wish?"

"Come on," said O'Brien, realizing her visitor must be drunk. "I'll show you the way."

"I'm not going anywhere," said the woman. "This is the address I was given. Do you want love or adventure or what? We don't do money."

O'Brien thought for a moment. Perhaps this was a new kind of singing telegram. She decided to play along, hoping to discover the sender.

"What can you offer?"

The stranger pulled out a photograph album. "In here are all the eligible men in London. It's indexed, so if you want one with a moustache, look under 'M,' where you will also find 'moles.'"

O'Brien had a look. She could think of nothing but those booklets of Sunny Smiles she used to buy to help the orphans. Seeing her lack of enthusiasm, the stranger offered her a second album.

"Here's one with all the eligible women. It's all the same to me."

"Shouldn't you be singing all this?" asked O'Brien, thinking it was time to change the subject.

"Why?" said the fairy. "Does conversation bother you?"

"No, but you are a Singing Telegram."

"I am not a Singing Telegram. I am a fairy. Now what is your wish?"

"OK," said O'Brien, wanting to go back to sleep. "I wish I was blonde."

Then she must have gone back to sleep straightaway, because the next thing she heard was the alarm ringing in her ears. She dozed, she was late, no time for anything, just into her red duffle coat and out into a street full of shoppers, mindful of their too few days to go.

At work, on her way up to the Pet Department, she met Janice from Lingerie, who said, "Your hair's fantastic, I didn't recognize you at first."

O'Brien was confused. She hadn't had time to brush her hair. Was it standing on end? She went into the Ladies and peered into the mirror. She was blonde.

"It really suits you," said Kathleen, from Fabrics and Furnishings. "You should do more with your make-up now."

"Do more?" thought O'Brien, who did nothing. She decided to go back home, but in the lift on the way out, she met the actor who had come to play Santa ...

"It's awful in the Grotto. It's made of polystyrene and everyone knows that's bad for the lungs." O'Brien sympathized.

"Listen," said Santa, "there's two dozen inflatable gnomes in the basement. I've got to blow them up. If you'll help me, I'll buy you lunch."

For the first time in her life O'Brien abandoned herself to chaos and decided it didn't matter. What surprises could remain for a woman who had been visited in the night by a Non-Singing Telegram and subsequently turned blonde? Blowing up gnomes was a breath of fresh air.

"I like your hair," said the actor Santa.

"Thanks," said O'Brien, "I've only just had it done."

AT THE VEGETARIAN CAFE where every lentil bake came with its own sprig of holly, Santa asked O'Brien if she would like to come for Christmas dinner.

"There won't be any roast corpse though."

"That's all right," said O'Brien, "I'm not a vegetarian but I don't eat meat."

"Then you are a vegetarian."

"Aren't you supposed to join something?"

"No," said Santa. "Just be yourself."

IN THE MIRROR on the wall O'Brien smiled. She was starting to like being herself. She didn't go back to work that afternoon. She went shopping like everybody else. She bought new clothes, lots of food, and a set of fairy lights. When the man at the stall offered her a cut price Christmas tree, she shouldered it home. Her landlady saw her arriving.

"You are early today," she said very slowly. "I see you are

going to get pine needles on my carpet."

"Thanks for the sardines," said O'Brien. "Have a bag of satsumas."

"Your hair is not what it was last night. Did something happen to you?"

"Yes," said O'Brien, "but it's a secret."

"I hope it was not a man."

"No it was a woman."

Her landlady paused, and said, "I am going now to listen to the Gospel according to St Luke on my wireless."

O'BRIEN PUT THE POTATOES in the oven and strung her window with fairy lights. Outside the sky was strung with stars.

At eight o'clock, when Santa arrived, wet and cold and still in uniform, O'Brien lit the candles beneath the tree. She said,

"If you could make a wish what would it be?"

"I'd wish to be here with you."

"Even if I wasn't blonde?"

"Even if you were bald."

"Merry Christmas," said O'Brien.

The Authors

Auster, Paul (U.S.A., 1947). Born in Newark, New Jersey, Paul Auster is a poet and a novelist. He has won acclaim for his New York trilogy: *City of Glass, Ghosts,* and *The Locked Room.* Among his more recent novels are *The Music of Chance* (1990) and *Leviathan* (1992). He is also the author of several screenplays.

Beattie, Ann (U.S.A., 1947). Ann Beattie is mainly known for her short stories collected in various volumes, such as *The Burning House* (1982) and *Where You'll Find Me* (1986). She is also the author of several novels, including *Chilly Scenes of Winter* (1976) and *Falling in Place* (1980).

Cheever, John (U.S.A., 1912–1990). Cheever's career began with his expulsion from Thayer Academy in Massachusetts, the subject of his first published story. In 1957, he won the National Book Award with *The Wapshot Chronicle,* which he followed with three other novels: *The Wapshot Scandal* (1964), *Bullet Park* (1969), and *Falconer* (1977). His numerous short fiction was collected under the title *The Stories of John Cheever* (1978).

Ford, Richard (U.S.A., 1944). Born in Jackson, Mississippi, Richard Ford won the Pulitzer Prize for his novel *Independence Day* (1995). His other novels include *A Piece of My Heart* (1976), *The Ultimate Good Luck* (1981), and *Wildlife* (1990). His stories have been collected in three volumes: *Rock Springs* (1987), *Women Without Men* (1997), and *A Multitude of Sins* (2001).

Gallant, Mavis (Canada, 1922). After working as a journalist for the *Montreal Gazette,* Mavis Gallant moved to Europe in 1950. The author of two novels, *Green Water, Green Sky* (1959) and *A Fairly Good Time* (1970), she is best known for her remarkable short stories, almost all of which were reissued in one volume under the title *The Collected Stories of Mavis Gallant.*

Gardam, Jane (England, 1928). Born in North Yorkshire, Jane Gardam is the author of three collections of short stories and many novels, among them *The Summer After the Funeral* (1973), *God on the Rocks* (1978), *The Sidmouth Letters* (1980), *Crusoe's Daughter* (1985), *Queen of the Tambourine* (1991), and *Old Faith* (2004).

Goldsworthy, Peter (Australia, 1951). After graduating from the University of Adelaide's school of medicine, Peter Goldsworthy began a second career as a writer. He has published poetry, short stories, essays, and opera libretti, and the novels *Maestro* (1989), *Honk If You Are Jesus* (1992), and *Three Dog Night* (2003).

Greene, Graham (England, 1904–1991). Graham Greene was one of the most popular novelists of the twentieth century. Among his best-known are *The Power and the Glory* (1940), *The Heart of the Matter* (1948), *The Third Man* (1950), *The End of the Affair* (1951), *The Quiet American* (1955), *Our Man in Havana* (1958), *A Burnt-Out Case* (1961), *The Honorary Consul* (1973), and *The Human Factor* (1978). He also wrote essays, plays, and two volumes of autobiography.

Head, Bessie (South Africa, 1937–1986). Though born in Pietermartzburg, Bessie Head lived most of her adult life in Botswana. She is the author of *When Rain Clouds Gather* (1968), *Maru* (1971), *A Question of Power* (1974), and *A Bewitched Crossroad* (1984). *The Collector of Treasures* (1977) and *Serowe: Village of the Rain Wind* (1981) are collections of traditional tales.

Hernández, Juan José (Argentina, 1931). One of the outstanding writers of his generation, Juan José Hernández is the author of three volumes of poetry, one novel, *La ciudad de los sueños* (1971), and two volumes of short stories, *El inocente* (1965) and *La favorita* (1977).

Lenz, Siegfried (Germany, 1926). He is a member of Gruppe 47, an association of writers opposed to both the politics of Eastern Germany and to the values of the Federal Republic. His novels include *Es Waren Habichte in der Luft* (1950), *Der Mann im Strom* (1957), *Brot und Spiele* (1959), *Stadtgespräch* (1963), and *Deutschstunde* (1968). Among his many short story collections are *Jäger des Spotts* (1958), *Das Feuerschiff* (1960), *Der Spielverdeber* (1965), and *Einstein uberquert die Elbe bei Hamburg* (1975). He is also the author of several plays.

MacLeod, Alistair (Canada, 1936). He is the author of two collections of short stories, *The Lost Salt Gift of Blood* (1976) and *As Birds Bring Forth the Sun* (1986). His novel *No Great Mischief* (2001) won the Dublin IMPAC Award.

Munro, Alice (Canada, 1931). Alice Munro wrote her first short stories for magazines and for the radio, collected later under the title *Dance of the Happy Shades* (1968). Since then she has published numerous collections, including *Lives of Girls and Women* (1971), *Something I've Been Meaning to Tell You* (1974), *The Moons of Jupiter* (1982), *The Progress of Love* (1986), *Open Secrets* (1994), and *Runaway* (2004).

Nabokov, Vladimir (Russia/U.S.A., 1899–1977). After having written several novels in his native tongue, Vladimir Nabokov emigrated to the United States and began writing in English. The author of two volumes of short stories, he is best known for his novels: *The Real Life of Sebastian Knight* (1941), *Lolita* (1955), *Pnin* (1957), *Pale Fire* (1962), *Ada, or Ardor* (1969), and *Transparent Things* (1972).

Odrach, Theodore (Ukraine, 1912–1964). In order to escape capture for having fought against Soviet rule as a member of the Ukrainian Insurgent Army, Theodore Odrach fled to Czechoslovakia toward the end of World War II. Later, after living in Germany and England, he settled in Canada in 1953. He is the author of five novels and two collections of short stories, only one of which, *Whistle Stop* (1959), has been translated into English.

Paley, Grace (U.S.A., 1922). Grace Paley began her writing career as a poet, but in 1956 decided that her real calling was in the field of the short story. Her collections have won her universal praise, notably *The Little Disturbances of Man* (1959), *Enormous Changes at the Last Minute* (1975), and *Later the Same Day* (1985).

Ramírez, Sergio (Nicaragua, 1942). Sergio Ramírez became vice-president of Nicaragua during the Sandinista takeover of 1980. Among his many books are collections of short fiction, such as *Cuentos* (1963), *De tropeles y tropelías* (1971), and *Catalina y Catalina* (2001), and several novels, including *Castigo divino* (1987), *Margarita, está linda la mar* (1988), and *Sombras nada más* (2003).

Seikoh, Itoh (Japan, 1961). A celebrated stand-up comedian, the host of a popular television program, a video artist, and actor, Itoh Seikoh is also the author of the bestselling novel *No Life King* on the "Nintendo kids" generation.

Spark, Muriel (Scotland, 1918). Novelist, poet, and short-story writer, Muriel Spark was educated at Gillespie's School for Girls in Edinburgh, which became the model for her novel *The Prime of Miss Jane Brodie* (1961). Her other books include *The Comforters* (1957), *Memento Mori* (1959), *The Ballad of Peckham Rye* (1960), *The Mandelbaum Gate* (1965), *Loitering With Intent* (1981), *Symposium* (1990), and *Finishing School* (2004).

Tournier, Michel (France, 1923). Michel Tournier has written both for children and for adults. His novels—*Vendredi ou les Limbes du Pacifique* (1967), *Le Roi des Aulnes* (1970), *Les Météors* (1975), *Gaspard, Melchior, Balthasar* (1980), *La Goutte d'Or* (1985)—have won him the reputation as one of France's major writers. *Le vent Paraclet* (1977) is his intellectual biography.

Trevor, William (Ireland, 1928). William Trevor was educated at Trinity College, Dublin, where he began writing his first short stories. His best-known novels are *The Old Boys* (1964), *Elizabeth Alone* (1973), *Felicia's Journey* (1994), and *The Story of Lucy Gault* (2002). His short-story collections include *The Day We Got Drunk on Cake* (1969), *The Ballroom of Romance* (1972), *Angels at the Ritz* (1975), *Lovers of Their Time* (1978), *Beyond the Pale* (1981), and *A Bit on the Side* (2004).

Winterson, Jeanette (England, 1959). Jeanette Winterson's first novel was *Oranges Are Not the Only Fruit* (1985). Since then, she has published five other novels, *The Passion* (1987),

Sexing the Cherry (1990), *Written on the Body* (1992), *Gut Symmetries* (1997), and *Lighthousekeeping* (2004), as well as one collection of stories, *The World and Other Places* (1998), and one of essays, *Art Objects* (1995).

Squ,
 (1991).
 (1993).